MW01615898

A LION OF A MAN

He was a Breed. The bastard of the human and animal species. His genetics were a mismatched collage of human and lion DNA that made him stronger, faster, more predatory, more vicious than any human should be.

His sexuality was hard, driven. If there was anything better than sex and a wild, hot woman, then he hadn't found it. It was better than a good bloody fight, and he loved those, too.

Adrenaline was the spice of life, be it sexual or life-threatening. But he had never taken a woman who wasn't a Breed. And he had never taken one as fragile as the woman sitting beside him. The one burning, slick and wet and ready for him.

Megan's Mark

Lora Leigh

BERKLEY SENSATION, NEW YORK

THE BERKLEY PUBLISHING GROUP
Published by the Penguin Group
Penguin Group (USA) Inc.
375 Hudson Street, New York, New York 10014, USA
Penguin Group (Canada), 90 Eglinton Avenue East, Suite 700, Toronto, Ontario M4P 2Y3, Canada
(a division of Pearson Penguin Canada Inc.)
Penguin Books Ltd., 80 Strand, London WC2R 0RL, England
Penguin Group Ireland, 25 St. Stephen's Green, Dublin 2, Ireland (a division of Penguin Books Ltd.)
Penguin Group (Australia), 250 Camberwell Road, Camberwell, Victoria 3124, Australia
(a division of Pearson Australia Group Pty. Ltd.)
Penguin Books India Pvt. Ltd., 11 Community Centre, Panchsheel Park, New Delhi—110 017, India
Penguin Group (NZ), Cnr. Airborne and Rosedale Roads, Albany, Auckland 1310, New Zealand
(a division of Pearson New Zealand Ltd.)
Penguin Books (South Africa) (Pty.) Ltd., 24 Sturdee Avenue, Rosebank, Johannesburg 2196, South Africa

Penguin Books Ltd., Registered Offices: 80 Strand, London WC2R 0RL, England

This is a work of fiction. Names, characters, places, and incidents either are the product of the author's imagination or are used fictitiously, and any resemblance to actual persons, living or dead, business establishments, events, or locales is entirely coincidental. The publisher does not have any control over and does not assume any responsibility for author or third-party websites or their content.

MEGAN'S MARK

A Berkley Sensation Book / published by arrangement with the author

ISBN: 0-7394-6779-4
ISBN: 978-0-7394-6779-4

BERKLEY SENSATION®
Berkley Sensation Books are published by The Berkley Publishing Group,
a division of Penguin Group (USA) Inc.,
375 Hudson Street, New York, New York 10014.
BERKLEY SENSATION is a registered trademark of Penguin Group (USA) Inc.
The "B" design is a trademark belonging to Penguin Group (USA) Inc.

PRINTED IN THE UNITED STATES OF AMERICA

For Daddy, because you believed in me when no one else did. I miss you. And for Mom, because you always wanted to read whatever I wrote.

For Tony, because you made the dream possible.

To Roni, the best sister a Shadoe could ever have. You make me laugh even when I don't want to.

To Tracy, because you brighten the day. Just because you are you, and I love you for it.

And to all the ladies of the Forum. You keep me sane and you keep me laughing. Thank you.

But most especially to my CP. For the long hours, the midnight chats, and for reading a dozen copies of the same characters in different settings. Without you, I would never have finished.

✦ P R O L O G U E ✦

They were created, not born. They were trained, not raised. They weren't meant to be free, to laugh, to play or to love. They were men and women whose souls had been forged in the fires of hell.

Jonas Wyatt stared at the files in front of him, the reports of the Breeds and their mates; men and women who had found something unique. A Mating unlike anything most humans could know or understand. One that may very well turn world opinion against them now.

They were Breeds. Genetic alterations that had somehow found the grace of God, or whatever deity existed. They had survived, not just the genetic alterations, but also the cruelties their creators had heaped upon them for de-cades.

The Genetics Council.

He ran his fingers over his short, military-cut hair and breathed out roughly as the tattoo on his scalp tingled beneath the short spikes of his hair. F2-07. His lab designation

and birth ranking that the Genetics Council had assigned
to him.

The Genetics Council had been created nearly a century
ago, a group of the greatest scientific, biological, physiolog-
ical and genetic experts in the world at that time. They had
funded the first Lab, started the first experiments. Monsters
with no conscience, no remorse and no compassion.

He grimaced as he pushed himself from his chair and
stalked to the wide window on the other side of his office.
There, he stared out onto the perfect, precise lawn of the
federal building the Bureau of Breed Affairs was located in.

He pushed his hands into the pockets of his slacks, staring at the image he cast in the glass. Military straight, his
shoulders thrown back, the silk gray slacks and white dress
shirt hung comfortably on his broad frame. He didn't look
out of place. On a good day, he didn't feel out of place.

Today wasn't a good day.

Below, traffic eased along the street next to the perfectly
manicured lawns and the wrought iron fence. Carefully
tended trees dotted the lawn, small white cement benches
sat in the lazy shade they cast. Summer was blooming across
the landscape, causing waves of heat to pour from the side-
walks and streets beyond.

The capital was as brisk as ever, the political mire he
had been traversing so effectively in the past months no
thicker than it ever had been. But he could feel it pulling at
him now in ways it hadn't before, tugging at his loyalties,
reminding him of his limitations. He didn't like being reminded of those.

He was a Breed himself. Two hundred and fifty pounds,
six feet, six inches of solid Lion Breed muscle and honed
instincts. He had been created to kill, not to negotiate. But
he had learned early in life the fine art of politics, of maneuvering, of lying within the truth. He had learned it so
well that he had taken to this position with an ease almost

worthy of concern. Was he what he had fought to escape?
A monster living as a man?

Perhaps he was.

The Lion Breeds had been the first created. The male
sperm and female ovum selected had come from strong,
fierce bloodlines. American Indian—mostly Apache or
Navajo—Irish, Scots, German. The list sometimes seemed
never ending. Once chosen, they had been altered. Gene-
ticists had thought they had finally isolated the DNA that
controlled certain aspects of behavior or weakness. Human
weakness was replaced with animal strength and instincts.
Exceptional hearing, sense of smell and primal awareness.
Advanced strength, endurance and muscular perfection.

They had created what they believed was the perfect
disposable soldier. And then they began to train them.
From birth they knew no love, no compassion. They were
tested, experimented upon, pushed to the limits of the
spirit and then beyond.

He ran his hands over his face, remembering the cruelties, the horrors of the Labs. Breeds killed for the slightest
infractions, abused to the point that many died screaming
in agony, their blood staining the hard stone floors of the
Labs. What they did to the men was bad enough. What they
did to the women . . .

Jonas shook his head, spun from the window and paced
back to his desk where he threw himself into the chair.

A century of hell was now behind the Breeds. And if he
wasn't extremely careful, they would all be thrown back
into it. The Feline Breeds, the Wolves, the small majority
of Coyotes who had managed to retain the humanity science had attempted to remove from their genetics.

The Lion Breeds were the forerunners. Their Pride
Leader, Callan Lyons, had opened the door to freedom
more than seven years ago with his Mating to Merinus Tyler, the daughter of an influential journalist and newspaper

owner. Of all the species, the Lions numbered highest, though those numbers were pitiful in the extreme. All totaled, all Breed species, there were less than a thousand.

And Nature, though kind in her determination that they would survive, had created a problem that could well see them all exterminated.

Mating.

He picked up the file sent that morning from Sanctuary, the results of the latest tests on the Mated pairs. There were under a dozen. And all those consisted of Breed and human.

Procreation was complicated, involving periods of sexual heat and, for the females, debilitating need. Felines conceived easily, but the results of those conceptions would be unknown for years to come. What was known was the result of the Matings.

Neither male nor female, Breed nor human had aged so much as a day once the hormones that bound them were balanced within their bodies.

Callan and Merinus had Mated seven years before and physically, their bodies had yet to show the stress of those additional years.

The Breeds were screwed if knowledge of this leaked into the general public. He could hear the Blood Supremacists screaming now, demanding their incarceration, their separation from the general public.

And to add to the problem, they had a disappearance at Sanctuary. A Breed couple suspected of having Mated, the female of which Jonas had been very interested in.

As he stared at the file, a slight knock on the oak door separating his office from his assistant echoed through the dark-paneled room.

He lifted his head as the door opened and his assistant, Mia, stepped in, closing the panel behind her.

"Senator Cooley is here to see you about the National Breed Registry, Mr. Wyatt." Her lips lifted in a little snarl, a short incisor gleaming briefly. "Should I tell him you aren't in?"

Mia's opinion of the National Registry was well known. The Breeds had been fighting it for months. The private registry held within Jonas's office was all that was needed for now.

"You can send him in." He laid the file on the desk as he leaned back in his chair. "And Mia, I need all the information you can pull on Mark and Aimee. Cross-check them against other Breeds for any shared assignments or tests as well as non-Breed contact."

"Yes sir. I'll get on that now. You also have lunch at one o'clock with Senator Tyler and his brother, and a cocktail party tonight at Drey Hampton's. Neither appointment can be canceled."

Jonas nodded; Mia was as competent at her job as he was at his. "Send Cooley in and get Braden Arness on the phone the minute the senator leaves. I have a job for him."

She nodded briskly before turning and stepping smartly back into her own office.

Jonas pulled the file on the Bill for Breed Registry free from the others on his desk and opened it casually. He had no intentions of agreeing to any part of it, but sometimes . . . Sometimes it was better to play the game.

He looked up as Senator Cooley entered the room, middle-aged, his naturally narrow eyes and sharp nose gave the appearance of a rat. A thin smile stretched across the senator's face, pretending to be jovial, to be comfortable.

Jonas contained a weary sigh. Another game. Another lie. And he knew, to survive, the lies could never end.

· CHAPTER I ·

SOUTHERN NEW MEXICO, 2023

Evanescence was blaring from the speakers of the four-wheel drive Range Raider, the new wave of law enforcement vehicles specially built for the rugged desert terrain. The gentle rock of the vehicle, attributed to the separate suspension on each tire, allowed it to traverse the terrain easily and was also a soothing comfort when added to the pulse-pounding music flowing through the interior.

The music was old, but it fit her mood. Dark, filled with energy and a quest for life. But beneath the beat, Megan Fields could feel threads of emotion weaving around her, pricking at her mind. Others' emotions, someone else's pain. The empathic talents she possessed were her curse; the desert was usually her salvation. Until now. Now the two had somehow managed to collide.

Desert patrol was never fun, and only on the odd occasions did it become dangerous. She knew that. It was the perfect area for the criminal element. Easily crossed and nearly impossible for law enforcement to adequately patrol, it was the perfect habitat for the two-legged variety of scavengers that preyed on innocent human beings.

Megan Fields ignored the music blaring around her as she adjusted the dark glasses that protected her eyes from the blazing sun and surveyed the land around her. Stark, with a blend of russets, golden-hued browns and darker tans with intermittent splashes of green, the land seemed empty, broken, forgotten.

Sometimes she wondered if she was the only one who could see the beauty in the land that surrounded her. The caverns hidden in shadowed buttes, the small, well-hidden areas of grassy splendor. It was a wonderland, secreted away amid the brush and bramble that first caught the eye.

And if she wasn't mistaken, she just might have company in her desert wonderland. She could feel the snaking sensations of disturbance tightening her skull, sending tension racing through her body.

She braked at the edge of a deep gully, her eyes narrowed at the tire tracks that led into it. They were fairly recent, cutting deep into the sandy soil, like a wound carelessly inflicted. A chill raced over her flesh at the sight of it, cutting through the peace that had previously filled her.

She turned her gaze to the report log scrolling across the small screen to the right of the steering wheel. There was a report of a missing hiker from Carlsbad, various APBs and stolen vehicles.

She scratched at the top of her nose thoughtfully before muting the music and flipping down the microphone that was attached to the transistor at her ear.

She couldn't ignore it. Adrenaline pulsed through her, heightening the already sensitive receptors in her brain. Something was in the gully. Something she could battle, could face without the presence of others. A chance to still the restless, driving energy that rarely had an outlet.

"Control, I'm at Gully B-4. There are signs of recent passage heading into it. Do you have a mark on any vehicles in or out?"

"Negative, Fields," Lenny Blanchard, satellite stats officer and general gopher answered with a lazy drawl. "We have no tracked movement in or out for the past month. GPS shows your vehicle only."

She tapped her fingers on the steering wheel, her lips in a thoughtful pout as she stared at the tracks.

It wasn't unusual for owners to disengage their GPS unless they wanted to use it, though it was heavily frowned upon and in certain areas could result in high fines. This was one of those areas.

Danger almost shimmered in the waves of heat that drifted over the vehicle.

Making up her mind quickly, she exited the Raider, moving to the front of it and bending down to inspect the tire tracks more closely. They cut deep into the ground, the off-road tires leaving a distinctive mark as they made their way down the steep slope into the narrow valley below.

She reached out, her fingers brushing over the tracks as she tried to focus on the impressions coming from them. Fear. Determination. She could feel the emotions from inside the vehicle on the impressions in the loose sand and dirt.

Staring at the area, she moved farther to the right, her fingers running over the edge of another print. Mountain boots. Someone had followed the vehicle in on foot. And they weren't there for the scenery either.

She rubbed at her chin, frowning as she tried to remember the lessons her grandfather had given her in tracking as a young girl. The tracks were at the least twenty-four hours old, no more than forty-eight. The mountain boots were more recent, within the past eight to ten hours.

She tilted her head then, her eyes narrowing at the lack

of emotion or sensation that came from touching the tracks. They were calm, centered. As though whoever made them had known no fear, no anger, no emotion as they made their way into the gully.

"Control, I'm heading in to investigate," she announced as she rose and moved back to her vehicle. "There's evidence of someone following on foot. It could be our missing hiker from Area Two."

"That's miles away, Fields," Lenny pointed out. "A good two-day hike."

"Yeah, but who the hell knows with some of these greenhorns." She sighed as she closed the door and attached her seat belt once again. "I'll check it out before heading home. Fields, out."

She engaged the vehicle's rough-terrain drive with a flip of the switch before heading down the steep incline into the sluicing path made by the millions of flash floods that had traversed it over the centuries.

Maneuvering slowly, she kept her eyes narrowed for signs of the vehicle or the hiker. The wide gully split into several smaller tributaries, some leading to secret caves that flooded easily during the rainy season, others cutting a course in the land before slowly narrowing to dead ends.

This gully was deeper than most, the steep walls easily reaching ten to fifteen feet above the sandy base. Rock houses and deep craters had been cut into the walls, proof of the incredible force of the water that had gouged a path into the gully. Through the center of it, the tire tracks continued until they disappeared around a steep bend.

Megan watched the curve as she approached it slowly. She could feel a building sense of danger as she drew closer, of something not right. The sun seemed too bright, the heat radiating off the hood of the Raider too intense. All her senses suddenly kicked in and spiked in strength. Wariness filled her, as did the sense of impending doom.

Rounding the curve, she braked slowly, staring at the black SUV sitting silently beneath the golden rays of the sun.

Damn. This wasn't exactly what she had expected.

The vehicle, while not as desert-friendly as her own, was definitely built for off-road maneuvering. The heavy, terrain-cutting tires were made to aid in pulling the vehicle from muddy or sandy ground. At least, when they weren't flat, as these tires were.

She looked across the gully walls, eyes narrowed against the sun as she enabled the Raider's vehicle security. The hum and vibration of the tire protectors sliding into place, along with the energized bulletproof shielding, accompanied the rapid beat of her heart.

Death. She sensed it now.

"Fields, we show security engaged on your vehicle. Are you in trouble?" Lenny's voice was suddenly alert.

"Negative, Control. Not yet, anyway," she answered as she checked her field gun, sliding an extra clip of ammo into her vest as she disengaged her seat belt. "I found the vehicle. It appears abandoned, all tires flattened, windows shattered. I'm going in for a closer look."

She breathed in deeply, fighting to block the remnants of horror that pulsed through the gully. Death. Her chest clenched, her lungs aching as she forced air into them, fighting past the pure grief that rolled over her.

I failed . . . She flinched at the sudden random emotion that drifted to her. It wasn't her thought, nor her failure, but she felt it pierce her soul.

This was why she hid in the desert. Because of this curse, she wasn't safe to work with, nor to work around. Because of what she felt now, she knew she could never do the work she had always dreamed of. The empathic abilities fractured her attention, drew her so deeply into the morass of emotions that flowed from others that her concentration and her control began to crumble.

She breathed in harshly, determined to push back the

pain and rage of another's emotions as she attempted to find the reason why it existed.

"Negative, Fields." The voice of her cousin, Sheriff Lance Jacobs, came over the receiver. "Get out of that gully and await reinforcements. All copters are out of range and unable to assist. I'll head out with Crawford now."

Megan snorted. She could hear the demand in his voice.

"I'm not the meter maid, boss," she drawled. "Regardless of your attempts to make me one. The tracks into the gully are at best twenty-four hours old. Whatever happened here is done and gone."

She hoped.

She activated the display board on her windshield, watching for signs of life within the gully. She couldn't trust her senses now; they were too flooded with the rage and pain that flowed from the vehicle in front of her. But she had a feeling she really wasn't alone.

"Display shows the gully clear of life signs. I'm going to do an initial investigation while I wait on you."

His curse was muffled, his frustration wasn't. He knew the problems she had experienced during training at the Law Enforcement Academy, just as he knew that it was the reason she had returned home rather than taking one of the offers from the larger cities that had come her way.

"Proceed with extreme caution, Megan," he warned her. "I don't like the feel of this."

Neither did she.

She stepped out of the vehicle, cocking her head at the silence of the gully. It was as though all life had deserted the area. Normally it would be filled with the whisper of birds' wings, small wildlife and insects fighting for food and survival. This gully was one of the few arcas that managed to retain moisture within the small caverns the water had carved from it. There should be life here.

There was only death.

A peculiar, horrifying stench filled the air as well. The smell of death wrapped around her, thick and filled with menace in the late afternoon stillness. She felt the tension thicken, and it wasn't just her own.

"Lance, it stinks here." She heard her own voice tremble as she stared at the SUV gleaming beneath the hot sun.

Her chest tightened as she glimpsed the presence of two bodies through the heavily tinted, mostly shattered glass.

"Goddamn, Megan. Get the hell out of there." Lance hissed, his voice heavy with dread.

Chills raced over her scalp, her shoulders, tightening her muscles as she pushed back the sensations and fought to get a better grip on what was there.

Releasing the light field Wounder from the holster at her hip, she held it confidently, her senses rioting and sending adrenaline coursing through her as she walked to the vehicle.

Damn, she wished she had a real weapon, rather than the Wounder used for lighter duty such as patrol. It only slowed down a criminal rather than incapacitating him. Its greatest plus was its extended range. One of its drawbacks was the inability to predict its effect in any given situation.

"The vehicle is riddled with bullet holes. We have at least two dead," she spoke into the microphone, relaying the information she found to the control center.

The windows of the SUV were punctured with bullets. The tires had been ripped apart by them; the cliffs rising from the gully were scoured with ammunition damage. The smell of death surrounded the area, the heat and carnage inside the vehicle twisted her gut as she surveyed the scene.

"Definitely two dead," she reported as she stepped back. "God, Lance, their mothers couldn't identify them." The bullets had torn through their upper bodies, ripping away much of their facial features.

"Megan, get back to the Raider now!" Lance ordered, his voice edged with steel.

She could feel the hairs along her nape standing on end as her spine began to tingle. Turning slowly, her gaze narrowed on the high gully walls as adrenaline rushed through her system and her senses began to riot. Someone was watching her.

"Infrared showed no signs of life . . ." she mused out loud. Somehow, something had interfered with the system's readings, because she knew someone, something, was out there.

She could feel the eyes watching her, malevolence following her.

Her finger tightened on the trigger of her weapon as she felt the danger intensify. Where? Where was it coming from? She could feel it watching her, tracking every move she made, yet the sensors in the vehicle showed no signs of life.

"I'm heading back," she agreed. "Something's messed up on the Raider, Lance. Check it out. It showed no life signs . . ."

Lance was cursing, screaming at Lenny to find the copters, to get his unit ready to roll. Backup. Yeah, she needed backup now.

Megan could feel the eyes trained on her. Even worse, she could feel the weapons.

She backed up, her eyes scanning the gully as her heart raced in her chest. Her mouth felt dry, her body tense with the need to turn and run.

She was halfway to the Range Raider when she felt the first shots being taken. She could actually feel the malicious energy pouring over her a second before she threw herself across the gully toward one of the small caverns that had been cut into the wall.

Violence exploded through the air. Bullets tore into the sandy ground, moving like lightning across the gully and taking chunks from the rock wall of the entrance of the cavern she had thrown herself into.

"Megan. Megan, report." Lance was yelling in her ear as she plastered herself against the dubious safety of a small indentation the water had cut into the side of the wall, keeping her body well away from the entrance.

"At least two," she snapped into the mic, keeping her eyes trained on the entrance and the sliver of outside she could see from her position. "How far away did you say the copters were?"

"I said they were too fucking far away." Lance snarled furiously. "Dammit, Megan, we're too far away from you."

Yeah. She remembered now. Damn. That sucked.

Holding her weapon ready, she moved carefully to peer around the protection of the groove in the wall to get a sense of the movement outside the cavern. She ducked back just in time to save her head as the bullets ripped around her once again.

"Give me an idea of what's going on. We're heading out there but we're at least an hour away."

She could hear the force of his breath behind his words, proof that he was running from the control center and heading to his vehicle.

An hour.

Boy, she was so screwed.

"I'm holed up in a small cavern. I have at least one assailant in clear view of the entrance keeping me hemmed in. I can't tell what's going on outside though." She swallowed tightly. "Lance, I'm not going to make it an hour."

Chills raced over her flesh, a premonition of increasing danger as the air thickened around her, growing heavier, hotter. Time seemed to stand still, to creep by at a turtle's pace. So much could happen in an hour.

Over the receiver, voices raged in the background, the sound of tires screaming as vehicles roared.

"Stay put!" She winced at the fury in Lance's voice. "Keep your weapon aimed at the entrance and fucking stay the hell where you are."

"Yeah, that was my intention," she answered as she breathed in roughly. "What the hell is going on out here, Lance? Why stick around after the killing?"

It didn't make sense. Whoever killed that couple should have been long gone, not waiting around to see who found the bodies.

And why hadn't she sensed the killers? She should have felt them, even if the sensors hadn't picked them up.

"Well, why don't you just ask them, Miss Nosy?" Lance snarled through the mic. "Dammit, I told you to turn back. Didn't I tell you to turn back?" Cousins. They were always saying "I told you so."

"Yeah, well, you tell me to go to sit tight and look pretty, too. Since when did I start listening to you?" Sweat rolled down her back as the need to move tightened her muscles. Bullets tore through the entrance again as she flattened herself further against the wall and tried to become one with the stone. Dammit, all she needed was a little bit more room.

"Shit." She wheezed. "Those were close. Hell, Lance, I really wish you would hurry."

She screeched as bullets ripped through the entrance again, hitting lower to the ground, spraying sand at her feet as she tried to crawl up the wall to prevent the deadly projectiles from tearing into her feet.

"Your girl needs to be spanked, Lance." The strange, arrogant voice coming through the receiver made her stiffen in shock as a tense silence suddenly filled the line.

Calm. Centered. There were no riotous emotions pouring over her as she heard the voice, no impressions of past pains or lost dreams. There was just an unbroken circle of peace.

She latched onto it. Felt it weaving around her, sensed the nearness of the voice despite the sardonic amusement within it.

"Where are you, Braden?" Lance sounded frantic as

Megan dodged another volley of shots. Whoever was out there had obviously moved for a better angle into the shallow cavern. The bullets were coming closer to her, tearing chunks out of the wall and pelting more sharp projectiles of stone.

"Close enough." The rough, growling tone of his voice sent shivers up her spine as she pushed herself closer to the stone at her back.

"If you're close enough then take a shot, dammit." She covered her face with her arm as more shots rang out, sending a rain of rocks exploding around her head.

Stooping, she leveled her weapon and fired twice into the gully toward the estimated position of her assailant before she threw herself to the other side of the wall and watched in horror as the wall where she had been standing took five hard bursts of gunfire.

Okay, that was about as close to death as she ever wanted to come.

"Politeness counts, baby." The humor in his voice almost had her lips twitching in response as she moved farther into the cavern. "Say please."

Shock washed through her system as a chuckle sounded through the earphone.

"Please?" she questioned furiously, her amusement quickly dissipating.

"There you go. See, that didn't hurt a bit, did it?"

She screeched as hard arms suddenly surrounded her from out of the darkness and the voice blew a breath of air across her ear.

Her elbow slammed back into a hard-packed abdomen as she attempted to hook her foot around his ankle and throw him off balance. All she got in reward was a sudden tightening of his arms and the breath whooshing from her chest.

Adrenaline surged through her like fireworks out of control. He was holding her, restraining her. Shock, fear, and the overwhelming instinct to survive were all she knew at that moment.

For the first time in her life, the emotions of others, the frustrations, fears and angers of those around her weren't flooding her brain. Only the need to survive.

"Settle down. The cavalry's here. Or a version of it, anyway." His soft laughter did nothing to still the rush of fear and the instinctive need to fight.

"Can you extract?" She was only distantly aware of Lance barking the question into the headset.

"Can and will, if she would stop fighting me like a little wildcat." She was lifted off her feet as the dark male voice deepened. "You have a claim on her, Jacobs? I think I might like to keep her."

Keep her? What the hell, was she a trophy now? She grunted as she tried to elbow him again, fought to throw him off balance.

"Get her the hell out of there. You want to risk the second, it's your head. We're on our way."

"Let me go." Satisfaction filled her when she finally managed to land a blow that caused him to tense, his hold weakening enough for her to tear away and turn on him.

Dark amber eyes stared back at her, the color intensifying in the shadowed expanse of the cavern.

Calm. It wrapped around her, soothing the ragged edge of her own nerves as it forced her to center herself.

"If you're going to shoot, hurry up and do it." A growl seemed to linger in his voice as white teeth flashed in a sun-darkened face. "Otherwise, we're going to be hamburger meat if we don't get to my Raider before they get to us."

She could hear the voices outside the cavern now. Obviously more than one, and getting closer.

She lowered her gun, breathing harshly as control slowly returned.

"I don't think I like you," she snapped as he turned and began leading the way through a dark, nearly hidden crevice

in the rock wall, the kind often formed when one of the tributaries of water cracked through the weaker portions of
the caverns. It was barely wide enough to make their way
through, deep and dark, stifling hot. Its confines wrapped the
scent of man around her rather than death.

And oh boy, did he smell good. Dark and male, and like
the land itself, hot and hard and rich with life. She liked that
smell. Too damned much. Because suddenly it wasn't the
danger following them that filled her; rather, it was the scent
of the man ahead of her and the sensual forks of sensation
it sent careening through her body. He made her think of
sex.

"Good. Conflict just makes life more interesting."

He was insane. She loved it. She could feel her heartbeat racing with the danger, adrenaline heightening her
senses, surging through her with a natural high that almost
made her giddy.

They moved quickly and within minutes the slender
threads of sunlight began lighting their way.

"We're out," Braden announced as they moved through
the entrance and ran to his Raider parked just in front of it.

"We're on our way," Lance replied. "Get her out of
there . . ."

"No!" She turned on the brawny, wild creature that
jumped into the driver's side of the Raider as she turned in
the passenger's seat.

For whatever reason she could no longer feel the rage,
the need to kill, the terror and the fear that had echoed from
the valley. With the arrival of this man, and the calm that
seemed to reach out from him like a shield that blocked
those jarring emotions, she was centered once again.

"I can do this." She needed to fight. To prove to herself
she could. "We can't afford to let them get away. They
killed, and they were waiting for me. We need to know
why."

He turned, his oddly colored eyes reflecting amused approval as a crooked grin tilted his hard, sensual lips.

"Let's get them then . . ."

"Hell no," Lance all but screamed then. "Damn you, Braden, get her the hell out of there."

She continued to watch Braden as he looped a length of leather around his long, tawny-gold hair and tied it at his nape.

"Megan Fields." She extended her hand as excitement poured through her.

"Braden Arness." His grip was strong, firm. It sent a pulse of energy whipping through her arm, echoing along her body. But there were none of the riotous emotions coming from him that she felt from others. Emotions that normally left her drained, unable to think clearly. She felt the remnants of the earlier violence dissipating, the horror of a death not her own easing, as though the calm he projected extended to those around him.

"Braden, she's not experienced enough. Get her back to Control," Lance ordered again. "We can handle this."

Braden's eyes narrowed as he watched her. Casually he disconnected reception by flipping the mic up while his eyes stared into hers.

"Do you like to live dangerously?" His eyelids lowered, a hungry, almost sexual expression crossing his face.

A smile trembled on her lips as she flipped her mic back as well. "I live for it."

Braden turned in his seat, revved the Raider's powerful motor and took off. No seat belts, no word of warning as he turned the wheel sharply, sending the Raider skidding along the sandy ground as it headed back toward the gully.

"Wheel protectors and bullet shield engaged." She activated the security settings before checking her weapon and lowering the window at her side.

The bullets would clear the security field with no problem, but anything shot into it would explode harmlessly before touching the vehicle. Most of the time, anyway.

"Wrong weapon."

Megan turned, her eyes widening as Braden reached to the floorboard between the bucket seats and pulled an automatic, laser-guided rifle forward. "Try this one."

Illegal to the max.

She loved it.

She opened her mind to the calm that reached out from him, centering on it, letting it merge with her own fragile shields and finding it easier than she could have imagined as she tested the weight of the weapon he handed her.

The trim-line, fully automatic laser-guided rifle fired a deadly accurate blast that left a hole in a man the size of the Grand Canyon.

As with the man, even the weapons he owned carried no residue of violence or rage. They were tools, nothing more.

"Dead men don't shoot back, sweetheart," he reminded her as she cast him a gimlet stare.

"Lance will shoot us both." She grinned in delight.

"Yeah, but his bullets don't kill." He grunted. "Damned police-issue crap. What happened to the good ole days?"

She turned, bracing the rifle's barrel on the window as they sped around the curve into the gully where her own Raider sat. Gunfire blasted against their shields.

"Three o'clock." He yelled out the position. "Give 'em hell."

Her finger tightened on the trigger as she further braced the rifle against her shoulder, allowing the weapon to pound against her as she held the trigger back and sliced an arrow of death through the gully wall.

Bullets ricocheted off the shield as they passed, a second before she saw the first body fall.

"One down." She let off the trigger, throwing herself

against the seat as Braden threw the vehicle into another turn for the second pass.

"Second one is on the run. There he is." Rather than pulling up the heat-seeking radar on the windshield, he pointed to where a shadow moved along a crevice at the top of the wall. "Are you going to wound or wipe?" Kill or capture.

"Wound. I want answers." She pulled her own weapon free. "Let's roll."

Exhilaration pumped through her as the tires bit into the ground and the vehicle shot down the expanse of the gully. She aimed, watching the laser sight on the weapon carefully.

"Get your eyes off that damned light." Braden snarled. "Use your gut. Let it tell you when to shoot. Those laser guides are for sissies."

She licked her dry lips nervously, took a deep breath and watched the assailant as he ran. She lifted the weapon a bit higher than the sight called for, letting her senses explode, reaching out to the weapon as her Navajo grandfather had taught her to rather than depending on the sights as her training had.

She fired the first shot, cursing silently as the bullet bounced away harmlessly just above her target's head. Quickly adjusting, she fired again, twice in rapid succession, and watched with a sense of satisfaction as the sniper shooting at her fell.

"Get ready." The Raider turned, slammed to a stop, and Braden exploded from the vehicle to secure him.

"Dammit, that was dirty pool." Megan raced out behind him. "I took him down, I get to cuff him."

A roar exploded from Braden's throat as he struggled with the assailant, who was growling with feral intensity. She stood back in shock, horrified as she watched the curved fangs flash at the side of the assailant's mouth a second before they sank into Braden's shoulder.

Braden's fist slammed into the side of his head, a furious roar leaving his chest as wicked, long canines were revealed by the animalistic snarl on his lips.

They were both Breeds.

Suddenly, the man who had been her co-conspirator in adventure was a primal, unknown threat. Discounting the fact that Braden seemed to know Lance, she couldn't be certain that even her cousin knew the man she faced now.

Shock transfixed her as she backed away, eyes wide, weapon raised. Braden's fist landed in the undefended underbelly of the shooter, taking his breath before Braden landed another hard blow to the face and then delivered an incapacitating strike to the vulnerable neck.

It was powerful enough to knock the other man unconscious. Powerful enough to send a pulse of terror pounding through her as she flipped her mic down. She reactivated the receiver at her ear as she leveled her weapon on Braden. He was powerful enough that the next blow he was drawing back for might very well kill the only thing alive capable of telling her what had happened here.

"Step away from him," she ordered, raising her voice above the animalistic growl rumbling from his chest. It would have been sexy if it didn't sound so damned dangerous. "Now."

She couldn't afford to trust him. She couldn't sense Braden, couldn't read him as she could others. And suddenly, she wasn't so certain that he wasn't the enemy as well.

"Megan? Megan? Is that you? Thank God!" Lance was screaming in her ear. "We're headed your way in a private chopper, ETA five minutes. What's your situation?"

She ignored his frantic questions.

"I thought you liked to live dangerously?" The canines flashed again as a growl rumbled from Braden's chest and he began to walk toward her.

Megan fired at his feet, causing him to come to a dead

stop as he stared back at her in surprise. His brow lifted mockingly.

"I wouldn't come any closer if I were you," she warned him firmly.

He flipped his mic down.

"Lance, your girl doesn't want to believe I'm one of the good guys. Reassure her, huh?"

Braden was laughing. The son of a bitch was staring at her and laughing. No anger, no rage, no desire for retaliation against her. "Sometime before she puts a hole in my toe." She aimed higher. "Or somewhere more important."

She felt his amusement. It eased around her like a caress as she breathed in deeply, forcing herself to release the edge of calm she had allowed herself to tap into. His calm.

"Do you two think this is fun and games time?" Lance was screaming as the sound of the chopper coming in from the distance could be heard. "Megan, if you shoot him, I'm going to tan your hide for sure. You'll never get out of booking. Do you hear me? Pull back, dammit."

She kept her gun leveled on him. Fine, Lance trusted him, but did her cousin know who and what they were dealing with here?

"The situation here is contained," she reported. "But I think I'll play it a bit safe and keep Puss in Boots in my sights until you get here."

Braden's eyes narrowed at the nickname as silence filled the receiver, confirming her suspicion that he was indeed a Lion Breed. Coyote fangs held a hard curve; the Lion Breeds' were straighter. He might not be the enemy, but he wasn't exactly safe either.

Lance groaned a second later. "Megan, sweetheart, you are digging yourself into a hole you won't be able to pull yourself out of here."

If the way Cat-boy was looking at her was any indication,

she already had. Anger swirled in the golden depths of his eyes as he flipped the mic up and crossed his arms over his impressively broad chest.

She didn't feel the anger though. It wasn't whipping at her head, shredding her nerves. It was contained within him. Damn, she really could have grown to like him. Maybe.

"You do like to live dangerously then." The rough timbre of his voice sent a chill up her spine. "Next time, I'll let you tangle with the Coyotes and I'll find a nice place to sit and watch."

"Yeah, you do that." She refused to let the gun waver so much as an inch.

She could feel the tension in the air, despite his apparent casual stance. He was waiting on an opening, watching her for a weakness. And she could feel it, feel his readiness consuming her, pounding through her blood.

It was exciting rather than painful. Exhilarating when it should have been terrifying.

He shook his head in mock sadness, the deceptively lazy stance of his powerful body almost deceiving her into relaxing her guard. Jeans loosely molded his powerful thighs, a gray T-shirt hugged his broad chest. He was a walking sex machine and the glitter of his unusual eyes showed her he knew it.

"We were making a great team." He sighed as the sound of the helicopter grew louder. "It's too bad, Megan. I was finally starting to have fun."

He jumped for her. Damn. No warning, no thought, no impression of what he was going to do before he did it. He just did it.

The gun flew from her hand as she hit the ground, the breath whooshing from her body as his heavier length covered her, heated her.

"Later baby." He nipped her ear before jumping to his feet and racing for his Raider. A second later, dust enveloped her as he sped through the gully and disappeared around a bend. The sound of the helicopter grew closer.

Geez, could this day get much worse?

WASHINGTON, D.C.

Senator Macken Cooley frowned in displeasure as the cell phone vibrated in his jacket pocket, forcing him to take his attention from the statutes of Breed Law he was currently reviewing. The mandates that governed the new species and gave them their special rights were a thorn in his side. They were creatures. They weren't animal or human; they deserved no rights.

As the special, secured cell phone continued to vibrate, he jerked it from his jacket pocket with a grimace that turned to a look of interest when he saw the number on the caller ID.

"Yes?"

"Arness was there," a low voice spoke into the phone. "Megan Fields has taken out one of the hunters and captured the other."

Braden Arness was becoming the problem he had predicted to the Genetics Council. He smirked at the ire in the voice on the phone, wishing he knew who his contact was; he would love to imagine the expression that went with the voice at the moment. He didn't sound pleased.

"I warned you it wouldn't be so easy." He couldn't help but gloat. "She doesn't hide in that desert because she doesn't know what she's doing."

He had tried to warn the Genetics Council of this when they decided to take the matter out of his hands. They didn't know the girl or her family as he did. Their special psychic powers would make it practically impossible to ambush one of them, especially Megan Fields. Her empathic abilities were stronger than most, harder to control, but definitely impressive.

"We're turning over two units to you, Senator," the voice rasped. "They're ex–Navy SEALs and dedicated to our cause. Don't mess up. We won't try to cover you if you're caught. You're on your own."

"And if I succeed?" He could feel his cock stiffening at the thought of the control he would soon have over the delicate little Megan.

"If you succeed, you'll advance to the next position," the voice promised. "If you fail, you'll die."

He wouldn't fail. And advancement within the Genetics Society was his ultimate goal. He craved the power that would come with the position of a section leader. One of the few that commanded their own units of Coyote soldiers. The spies would come to him then, their lives would be in his control. The thought of that power was almost orgasmic.

As the phone connection was severed, he allowed anticipation to begin building within him.

He didn't see the Breeds as human or as animal; they were creatures. Tools to be used and nothing more. And Megan, by sheer chance, would become no more than a pawn in his efforts to see the creatures placed once again where they belonged—within captivity.

He would play with Megan a bit first though, see if she was as good as her father had always claimed she was. He could take her out at any time, but he wanted to see her fight. He wanted to see her scared. And he wanted that damned arrogant Jonas Wyatt to come to the realization that the Breeds were nothing compared to the Council. Nothing compared to Senator Macken Cooley. Wyatt was always so arrogant, so sure of himself and his power. Mac would show him once and for all the reality of true power.

Of course, Wyatt would attempt to save Megan. He might even have her placed in Sanctuary. It wouldn't matter. No matter where she went, Mac knew his people could get to her. He wanted Wyatt to know that as well.

And maybe, just maybe before he killed little Megan, he would tell her why he had marked her for death. Not that she would remember at first. He knew her. Knew how her powers worked. David Fields, her father, had often confided in Mac as he worried for his daughter and her inability to process the empathic signals she received.

No, she wouldn't remember that night; not until he took her life. He would have her, and then he would kill her. But in the meantime, he could play, just a little bit. The thought had him smiling as he turned back to his research, his dedication renewed, his determination to find a way to destroy those damned Breeds energized. He would succeed.

· CHAPTER 2 ·

Damn, she made him hard. It was the first thought that
popped into Braden's mind the next morning when Megan
stepped into her cousin's office and stared at him with instant suspicion.

She was dressed in tight, sexy jeans tucked into calf-
high boots. A khaki shirt was buttoned just over the rise of
her breasts; a wide belt cinched her waist and held the holster for her police-issue Wounder that lay just behind her
left hip.

A fine film of perspiration dotted her brow as her dark
blue eyes gleamed with amusement and a spark of menace.
She would not be an easy woman to control, but he had already guessed that.

And she was aroused. That was his second thought. It
slammed into him as the subtle, unmistakable scent of
female heat reached his sensitive nostrils. He sat up
straighter at the scent, narrowing his eyes in complete pleasure so he could relish it.

Who had aroused her, though? The prick to his male pride suddenly had him frowning at her. She lifted her brow, her expression mocking.

He restrained his chuckle, just as he restrained the need to meet her challenge. One thing was for sure: It wouldn't be long before he had those pants off her ass and his cock seated snugly in that hot little pussy.

"You wanted to see me?" Megan prompted her cousin with a mocking lift of her brow as she closed the door behind her.

Braden turned his gaze back to Lance, quirking his brow when he caught the other man's less than pleased expression. Lance hadn't been thrilled by the order that came from his superiors, nor by the information Braden had given him on the Coyote's interrogation the night before. Not that much had come of that.

"Take a seat, Megan," Lance sighed.

Slouched back in his chair, his ankle propped on his knee, Braden turned his head once again to watch her walk across the office. She moved like a spring rain, smooth and silky. And damn if the smell of her didn't have his mouth watering.

"Okay, so here I am." She stopped at the desk, eyeing the chair beside Braden with no small amount of suspicion and a glint of humor as a smile was quickly controlled. "I don't want to sit next to him. He bites."

She crossed her arms over her breasts, nice, compact little breasts with just enough fullness to tempt him. Her mock frown informed him that yesterday's little adventure hadn't really angered her. Those winged black brows lowered over ocean blue eyes that looked deep enough to drown a man, and challenged at the same time. He loved a challenge.

"She shoots." He restrained his smile as he turned back to Lance and nodded in her direction. "I needed some sort of defense."

Lance wasn't amused. He wiped his hand over his face and muttered something about "damn stubborn women." Braden completely agreed with him.

"Why is he here? Don't we have enough problems to deal with?" she asked.

"Sit down, Megan," Lanced groused, obviously not in the mood for this little meeting. "Even if it means moving the chair."

She did just that. Braden smiled at her slowly, wickedly, as he watched a light flush color her bronzed flesh. The information he had on Megan had been as clear, concise and well put-together as Braden had come to expect from Jonas.

Her relationship with her cousin had been part of the report. It seemed she and Lance had been sniping at each other for months due to her insistence on taking the desert patrols rather than the safer assignments in town. But they were closer than most brothers and sisters, let alone cousins.

"I do have work to do today," she finally pointed out a bit impatiently when neither of them spoke.

"No, you don't." Lance sat forward then, bracing his arms on his desk as his frown darkened. "You're about to get exactly what you've been wanting for the past two years. Congratulations." He wasn't pleased, but Braden was already aware of that fact. Lance was madder than hell, not just at Braden and the Bureau of Breed Affairs, but also at Megan.

"Really?" she drawled in mocking amusement. "That's interesting. So, does this mysterious want of mine include a gun?" Evidently that was one argument she hadn't managed to win against her cousin. She hated the police-issue Wounder and had been harassing him to requisition a more powerful gun for her.

"Use one of your own," Lance harrumphed rudely. "You have enough of them, and since you're no longer on official duty, I can't stop you. Or use one of his. You seem to have done fine with it yesterday."

Megan cast Braden a look from the corner of her eye.

Braden gave her a smug, satisfied smile as her gaze moved fully to his. Finally, she turned back to her cousin rather than voicing the mocking retort he sensed lay on the tip of her very pretty tongue.

"Are you going to tell me what it is I'm getting? I have a lot of wants, you know. Or are you going to let Mr. Arness do your talking for you?"

Spicy. That's what she was. Just spicy as hell. He loved it.

He lifted his foot from his knee and set it slowly back on the floor before straightening in his chair. He never took his eyes off her, staring back at her intently, loving how she met his gaze and hid the nervousness he could feel growing inside her.

Sometimes the animal DNA he possessed came in damned handy. The natural empathic abilities easily picked up the emotions of those around him, filtered them and came across without the emotional impact on his own psyche that a normal person would experience. He knew what she was feeling, but he didn't feel it himself.

He growled, a deliberate, rough vibration that rumbled dangerously from his chest as he lowered his eyelids and let his gaze rake over her.

Heat flushed her face and he'd be damned if the soft, spicy-sweet smell of her sex didn't have him ready to jump her then and there. He wondered if she had glimpsed his hard-on. It would be damn hard to miss if her gaze slid down just an inch farther.

"Menace," she muttered, clearly not intimidated as she turned back to Lance. "Why is he here again? You haven't explained that one yet, Lance."

"Making my life hell," Lance grumbled as he flicked him an irritated glare.

Braden tilted his head in mocking acknowledgment.

"Fine, he can make your life hell and I can leave." Megan moved to rise from the chair.

"Sit down, Meg." Her cousin sighed then. "This involves you, too. Too much. Braden, as you know, is a Feline Breed. Lion, to be exact. His assignment here is a bit complicated."

"And involves me how?"

Before Lance could speak, Braden broke in.

"In the fact that the Breeds you found dead in that gully were here looking for you. As were the Coyotes. Would you like to explain that?" He tilted his head, watching her closely, sensing her confusion.

"Me?" She shook her head, staring back at him, perplexed. "Why would they be looking for me?"

"I was hoping you could answer that one."

"Lance, what's going on here?" she asked. A subtle scent almost of fear reached out to him, made him want to shield her, protect her.

"Our interrogation of the Coyote you wounded yesterday revealed they were here to kill Mark and Aimee . . . and you. They were to murder them in your area, where you would be drawn to them . . ." His choice of words had to be a mistake. "From there, they were to kill you, Megan."

She licked her lips nervously as she shook her head in denial. "But I didn't know them. I've never been in contact with Breeds or any part of the Council. Why target me? Why would they want me dead?"

Megan stared at Braden with the heavy weight of fear in her chest. She couldn't imagine why the Council would want her dead, or why two Breeds would have been searching for her. She hadn't been part of the Breed rescues, nor the investigations that had taken down the various Labs. She had left the Law Enforcement Academy and come straight home to her job within Lance's office.

"I was hoping you could tell me." Braden sat back in his

chair then, watching her with eyes that mesmerized and seemed to see too much, too easily.

"I don't know." She shook her head. She was confused. This couldn't have anything to do with her empathic abilities. It had to be something else.

"I'm here to find out why, then." His voice hardened, as did the amber glow of his eyes. "I've been placed with the sheriff's department to learn the reasons why our Breeds are dying here and what the Council wants from you. To do that, certain steps have to be taken."

Why did she have a feeling this was the kicker? She could see it in his eyes, hear it in his voice. And if that wasn't enough, her stomach was rioting with nerves, a sure sign that she was not going to like what was about to come.

"Such as?"

"A Rep." Satisfaction filled his voice. "I am required to live with, and to work with, a representative of the local law enforcement department. One who is aware of what I am, but will tell no one else. Since you are also part of the investigation, it's been decided by the sheriff and the Bureau of Breed Affairs, that you will be that Rep."

Oh, it was decided? As though she had no opinion? No say in how she was maneuvered?

"Oh, I don't think so." She came out of her seat, instantly rejecting that idea. There was not a chance in hell. "We have great motels here. Hell, Lance lives alone. Stay with him."

Braden rose slowly to his feet, and she just couldn't help it. She just couldn't help checking out those powerful, long legs encased in faded denim and sitting in dark, scratched leather boots. She jerked her gaze back to his, her face flaming at the knowing smirk on his lips. Not to mention the more than impressive bulge between his thighs.

"Lance isn't an option," he drawled. "You are the reason they are here. They won't stop until they kill you, Megan."

"Bull. Shit," she snarled. "If they wanted to kill me they

could have done so at any time. Your Coyote is lying to you, Braden. Have you thought of that?"

"I thought of it." He nodded slowly, that damned smile still in place. "I prefer to err on the side of caution. So, roomie, when do we head home?"

Megan turned slowly to Lance. Her cousin had been watching the argument silently, which wasn't like him. The look on his face wasn't comforting.

"Do something," she snapped.

"I did." He sighed, his look intent, determined. "I approved it."

Like hell.

"Then you can disapprove it." She could feel herself shaking, and knew she was making a mess of this meeting and she couldn't help it. "You can't make me let him live in my home, Lance."

Her response to Braden Arness was too strong, it went too deep. Every cell in her body was tuned to him, and she didn't like it. She didn't want it.

"Megan, sit back down." Lance sighed wearily as he stared up at her, his eyes, nearly the same blue as her own, darkened with worry.

"I don't want to sit down," she explained with mock patience. "And I definitely don't want that fang-toothed Neanderthal as a roommate."

She ignored the little growl, subtle and warning, that came from Braden. Just as she tried to ignore the fires that the sound set in her body.

"Your cousin has a sharp little tongue, Lance." The rumble in Braden's voice was deepening. "She's going to meet someone capable of dulling it, soon."

"That'll be the day," Lance grunted, appearing less than pleased at the subtle warning.

"Lance." Megan leaned forward, bracing her hands on his desk as she met his gaze. "We don't know him. He could be behind all this himself." Of course, she knew better. She could feel it. "How can you trust him far enough to order me to let him stay at my home?"

"Because those Coyotes are trying to kill you, Megan." Lance leaned forward, his voice guttural, filled with anger. "Because I'll be damned if I'll sit back and watch you walk into a fucking ambush. So get used to it. You can cooperate in this or I'll contact the family and we'll all move in with you. How does that one sound?"

She jerked upright. Contact the family? Her eyes widened at the threat, then narrowed furiously. It wasn't helping that she could tell Braden was enjoying every moment of the confrontation.

"Like hell." She tried to keep her voice reasonable as she cast Braden an accusing stare. She was definitely going to blame him for this.

She hadn't lived with anyone since she had left the Academy. She couldn't handle the emotions that vibrated between the walls from others, the resonation of nightmares, dreams, hopes and fears. And God knew, Braden had to have plenty of nightmares. And that was beside the fact that he made her jittery. Well, maybe jittery was the wrong word. Nervous, uncertain, not comfortable in her own skin. The thought of him was enough to arouse her, and the memory of that little nip to her ear was enough to set flares of sensation racing through her sex.

"Megan, what the hell is wrong with you?" She could tell Lance was as confused by her outbursts as she was. "You know you're not safe."

She flashed him a severe look. He knew what was wrong with her.

"I can't do it," she retorted, reminding him of the problems she had living with others, dealing with their fears, their emotions. "You know I can't."

His expression hardened. "You don't have a choice."

She turned on her heel and stalked to the door, refusing to argue the point further, refusing—period.

"Megan, dammit, come back here." Lance's anger was like a whip stinging her sensitive mind.

She shook her head as she gripped the doorknob, glancing back at the two men disdainfully.

"I don't think so." She smiled coldly. "Find him another bed. I don't have one free," she informed them with a calm she didn't feel before jerking the door open and fleeing the room.

She stomped the short distance to her own office, determined to collect what she needed before heading to the desert. Patrol was mostly boring as hell, but at least there she had a chance to calm her mind, to think logically. She really needed to think logically right now.

As she stepped into her office, without warning, she was pushed against the wall as the door slammed closed and a distinctive, warning growl sounded from the chest her face was currently pressed against.

Struggling didn't help. She tried to kick, to bite, to slap, and each move was countered until she stilled, silent, fighting to ignore an instinctive burning arousal that began flaming in the hungry depths of her pussy.

Son of a bitch. She wanted him. She stared up at him in realization, feeling a flush of pure pleasure racing over her flesh as he held her to him. Had she ever felt this? Ever known such intensity of sensation from so little?

"Finished now?" Braden's voice was calm, infuriatingly amused but tinged with dark hunger.

She refused to answer. He moved back enough to stare down at her. Megan refused to speak. If she did, she might have to do something stupid. Something irrational. Something guaranteed to get her into trouble. And . . .

He had a hard-on.

Her eyes widened in shock as she felt the thick wedge of flesh pressing against her lower stomach, hot and hard, and if she wasn't mistaken, more impressive than the bulge she had glimpsed the day before.

"Let. Me. Go." She forced the words from between her clenched teeth as her clit screamed in protest. She wanted to rub against him, feel her nipples raking his chest, and that just made her madder.

"You're not going to win." He held her arms behind her back with one broad hand, refusing to release her as he arched her closer. The other hand gripped her braid to pull her head back.

His eyes were dark gold, staring down at her with a latent sensuality that had her womb spasming and her sex creaming furiously.

Yes, she hated him. She did. She hated him bad.

"Don't bet on it." She narrowed her eyes, staring up at him furiously even as her body screamed with the pleasure of being so close to him. "I don't want or need you. And the next time you manhandle me, I'm going to shoot you."

His lips quirked in amusement.

"You try to shoot me, and I might have to bite you again." Her eyes widened in shock as his head lowered, his lips settling at her abused ear lobe to draw it into his mouth and lick it.

She jerked her head to the side, trying to slam it into his. Moving back, he chuckled, the sound rough and heated as he stared down at her once again.

"Keep your damned vampire teeth to yourself," she snapped. "And let me go or I'm going to scream bloody murder on your ass. This is called harassment, you know. Sexual harassment."

"Hmm, that's not sexual harassment, baby. When I decide to get sexual, trust me, you'll know it." He did let her go though. Slowly. Too damned slowly. "Now sit down and we'll talk this out." The latent warning in his tone caused her to tense.

"You talk it out." She drew herself up stiffly, staring back at him indignantly as the urge to scream became almost overwhelming. He had to be the most infuriating,

most stubborn man she had ever met in her life. "I am going to breakfast. A nice quiet breakfast. Without you. Then
I am going on patrol. Without you. I do not need your help.
I do not want it. Do you understand this?" Damned dimwit-
ted male that he was, he probably hadn't even heard her.

"We'll see if we can reset your schedule while we're at
it. For the moment, all patrols are out. Lance rescheduled
you for today, but I thought you might like to have some input on the rest of the week."

Shock shuddered through her. He was ignoring her, but
even worse, he had her schedule reset?

"You reset whatever the hell you want to." She snarled,
shaking, on the verge of a violence she had never imagined
herself capable of. She couldn't believe he was running
over her like this, or that Lance was allowing it. This was
her life, dammit. She had enough problems dealing with
the curse she fought daily. She did not need this. "I'm finished with you and my Benedict Arnold of a cousin. Go
sleep in his bed, because none of mine are free."

Before he could stop her, she jerked the door open and
stalked down the hall. Reset her schedule, did he? Canceled
her patrol, had he? Screw him. There was always something to do, even if it meant going home. She would be
damned if she would stand there and put up with his high-
handed attitude. No matter what her body wanted to do.

• C H A P T E R   3 •

Megan knew she was in trouble. She wasn't stupid; she wasn't being stubborn just to be stubborn. She was terrified, and that fear wasn't directed where it should have been. It wasn't the Council or their beasts of war that terrified her. It was her response to one arrogant, too-sure-of-himself Breed.

She wanted him. And it didn't make sense. She had given up on physical pleasure years ago, preferring to do without rather than suffer the thoughts and emotions that poured from her partners during sex. The stress from that alone was enough to pull a woman back from any orgasm she may be nearing at the time.

Yet her heart was racing, her flesh heated, the soft folds between her thighs were tender, sensitive, swollen with need. And she was wet. And not just from the hot water that covered her as she stepped into the steaming water of her bathtub.

Her ear was tingling, burning. Megan pulled at the offended lobe as she relaxed in the huge claw-foot tub, fuming over Braden's complete arrogance.

She hated arrogant men. And she hated how easily her body betrayed her when Braden was anywhere near. One day. She had known the jerk one freakin' day, and her body was clamoring for his touch.

Let the bastard just try to move in with her. She would show him exactly how fast she could shoot. She would blow his balls to dust.

Steam enveloped her from the hot water, soaking into her flesh to ease the aches and pains of the numerous bruises that marred her upper body. Her ribs looked like Christmas decorations, abraded red, deep blue bruises and a multitude of scratches that burned like hell from yesterday's battle.

She was pissed off and worried. The worried part was going to keep her awake for a while, she knew.

"Woof." The soft snuffle of the shepherd/chow mix was a soothing comfort. It also helped to pull her thoughts away from a certain Lion Breed and back to the present.

Mo-Jo had refused to allow her to touch him when she first stepped up on the porch. Again. As though yesterday hadn't been enough. The smell of the Breed had been an affront to his canine pride. Or something.

He had taken one sniff and growled at her as though she was the enemy and it was his job to dispose of her. Baring the wicked, sharp, perfectly white teeth in his mouth, he had made her wonder why she even kept him around as she snarled back at him. She had earned herself a doggy sneer as she unlocked the door and he pushed past her. He plopped down on the air-conditioning vent as she fixed herself snack. Well, fixed him a snack that he allowed her to share.

Now he lay at the bathroom door, watching her with that confused doggy expression as she bitched and raged about

Lion Breeds for the last thirty minutes. He was a good dog when he wanted to be.

"Mo-Jo, go get me a beer." She sighed whimsically as she glanced over at him, wishing he were a little less temperamental and stubborn. If he had been, then that school for stubborn pooches might have worked out for him. He would have known to go get her a cold one instantly.

Instead, he tilted his head and lifted his nose disdainfully, as though she had asked him to do something distasteful. She reminded herself not to share the next beer with him.

"Must be an animal thing," she muttered, thinking of Braden's expression when she had sneeringly referred to him as Puss in Boots the day before. That brought a smile to her face. Pure male outrage had reflected in his expression. Score one for the female deputy; she mentally marked the invisible scoreboard of life. She deserved that mark after the shock he had attempted to give her today.

Move in with her? She didn't think so.

Mo-Jo heaved a sigh when she glanced back at him, his big brown eyes drowsy as he enjoyed the climate-controlled coolness of the house. The temperature outside had reached a hundred, and though he survived just fine in the higher temperatures, he still preferred it inside.

"Are you lying on the vent again, Mo-Jo?" she asked, pretty damned drowsy herself now as she noticed the position of his body.

He gave her a disinterested growl.

"One of these days, I'm going to trade you in for a poodle." She yawned.

Or a lion. She grunted at the image that suddenly appeared before her mind's eye. Six-four. He had to be six-four. Height was her weakness in a man. Height and those wide, strong shoulders, and the thick, long golden-brown hair. Broad hands. Boots. He had worn boots and jeans and a black T-shirt that stretched across that amazingly broad chest as the material strained around the bulging biceps of his arms.

Snug jeans had hugged those long powerful legs, cupping an impressive bulge she had made certain to check out when she aimed the barrel of her police-issue Wounder at him yesterday. It had been just as impressive today.

Not that she would have shot. Not there, anyway. Some things were just a crime to destroy, and if that bulge was any indication, that was prime male flesh.

The thought of it made her mouth water and a moan tremble on her lips. How long had it been since she had actually had sex?

"He was fine, Mo-Jo." She sighed then. "Really fine. And he knew it. Damned Tomcat."

That one sucked.

Not that she had anything personal against the Breeds. Hell, she had even campaigned for the Human/Breed rights law when it had come up the year before. She wasn't prejudiced. Just cautious. That was all.

He was wild and untamed. She could see that in his devil-may-care smile and in the brilliance of his dark amber eyes. He was an adrenaline junkie, not the stay-at-home type, or the happily-ever-after kind. He could, and if she let him, he would break her heart.

But he had let her fight. For once in her life she had been able to join the action. She had personally battled the bad guys and won.

The rush of pleasure that suffused her at that thought was nearly sexual. She had trained for this job most of her life. She had fought for it only to have her curse rear its ugly head.

Her empathic abilities had shown themselves during her last year of high school, and had only grown steadily worse. To the point that working in the field she had dreamed of was now denied her. She was a hazard to a team, and to herself. The stronger the emotions of the people around her, the worse they seemed to affect her.

"Maybe I should have gone into day care." She sighed with a grimace before groaning in resignation. Day care would not have done at all.

She shifted in the water, sighing as the heated liquid caressed her sensitive body.

"Woof." Her head jerked around as Mo-Jo came quickly to his feet, turning to the door as he watched it suspiciously.

He might have flunked Politeness 101 at that expensive canine school, but he had excelled at defensive/protective training. And what he was displaying now was pure male aggression. His territory was being invaded.

The most terrifying part was, she couldn't sense it. As she tried to sense a presence, all she felt was cold, dead space.

Coyote Breeds. It had to be. She might not be able to sense Braden's emotions, but she would have recognized his warmth and comfort reaching out to her. The only time she had felt *nothing*, not even echoes of awareness, had been yesterday when she stared into that Coyote Breed's eyes. She had felt them just before they attacked. The evil and the malevolence.

Shit. Shit. She didn't need this. She couldn't afford for Braden to be right. Dammit.

Megan moved silently from the water, grabbing the long, thin silk robe that hung on the wall and pulling it on quickly. Next came the gun she had left lying on the back of the commode. The forty caliber Glock 22 handgun was a little heavy in her hand, but comfortable, secure. The Glock was a bit outdated, but reliable. She liked reliable. And the clip was full and ready to fire.

Mo-Jo was in stalking position at the door, his body tense with the need to attack whoever or whatever was invading his self-proclaimed territory.

One thing the canine school had taught him was how to

defend Megan and her home. One of the major reasons she kept the ill-tempered bag of fur. That, and the fact that she secretly loved the hell out of him. Especially now.

Following his body signals, she gripped the doorknob and opened the door slowly, allowing him to move through the entrance first as she followed silently. She kept the gun braced at her shoulder, her opposite hand gripping the wrist that held it as she moved into her bedroom.

Mo-Jo was at the door now, silent, nearly quivering.

She turned the doorknob carefully, cracking it slowly as Mo-Jo began to force the opening wider to allow his broad body freedom.

Megan was more cautious. She peeked around the door-frame, lowering the gun and flipping off the safety as she surveyed the silent hallway. Mo-Jo stood at the stairs, crouched and ready as he waited on her.

She was moving silently toward him when he suddenly turned, a look of canine calculation on his face as he stared back at her. She couldn't hear anything, not the squeak of a floorboard or a whisper of sound. But she felt it.

Malice. Evil. Just as it had been at the gully. As though the destructive energy of the Coyotes drifted on the air it-self. It wasn't emotions. No fear, hopes or dreams. Just cold, deadly intent instead of dead space. It wrapped around her, tightening at her throat and her chest until she was forced to regulate her breathing and stamp back the fear. They were closer, in her home, moving in for the kill. She felt it, just as she had felt it in the gully.

She backed up, watching as the dog followed her. If Mo-Jo didn't want to tackle whatever was downstairs then she would be damned if she was going to.

She flicked her fingers to the bedroom door, command-ing the animal to follow her. They moved quickly back to the room. Locking the door silently, she raced to the win-dow, threw it wide and slipped over the windowsill to the porch roof.

Mo-Jo followed as she closed the window and moved back from it an instant before gunfire blasted through her bedroom door and the sound of shattering wood sent Mo-Jo jumping from the porch roof to the thickly padded sandbox she kept for him.

Megan quickly followed, landing hard and cursing silently at the impact of the ground on her bruised body.

"I'm going to kill them," she muttered as she came to her feet and raced to the front of the house, following her furious canine as he ran to the open front door. There were no vehicles in the drive; the lock had been lasered. Whoever was in there knew what the hell they were doing.

She slid into the kitchen as Mo-Jo moved to position himself at the entrance of the short hallway that led to the staircase. When he moved, she moved, until they were beneath the stairs, silent and waiting.

"The bitch was here. Water is still hot. She went out the window."

She crouched close to Mo-Jo.

"All I smell is that stinking dog," another voice growled. "People should learn to bathe their fucking animals."

They were at the top of the stairs. Megan narrowed her eyes, her fingers clenching Mo-Jo's ruff as she waited. Yeah, so getting the mutt smell off him wasn't always easy, but he was about to show these bastards exactly why she put up with it.

They were coming down. Her fingers tightened. Wait. All she had to do was wait. Mo-Jo would surprise them and she would take them out. Simple. Easy.

"Outside." The animalistic growl had the hairs at the nape of her neck rising in alarm. "She's on foot. We'll catch her."

They ran down the stairs, nearly silent in their pursuit of her. She released Mo-Jo's ruff and waited on him to make the first move.

When he did, he went out snarling as they made the

landing, while Megan rolled across the floor, lying flat and firing. She took out the first intruder with a deadly blow to the chest while Mo-Jo took the other man down. Rushing to her feet, she raced to the confrontation to kick the assailant's gun across the floor.

"Jo. Move!" she yelled as she watched the flash of a knife heading for the dog's exposed belly. She couldn't get a clear shot, but she didn't have to.

She turned her head as wicked, sharp canines tore into the Coyote's throat no more than a breath before the knife touched vulnerable flesh.

Mo-Jo wasn't a neat animal. Blood splattered around her as he shook the neck of the assailant viciously before letting it go and jumping protectively to her.

She went down in a surprised heap, rolling to her stomach and coming up with her gun aimed at the door. The dog set off a round of snarling, furious barks as Lance and Braden skidded to a shocked stop at the doorway.

"Fuck!" Lance stared at the scene, his expression blank as he blinked at the sight.

"Where did you come from?" she snapped, blinking back at him in surprise.

"We drove up as the shots were being fired." Lance shook his head as Mo-Jo snarled in warning.

"Down, Mo-Jo." Megan pulled herself to her feet, almost groaning in pain as her body suddenly began to protest the additional abuse. "Down."

The two men stared at the dead bodies at the foot of the stairs. Lance shook his head in amazement as Braden turned back to stare at her, his brows lifting in question.

"Hope you have a good cleaning service," Braden drawled as he leaned against the doorframe. "Blood stains old hardwood like that fast, Megan. Might want to go ahead and call them."

A sharp burst of laughter escaped her lips, not hysterical but not exactly calm either as she stared at the mess.

Blood pooled around the bodies, the stench of death nearly overwhelming in the closed area of the house.

"Now this just sucks." She felt her knees buckling as she stood up and moved quickly to the steps. "They're Breeds." She sat down.

"Coyotes. God dammit Megan, we warned you. Didn't we warn you?"

Lance's fury slammed through the air around her, but this time, it didn't touch her, didn't assault her mind. Instead, that aura of calm stability reached out from Braden and wrapped around her.

She looked at Braden. He moved slowly from the doorframe, careful to avoid the blood as he stooped next to the man she had shot and lifted a lip cautiously.

"Coyote," he agreed.

Braden did likewise to the other before jerking his cell phone from his belt and pressing a button quickly.

"We have two more. Area Four B, Megan Field's residence. Get your ass out here."

Megan turned to Lance in numb confusion.

"Are you going to call this in?"

He stared back at her, his expression livid.

"Hell no!" he snapped. "They can have this one too. We don't need news of this hitting the streets in town." He wiped his hands over his face before staring at her worriedly. "Are you okay?"

"I'm fine," she sighed before lifting her eyes to stare at the dog. He was whimpering at the doorway, having lain down, watching her with miserable brown eyes. He didn't move.

"Mo-Jo, come here."

He didn't attempt to move, only whined miserably.

"Oh no." She struggled to rise to her feet as Braden turned to the animal. "Don't touch him, he'll take your face off," she warned the Breed as he moved to check the animal. "Lance, call Dad. The Coyote had a knife."

Evidently the assailant had managed to land a blow after all.

"Are you crazy?" Lance stiffened in rejection. "We'll take care of him. If Uncle David sees this, Megan, he'll jerk you off the force so fast it will make both our heads spin."

"You're just afraid he'll hit you," she sniped.

"You keep thinking that." He grunted in frustration.

She shot him a furious look as she jerked the phone from the wall and knelt beside Mo-Jo. She punched speed dial.

"Meg. Dad and Granddad are on their way. Are you okay?" Her mother's voice was frantic as Megan inspected the deep slice along Mo-Jo's underbelly.

Her mother, bless her heart, had always known when her children were in trouble even if her empathic abilities weren't as strong as her daughter's.

"Fine, Mom. Jo is just hurt." She rose, jerking a dish towel from the counter to apply pressure to the wound. Leaning close to the animal, she cradled his head as the decrease in adrenaline began to leave her weak. "He'll be fine until they get here."

"You're sure?" Her mother wasn't fooled. She had been waiting on Meg's call, proof that her father and grandfather left the house at a dead run.

Her grandfather would have known something was wrong as well. He said the winds spoke to him of her. She shook her head at the thought. Empathy ran on her grandmother's side. She had never been certain what ran on her grandfather's, but Megan knew it was just as powerful as the talents she possessed, if not more so.

"I'm sure, Mom. I love you but I have to go now."

She disconnected the phone before staring up at Braden.

He was watching her with concern, and she realized she was definitely going to be stuck with him. Lance would not let this little event pass without having a stroke, or at the least without calling the whole damned family in.

"You know, Braden, we're really not going to get along. As a matter of fact, I don't even think I'm going to like you."

She turned away from him before he could speak, the sound of a vehicle pulling up in the drive drawing her attention. She moved to the back door, breathing a sigh of relief as her father and grandfather moved quickly from the truck and headed for the house.

"You okay Meg?" Her father hugged her tightly.

"I'm fine. Mo-Jo is down though. He took a knife to his underbelly." She was shaking, trying to avoid her father's gaze and the concern that always made her feel smothered.

Her father was dressed in his customary jeans but wore a dress shirt and silver string tie, indicating he had been preparing to go out for the evening. His thick black hair was peppered with gray, his black eyes hard and probing as he moved through the kitchen to the hall entrance and glanced over at Lance.

"It looks pretty deep, Dad," she sighed, staring at her grandfather in resignation as she let him help her up and lead her to a kitchen chair.

"Uncle Dave, meet Braden Arness," she heard Lance mutter from the hall.

She was aware of Braden watching her, his head tilted, taking in every movement, every expression, as he watched the scene before him. But even more, that calm that was so much a part of him weaved around her as well, sheltering her. A girl could get used to that. Too used to it. It would be a bitch when it was gone again.

His eyes were questioning, almost confused, as her grandfather, stooped with age and shuffling from his stiff joints, patted her on the shoulder.

"You sit still, little warrior. I'll fix you tea." His voice was filled with concern, his weathered expression lined with worry.

"Coffee."

"Tea," her father and grandfather spoke firmly.

She grimaced. The tea wouldn't even be caffeinated.

Despite their calm, she sensed the fear. She didn't feel it, thankfully. But she sensed it thickening the air around her.

"What happened here, Lance?" Her father was bent over Mo-Jo, a small, black medical bag at his side as he checked the wound.

"Why are you asking him? He wasn't here." She hated the protective coddling she could feel beginning to wrap around her. Why hadn't they just brought her mother along with them? That would have finished up the wool wrapping nicely.

Her father glanced back at her, and for a second she glimpsed a fury and fear that she knew shouldn't have shocked her. Yet it did, because she only sensed it, she didn't feel it. It wasn't washing over her in blinding waves or taking her breath. She also noticed Braden had moved closer to her, making it easier for her to pull that shield around her.

"Because I'm tending a wound to your animal that could have been inflicted on you." He didn't snap at her, but she could feel the anger vibrating from him. "I don't know if my nerves can stand hearing a report from you, Daughter."

Her shoulders drooped. How did you battle that kind of love, dammit?

"I don't know what happened, Uncle," Lance finally answered. "I was bringing Braden Arness here to talk to her. We walked in as Mo-Jo was ripping out a throat."

"And what of yesterday?" her grandfather asked then. "The winds blew through the land with a warning, her name echoing on the breeze."

Megan wanted to groan. "You guys are smothering me."

Braden leaned against the wall, watching it all, never speaking. Sexy and silent. Okay, so he had a few things going for him.

"Get used to it." Her father's voice brooked no refusal. "Until I leave this world, you are still my daughter and still under my protection."

"Protect Lance." She waved her hand at her smirking cousin. "He's in more danger than I am if he keeps pissing me off. Share the love, Dad."

Her father only snorted as he applied a thick coating of skin repair to Mo-Jo's underbelly.

"The dog will be fine." He closed the bottle of flesh-simulating latex and returned it to his bag. "The wound wasn't too deep; he's just a big baby." He patted the dog's head before filling a syringe and injecting it into the thick shoulder muscle. "There, something to ease the soreness. He'll be good as new in a few days. We'll take him back to the clinic and put him on some antibiotics to be certain."

At the same time, her grandfather set tea and ginger cookies in front of her. She could still smell death all around her. There was no way she was eating.

"Your blood sugar is low, Granddaughter. Eat as well." He shuffled around the table and, of course, put on coffee for everyone else. Sometimes, she wished she smoked. If any situation called for a cigarette, it was this one.

"Explanation time." Her father stood up, his broad body tense, his roughly hewn face matching the anger in his eyes as they met with Braden's gaze. "Who the hell are you and what do you have to do with this?"

Braden stiffened.

"Enough, David," her grandfather came to the rescue. She hoped. "Come, all of you, sit down at Megan's table and speak with respect in her presence. She has defended herself well today. She has done what no man could have done for her, and satisfied her warrior's soul in her own protection. It is time to celebrate, not to berate her or those who defend her."

Her grandfather's pride in her never failed to fill her with warmth.

Her father flashed him a disgruntled look.

"David . . . husband of my daughter." He sighed. "I feel your worry as it is my own. But I have warned you, her destiny is not as you would have it."

Argument time. Megan knew if she didn't change the subject quickly then her father and grandfather would end up fighting again.

"Someone has to clean up the mess," she sighed, pushing away the cookies and tea. "Has everyone forgotten the two bodies in my hallway?" she asked them all with an edge of incredulity. "They are staining my hardwood floors. Ask him, he knows all about it." She waved to where Braden still stood silently, watchfully.

Too many men were crowding around her. She was wearing nothing but a robe and reaction was starting to tremble through her as all the testosterone began to brew in a furious cauldron. She did not want to be here for the fight.

"My people are headed back in." Braden moved into the kitchen and before she could gasp or anyone else could protest he lifted her into his arms and strode from the room.

God, he was warm, secure. Her arms gripped his shoulders in instinctive response as she fought the need to get closer, to absorb more of the natural shield that enveloped her as well.

"I'm not a baby," she tried to snipe despite the sudden desire to curl against him.

"No, you're not. But the floor is bloody and you aren't wearing shoes." He set her down on the stairs. "Sometimes you see the bloodstains when you least expect it." He stared back at her, his golden eyes solemn. "Go. Dress. My people will be here and there will be a clash of tempers that you don't want to deal with half naked." His voice lowered. "And I sure as hell don't want anyone else seeing those perfect nipples shining through that damp cloth as they are now."

Her face flamed as her horrified gaze went down. Her nipples were hard. Spike-hard, pressing against the silk of her robe like signals.

Her head raised as arousal and embarrassment coursed through her. It wasn't him, she assured herself. He was not turning her on. She didn't even know him and she didn't want to know him.

She sniffed disdainfully, refusing to even attempt to explain or protest her body's response.

◆   ◆   ◆

Braden watched her stalk to her room, his chest tight, his heart racing. God, he wanted to wrap her up just as much as the three men behind him did. Seeing her in that chair, looking so forlorn, had nearly been more than he could stand. He had picked her up and moved her to the stairs for his own mental well-being. The thought of her having to step around the death in that hallway, that it could have been her lying there rather than two Coyotes had his guts clenching in fury.

He hadn't realized how small she was, how light, until he picked her up in his arms and felt the frailty of her body. How the hell had she managed to battle two Coyotes and survive?

Dark, midnight-blue eyes, nearly black, had seemed overlarge in her pale face, filled with excitement and an edge of confusion. But there was no fear. She was pissed. Quickly falling from an adrenaline high and aching with the demands she had put on her body in the past two days. But she wasn't scared.

And he couldn't wrap her up. He couldn't shelter her from the danger. He could only stand behind her and pray he could help her. The world wasn't a playground filled with laughter and games. At least, his world wasn't. It was bathed in blood and cruelty and only the strongest survived. She was being thrown into the middle of his world for some reason he couldn't fathom. He couldn't protect her from that. He could only guide her through it.

"She's a warrior." The old man, her grandfather, spoke behind him.

"She's a woman," the father snapped furiously. "Dammit, Lance, what the hell is going on?"

"She's crazy, is what's going on," Lance argued. "She drove right into a murder scene yesterday afternoon with me screaming at her to back off. The woman is looking for trouble. This time, it found her."

"She searches for justice . . ." Joseph murmured.

And they were all searching for a way to protect her. Their need to shelter her was slowly smothering her. Braden could feel it, could see it in her face. She needed to fight, and now she had no choice but to do just that.

"No." He turned to face them all. "She's a fighter and a survivor and if she's going to survive this in any way, then you'll have to let her fight. Until we find out why the Genetics Council marked her, we have to let her fight, or you'll all lose her."

Silence, waves of fury, confusion and one old man's knowledge seemed to flow around him. He met the sharp, ages-old gaze of the old Navajo who stared back at him, his graying braids framing his square, stark expression.

"She is a warrior," the old man said, raising his head in pride. "But beware, my young Lion, she is also a woman. And that is most often every male's greatest weakness. Even your own."

How the old man knew who and what he was, Braden didn't know and he didn't care. Now, as earlier, confusion swamped him. The Breeds, except for a very select few, had no children. No mothers, no fathers, uncles or cousins. They were created in a Lab, trained rather than raised, and now fought daily for survival in a world that wasn't certain exactly what to do with this new species.

Braden had never experienced the emotion, the sheer

protective fury and determination to protect one's family. He could easily see the three men slowly smothering the woman's fighting spirit with their love.

"You'd better come up with a plan before she gets back down here." Lance hissed as he stared at his uncle and grandfather. "I'm not firing her. She'll never forgive me. Besides, she just ignores me when I try."

"I told you to do that three months ago," David, the father, snarled furiously. "The very day he"—he jerked his thumb at the old man—"heard her name on the winds. 'But no, wait, Uncle . . .'" he mocked the younger man. "'Don't hurt her. She'll leave Broken Butte.'"

"Or shoot me," Lance snapped. "Dammit, Uncle, she's had three offers from the larger cities but she stays here instead. Push her too far and she'll leave."

"I won't allow it."

"You cannot stop it, my son . . ." the old man said.

"Bloody hell, she's going to find trouble no matter where she goes . . ." Lance argued.

Braden cocked his head, watching as the three argued. How interesting. Personally, he thought it was a bit delayed and definitely the wrong time for accusations, but interesting all the same.

The three males were obviously well used to arguing over how best to protect a woman who wanted nothing more than to be who she was, to fight as she was needed. It defied logic. Women were as fierce and often less merciful than any man. They were excellent fighters when they cared for the battle they were engaged in or for those they fought for. And Megan was all woman. In that moment, he decided, she was also his woman.

◆ CHAPTER 4 ◆

Megan was in no better mood the next morning than she had been the night before when Braden and Lance dragged their sorry butts into her guest rooms to sleep. The dead bodies had been cleared out of her house by ill-tempered Feline Breeds, one of which was a scary, silver-eyed son of Satan she was really glad didn't stick around long.

Her father and grandfather had finally left around midnight, under protest. Braden and Lance had stayed, which meant sleep had been next to impossible knowing that the object of her arousal was so close. She had ached for his touch, her skin so sensitive that even the sheets were an irritation against it.

Now, with the breakfast dishes cleared away and coffee sustaining her, Megan stared at Lance and Braden. Fighting this wasn't going to work, and she knew it. As much as she hated it, she needed Braden in this fight.

She glanced over at him, aware that he was watching her closely, his gaze hooded, his body tense. Was he aroused as well? Was he tormented by the same desire she was? One as confusing as it was strong?

She gave herself a mental shake before confronting both men.

"Now what?" She leaned against the counter and sipped at her coffee as they stared back at her.

Lance got to his feet with a sigh. "I have to get back to the office." The coward. He wasn't even going to hang around for whatever fireworks he expected to result from their discussion. "You're off today. I'll see both of you in the office in the morning . . ."

"No. She's off indefinitely." Braden spoke as though his word were law. Her eyes narrowed at the tone, her lips flattening in irritation as she glared back at him.

"That is my job," she snapped. "I can't just lie around . . ."

"Your job is to stay alive." He walked over to the coffeepot to refill his cup. Megan made certain she moved far enough away to keep from so much as brushing against him. "We'll get organized and see if we can figure out what the hell is going on. You're the link . . ." The look he gave her when he turned back was hard, cold. "That means you have the answers."

Which made sense. But that didn't mean she had to like it.

She glanced at Lance then, noting the tension in his muscular body, the merciless anger that glittered in his blue eyes. Damn, she was glad she wasn't feeling that. She couldn't have handled it. It destroyed her, the fear and worry that filled her family because of the job she had fought for so desperately and the weakness the empathy caused within her.

"Well." She breathed out roughly, containing the shiver that worked up her spine. "So much for our complaints that Broken Butte is too quiet."

Lance snorted at that.

"Those are your complaints, Meg. Not mine. I had enough excitement when I worked in Chicago," he snapped.

He was angry. Really angry this time. She stared at his closed expression, the haunted pain in his eyes, and felt her chest tighten.

"I'm sorry." She stared back at him directly, hating the fact that he was worried enough about her to be so furious.

"Dammit, Meg, I don't blame you." He reached out, his arm looping around her shoulders as he pulled her close for a brief, hard embrace. "Check in on schedule," he told her roughly then. "And watch your butt."

She hugged him back. Hard. Then watched as he left the house. For some unexplained and upsetting reason, his touch rattled her. As though her body was faintly protesting, uncomfortable with the once comforting embrace of the cousin who was more like a big brother.

She listened until the sound of his Raider faded into the distance, leaving a deafening, tension-filled silence between her and the Feline watching her closely. She turned to look at him, seeing the curious gleam in his eyes, the quizzical look on his face.

"What?" she asked with mock impatience, controlling her breathing, mainly to control the abrasion of her sensitive nipples against her lace bra. What the hell was wrong with her? She had never been aroused by so little in her life.

He inhaled slowly. What the hell was he sniffing for?

"Nothing." He finally shook his head slowly. "Get ready. I want to make a trip back out to the gully to look around and I want you to stick close. From now on, baby, just call me your shadow."

"Puss in Boots." She glanced at the boots. The man had some fine legs in between, too.

Tension filled the air. It wasn't angry tension; it was hot, blistering in intensity. He set his coffee cup on the counter, moving closer, his shoulder brushing against hers as he passed her, moved behind her.

Megan stood completely still, feeling the displacement of the air around her, the way he moved, turning until his chest nearly touched her back, his breath wafting over her sensitive earlobe.

"You know, Meg," he breathed out softly, his voice rough, growling, "you'll call me that one time too many, and then I'll have to show you which of us belongs on top. And it isn't you, sweetheart. I'd be careful pushing me, if I were you. The scent of that sweet, hot little pussy has my mouth watering and my cock pounding. I might show you not just who belongs on top, but exactly how a Breed teaches dominance to his woman."

She felt herself pale then flush, her eyes widening at the realization that he could actually smell her arousal. That he knew she was wet, hot. Ready to take him. That he fascinated her more than any man ever had. It was a fascination that scared her to death.

"Get your vaccinations first," she snapped, moving away from him, covering her embarrassment with snide anger rather than dissolving in his arms the way she wanted to. She would be damned if she would. Just what the hell she needed—the hots for a Breed, and he hadn't even kissed her yet. Could life get more complicated, please?

"Megan, the snide Breed remarks don't become you," he finally chastised her as she moved to place more distance between them. He only followed her. Stalking her. "If you want to insult me baby, then keep it personal."

He was right, her insults weren't fair. Megan turned her back on him, forcing herself to breathe, to find just a moment of stability amid the conflicting needs surging through her. She wanted him so badly the ache was a pit of fiery longing in her womb. She had forced herself to keep distance between her emotions and the men that existed in the periphery of her life. But she wasn't maintaining distance with Braden. The irresistible draw he was becoming made her angrier at herself than at him.

She turned to face him again, her eyes widening as he came flush with her body, trapping her against the counter, his thighs pressing against hers, his erection cushioning itself in the soft warmth of her abdomen. Her womb clenched, spasming with a sexual hunger that nearly took her breath.

"Don't." She pressed her hands against his chest, shaking her head, certain that if he touched her she wouldn't be able to fight.

"Sweet." He inhaled deeply, bracing his hands on the counter, his arms holding her in place as her hands flattened against his chest. "You're hot and wild, Megan. I could make you hotter. Wanna try me?"

She shuddered as his head lowered, his lips catching the sensitive lobe of her ear, licking it with a slow, seductive move of his tongue. A hard shudder raced up her spine as heat began to envelop her.

Her clit swelled in a resounding yes to his question; her breasts grew heavier, her nipples harder.

A shiver streaked up her spine, then back down again before a tremor of need sliced through her sex. She knew she couldn't hide it. As his head raised, his gaze meeting hers, she knew the hunger filling her was reflected in her eyes. It wasn't just a need for sex. It was a need for everything. To curl in his arms, to rub against him, to find a place to rest. And she knew the illusion that she could do just that couldn't be real.

He inhaled deep, his eyes darkening as sensuality suddenly darkened his expression.

"Get ready to ride," he growled rather than touching her further as she expected. "We either get this show on the road or we head to the bedroom. Your choice. Otherwise, you're going to find out exactly how a Breed fucks the fight out of tempting little wildcats like yourself. Now get moving. One way or the other."

He kept trying to remind himself that he wasn't like her.

Not really human. Not the right man to start an affair with a woman who had no idea what she was getting into with him, sexually speaking.

His lips quirked at the thought. Her snappish little comments against his Breed birth hadn't bothered him. He saw more than he was certain she wanted him to. The clash of emotions inside her was clearly felt, as was the arousal, hot enough, deep enough to burn a man to his soul. And it frightened her.

◆   ◆   ◆

He drove across the desert, the gentle rocking motion of the Raider making the silence inside the vehicle seem all that much deeper. It was hard to forget what he was, who he was, when the heat of her arousal scented the cool interior of the closed vehicle.

He was a Breed. The bastard of the human and animal species. His genetics were a mismatched collage of human and lion DNA that made him stronger, faster, more predatory, more vicious than any human should be. He was identified by the genetic marker of a lion's paw on the inside of his left thigh, and by the longer, sharper canines at the sides of his mouth. Not that those were the only anomalies, but they were the most apparent.

His sexuality was hard, driven. If there was anything better than sex and a wild, hot woman, then he hadn't found it. It was better than a good bloody fight, and he loved those, too.

Adrenaline was the spice of life, be it sexual or life-threatening. But he had never taken a woman who wasn't a Breed. And he had never taken one as fragile as the woman sitting beside him. The one burning, slick and wet and ready for him.

From the corner of his eye he watched her rub at the earlobe he had nipped the other day. He had broken the skin. The small curve was abraded, though it didn't look as

though it should cause her any problems. But she kept rubbing and tugging at it as though it bothered her.

"I didn't bite you that hard," he grumbled as she continued to toy with it. "You're not making me feel guilty for it."

"Think what you want to." She glared back at him. "It's
still sensitive."

He flashed her a lazy smile. "That little nip was nothing.
You need to toughen up, sweetheart."

It was nothing compared to what he had ached to do to
her earlier. As his tongue had licked over the little abrasion
on her lobe, he had longed to move to her shoulder, to taste
the sweet flesh there, to rake his teeth over it, to mark her
in a way no other man could ever mistake.

That need surprised him. He had never known a desire
to mark a woman. This woman he wanted to mark in all
ways, so that no other male could ever mistake to whom
she belonged.

"You need to refrain from biting," she parried with an
edge of nervous arousal. Oh yeah, she felt it too. The need
was burning inside her just as hot, just as fierce as it was
burning in him. He could feel it, could smell it.

He shifted in his seat to relieve the pressure against his
swollen cock. The scent of her arousal was driving him
crazy. He wanted nothing more than to hold her beneath
him, his teeth gripping her sensitive shoulder as he worked
his engorged cock as deep inside the melting depths of
her pussy as he could go. And she was melting. So hot, so
wild that her frustration was making her angry. Making
him impatient.

"I'll see what I can do about that," he grunted as he
turned and made his way down the inclined entrance into
the gully. The same path Megan had taken the day before.

"You stopped here before coming into the gully the
other day," he remarked, determined to do the job he had
been sent to do before he did the woman. "Why?"

He watched her as she stared into the entrance to the

deep gully, her gaze reflective. He could feel the subtle tug of her ability to pull his natural shield around her. It was . . . intimate. As it enfolded her, shallow though the protection was, it bonded him to her, made his spirit a part of hers.

"Someone followed the jeep down on foot, wearing hiking boots. The tracks were fresher than the tire tracks. Did you see who it was?" she asked then, peering from the side window as she pushed the dark shades above her eyes to see the ground clearly.

He shook off the knowledge of the deepening bond, relaxed his guards against her and allowed her to pull the shield further around herself.

"That was me." He eased the Raider into the wide gully before coming to a stop. "I found the jeep about six hours before you came through. I made it to about here, smelled the stink of the Coyotes around the bend." He pointed to a fissure at the other side of the gully. "I noticed this area is riddled with fissures and caverns. They're like a maze inside, many of them connecting together. I was able to slip through those to work my way closer to the cavern they were hidden within."

Megan nodded. "We had a particularly hard rainy season about ten years ago. The gullies stayed flooded and many of them washed out deep grooves into the stone. This is one of about a dozen of the hardest hit areas. The floods in these washouts would come hard and fast, many revealing small caves that go deep beneath them and now collect water when it does rain."

"I worked my way through those washouts until I found a way to get around them," Braden continued. "I wasn't far from you when I heard you call in to Lance. They were waiting on you."

"But why me?" That was the one she didn't understand.

As he started the vehicle forward again, she lowered the window, staring up at the steadily rising walls that grew steeper as they moved deeper into the gully.

He didn't answer her. There was no way to answer her until they found out the reason for the Coyotes' arrival.

He drove around the steep bend, pulling to a stop behind the black SUV Mark and Aimee had driven.

He watched as she glanced around the area, her eyes narrowed, almost distant as she seemed to listen to something he couldn't hear. Finally, she gripped the handle of the door and stepped out of the vehicle as he set the security controls and followed her.

He continued to watch her. Leaning against the front of the Raider, testing the wind every few seconds for the rancid scent of Coyotes as she stared at the SUV, her expression solemn, intense.

"They looked so young." Sadness washed over her, regret for the lives wasted before they could be lived.

"Aimee was twenty-three. Mark was twenty-four," he told her. "Neither had been out of captivity long enough to know freedom."

She moved to the open doors of the SUV. The smell of death was thick, the blood-soaked interior boiling with heat beneath the afternoon sun. She didn't throw up as he would have expected her to. Her expression tightened as she leaned in and bent forward, checking beneath the driver's seat, then in the console beside it.

She flinched every few minutes as though she were in pain. Or feeling that of another.

"Did your people have time to go over it?" she asked him then.

"Thoroughly." There was nothing to be found. A few fast-food bags, gasoline receipts. No notes, no letters, nothing to indicate why they had left or why they had died.

"So why are we here?" She moved back, turning to face him with a frown on her face.

"Because those Coyotes waited here for almost twenty-four hours for you to arrive. We checked the SUV. This canyon is another story. We're going to go over it, inch by inch. Every tributary leading into the rock wall, every cavern. We're going to go over it. Because the Coyotes that are dumb enough to stay with the Council are the ones too stupid to cover their tracks well. They've left something here. They were here for too long not to. Now it's up to us to find what they left and to figure out why they want you. And they do want you, baby. Real bad."

Fear flashed in her eyes but only for a second. It was followed closely by anger, then determination.

"They can want on then." A cool little smile curved her lips. Calculating, filled with cold purpose. "So where do we start?"

· CHAPTER 5 ·

They started with a perilous climb from the bottom of the gorge to the uppermost section of the cliff that rose above it. More than ten feet from the ground, handholds were few and far between; and though a fall wouldn't kill her, it would sure as hell hurt.

Their destination was the grouping of small, narrow openings into the cliff houses above. Weathered by sand and rain, the openings created dark, shadowed crevices with a narrow ledge running between them.

In the heat of the day, the climb sapped her energy as perspiration poured from her even before they reached the first set of small caves. Megan had been amazed that the large, brawny Coyotes could have existed for more than a few hours inside them, until she flattened herself against the stone floor and scooted in.

"The cave is much larger inside," she called back as she flipped on the flashlight she carried before moving further inside.

The risk of rattlers was high in the area, not to mention a dozen other poisonous denizens of the desert. The caves were cool in the heat of the day, and warmer in the cold of night—the perfect hidden shelter for wildlife.

There was nothing to be found but a lingering, subtly noxious smell. Her senses detected no danger, no presence of life. Only the cold, evil intent that had filled the Coyotes.

"Those boys stink," she muttered as she pushed herself farther into the cave and made room for Braden's larger body.

"Yes, they do at that." Unfortunately, the distracting scent of the remnants of the Coyote Breeds' body odor was instantly overshadowed by the smell of manly heat that tempted the senses and made her erogenous zones wake up and howl. She clenched her thighs, feeling the wet proof of her attraction to him dampening the outer curves of her cunt.

And he wasn't exactly uninterested. She flushed as his gaze touched her; the heavy-lidded, sensual awareness moving over his expression was less than comforting.

Rather than staring at the hard body moving across from her, she moved the light over the cave walls. The cave extended well back into the ridge, easily ten feet wide and perhaps twelve long, with several wide fissures opening into the wall and leading further back into the cliff.

"I had no idea the cliff houses were this large," she murmured, directing the beam of light to the widest fissure. It looked like a doorway opening into stone.

"That fissure leads to another inner cavern at the base of the cliff. I tracked them that far before I found the tunnel that led to the one they had trapped you inside. I don't believe they had explored far though; the tunnels are like a maze as you get deeper into the ridge."

She glanced at him as he spoke, watching the confidence in the way he began to move about the cliff house.

"So what are we looking for?" She rose to her feet, the ceiling barely high enough to allow her to straighten.

Braden's shoulders were stooped, his head lowered as he glanced back at her.

"Jonas and his men didn't have time to go through the two upper caverns fully," he said. "I just want to be certain nothing was missed."

"How did you manage to keep from getting lost in the tunnels?" The thought of an inner maze within the stone was daunting, and she didn't care to attempt to search one.

"A good sense of direction." Amusement laced his voice. "Don't worry; the tunnels shouldn't pose a problem. They wouldn't have left their vantage point to search them. They were waiting on you, and knew you weren't likely to use them."

She inhaled roughly before moving to the opposite wall and shining the light closely on it. She didn't want to think about the Coyotes waiting on her, watching for her.

"These haven't been here long." She ran her fingers over the stone, marveling at the forces that had created them. "The storms that washed out this gully were horrible. Before it was nothing more than a small chasm. Now it's almost a secret stone wonderland. I'll have to let the cavers' association know about these tunnels so they can explore and map them."

It was imperative to get the proper GPS trackers within the tunnels and caves in case the unwary became lost within them.

"And another of nature's secrets becomes unraveled," Braden murmured.

"But lives are saved." She shrugged at the faint condemnation. "Especially the children who lose their way so easily."

How many times had she done exactly that as a child? Too many to count. Her father, even now, told the hair-raising stories of attempting to find her during the times she had disappeared into a cave or an unknown part of the desert.

"Some secrets were meant to stay hidden." His voice was tight now, tense with a deep-seated anger as he investigated one of the ledges on the other side of the cave.

She assumed he meant the secrets the scientists had unraveled in creating the Breeds. From the news stories she had watched, she knew the controversy over Breed Rights was fueled by the Purists' beliefs that their animal DNA disqualified them from the description of human. As though the human DNA had no significant value.

It was insanity, the racism and prejudice that was growing against the Breeds. And though she could hear his anger, feel it distantly, it wasn't beating at her head, raw and painful. It was just there naturally. Allowing her to breathe and to function. The anomaly was comforting—confusing, but comforting.

"Nature does what she believes is right." She leaned against the rock wall, staring at his broad back curiously. "Do you think you would be here if you weren't considered a worthy life, Braden?" She tilted her head as he turned back to face her slowly.

His eyes were narrowed in the dim light that filled the cave, his expression pensive.

"I wouldn't fight for it daily if I didn't consider it worthy," he assured her, his lips quirking into a mocking smile before he turned back to whatever he had been investigating. "I just believe some things were not meant to be tampered with, Creation being but one of them."

He was accepting of who he was, of what he was. But she heard the regret in his voice as well. Perhaps it was the world in general that disappointed him. As it did her.

She cleared her throat, nervous. "Sometimes tampering creates something beautiful," she finally whispered, staring back at him, licking her lips as his gaze flickered with surprise.

"Back to work," she muttered, turning away from him

before she let her wayward emotions get her into trouble. Hadn't she learned better more than once?

Shaking her head, she turned back to the job at hand, shining the light deep into the opening that led farther into the land. The light beam caught on a piece of folded paper, tucked beneath the outcropping of a rock.

Moving into the tunnel, she bent and pulled it free before aiming the light on it. The computer-printed schedule was damning.

Fields, Megan.

Patrol Schedule.

Her fingers rubbed over the paper as hatred poured from it. Personal hatred. This wasn't the impersonal evil of the Coyote Breeds. It was closer. Familiar. She knew the feeling, the psychic imprint left by all creatures once they touched something. She bit her lip, frowning down at the paper as she continued to rub her fingers over it.

The emotion was faint, but vicious. Whoever had printed out this schedule had known what awaited her. Known and enjoyed the feeling of power that came from the knowledge.

"What is it?"

Megan jumped in startled awareness as she heard Braden's voice at her ear, only then realizing how easily he had slipped up on her.

"This is from the computers at the sheriff's office." She frowned down at the locator numbers at the top of the printout. "The printer automatically sets the locator numbers to display the location of the office printing it."

"Are they printed out often?" Braden reached out, lifting the paper from her hand as she turned to face him.

Megan shrugged. "Not that often. I get a copy and Lance has his copy. Unless someone prints out more. But you need the password to get into the system."

"It's still not a foolproof system." He shook his head slowly, staring down at the paper a moment longer before refolding it and tucking it into his pocket. "I'll send it to the labs and see if they can pick up any prints from it. Though I doubt any but those of the Coyote who carried it show up after all this time."

"From what I've heard of the Council, they don't go after high-profile or well-guarded women," she said then, remembering the reports she had watched over the years. "They kidnap runaways, or women who are destitute, with no family. And they don't just mark one for death. Why change their routine now?"

She wasn't stupid. There had to be something more that they were after.

"You're right." He reached up, pushing back the fringes of hair that fell over her face, his golden eyes narrowing as she stared back at him. "There is something more they want. Unfortunately, I have no idea what it is. Until I learn, we'll fight together. No going off alone, Megan. Trust me to let you fight and to live."

Her lips parted at his statement while her heart began to race at his nearness. She should be excited about the opportunity to fight, not about the chance to be a part of this man's life.

His lips quirked, a soft smile softening the features of his face. "You're surprised?"

"A bit," she admitted, aware that his hand now cupped the side of her neck, his thumb smoothing over the tender flesh just beneath her ear. The intimacy that wrapped around them seemed to invade every cell of her body.

"Why?" He tilted his head.

She shrugged, uncertain within the morass of arousal and emotions she could feel building within her. Braden, as maddening as he could be, drew her to him in ways she found impossible to fight. She wanted his arms around her, wanted his touch and his kiss; but even more, she wanted the man.

"Why have you stayed here?" he asked her then. "I see the wildness in your eyes, Megan, the need to run free, to fight and to dance within the flames of life. You let Lance give you a Wounder rather than a weapon, and allow yourself to be smothered in this corner you exist within. Why?"

A frown snapped between her brows as the shame of her failure to fight and control her Empathy filled her once again. "This is my home." She tried to shake off his touch.

"This isn't your life." He spoke the words that she shied away from daily.

"This isn't your business." She stepped away from him, ignoring the instant chill to her body as she lost his warmth.

"This is a lot of my business," he assured her, still blocking the exit of the tunnel. "I see a very strong woman. One with enough fire to warm the coldest nights or to fight the bloodiest battle. Yet you're here, sedated, bored out of your mind."

His voice was gentle, comforting, and yet at the same time the dark, rich baritone had her blood pressure rising to a heated pitch of arousal. She would have been amused if it didn't scare her silly. She could love this man, even knowing he couldn't stay.

"Bored?" She arched her brow mockingly. "Now, Braden, how could you consider this little corner of the desert boring? Surely you aren't ready to head back to battle so soon?"

He was hitting too close to the mark, bringing to the surface too many things that had been tormenting her with each passing year.

"I found a battle here," he responded softly, crowding her closer to the stone wall at the side of the tunnel. "Now I just have to figure out why there's a battle to begin with. Why would a beautiful, seemingly normal young woman suddenly be targeted for death by a Council that shouldn't give a fuck about her one way or the other. What did you do, Megan? What have you seen?"

She inhaled roughly, staring back at him with a remnant of fear as he asked that question. What had she done? What had she seen? Why had she run back to the safety of her home, her family, and hid within the desert she so loved, when she really wanted nothing more than to live the life she knew she had been destined to live?

Because she was scared. She had learned in the crowded setting of the Law Enforcement Academy that working within a team, dealing with the various emotions, dark, often agonizing emotions, fractured her attention to the point where concentration was impossible.

She had passed the courses with honors. But when it came to training maneuvers, she had often endangered the team as well as herself. And yet that had nothing to do with the Council.

"I haven't done anything, or seen anything that the Council would be interested in." Her fists clenched at her sides as she assured him just how wrong he was. "I'm here because it is home. I want to make a difference here."

"There's no battle here." His eyes were deceptively gentle; she could see the cool, calm calculation that rested beneath the purity of the amber color. "There is no fire here, Megan." He moved closer, his body brushing against hers until she retreated against the cool wall behind her. "There is no excitement, nothing to stimulate your very agile mind and body. You hunger for justice. For adventure and excitement. You hunger and yet you steer clear of the banquet waiting beyond your own borders. Why?"

"Maybe I'm scared?" She arched her brow mockingly as she felt her mouth go dry with nervousness. He was too close, too intent on learning secrets that she revealed to no one. "Broken Butte is safe—"

The rumbled growl of warning that sounded from his chest stopped her words as nothing else could have.

"Have I ever mentioned that lies have a scent?" he

asked her, his voice soft as he pressed closer. "Such a shame to mar the smell of sweet, aroused female with the rancid tint of a lie. Don't piss me off, Megan."

He flashed those incisors as though she should be frightened of them. She wasn't frightened of his bite; it was his touch that threw her off guard, that destroyed her equilibrium. That was what she feared. And it made her angry at herself and at him.

"Don't piss you off?" She pushed against his chest as she wiggled past him, stomping to the main cave as he followed her slowly. "No, Braden." She turned on him warningly, pointing her finger at him imperiously. "Don't piss *me* off, and don't poke your nose where it doesn't belong. Concern yourself with the problem at hand and leave me the hell alone."

Now she remembered why she didn't want a damned Feline Breed on her heels every damned minute of the day. Arrogance was as much a part of them as the steel-hard muscles and exceptional, savage beauty.

And let's not forget the strength. Before she could do more than gasp he had gripped her upper arm, turning her and pushing her against the wall again, his larger body holding her in place as his erection pressed against her lower stomach.

Arousal swamped her. It ripped through her; not just her senses, but every cell of her body seemed to open up, begging, pleading for his touch.

Damn, she didn't need that. She could feel her womb clenching. And he didn't miss a second of it.

His nostrils flared, his eyes darkening as he held her wrists in one hand, high above her head.

"Do you mind?" She struggled against his grip.

"I don't mind a bit," he murmured, lowering his head to her already abused ear as his teeth raked over it.

Okay, she was screwed, and not in a good way.

She shuddered at the caress. That just felt way too good.

Good enough that she couldn't still the hard exhalation of breath that nearly turned into a whimper of greedy need. Talk about a banquet. A smorgasbord of hard, tight male flesh. And if the erection pressing into her stomach was any indication, he was built like a damned tank and loaded.

Her hands strained against his grip as she arched against him, knowing she should be struggling to be free of the sensations that flooded her at his touch. But she wasn't. She was straining closer to the power, the heat of him, needing more. She forced back the need, panting for air as the blood raced through her body.

"Why are you doing this?" She tried to shake her head, but her eyelids only fluttered in pleasure as he drew her earlobe between his lips and caressed it.

"Be still." He growled, pressing his cock tighter against her belly.

"You're not being fair," she protested, her nails biting into his shoulders as she fought the attraction pulling her to him. She couldn't afford to let herself feel this, to need this. "You know this can't go anywhere."

"Who said I'm trying to go anywhere?" Amusement and pure male lust thickened his voice. "But if you don't stop rubbing that hot little body against me, then I'm going to fuck you here, in the middle of this damned cave. Now stay still."

His other hand locked on her hip as he eased back, his head lowering to allow his lips to graze her neck.

Damn, it had just been too long since she'd been with a man. That had to be all it was, because if it wasn't, then she was in more trouble than she could have ever imagined.

"Just blame it all on me, why don't you." She tried to be snide, she really did. But the smile that trembled on her lips fed to her voice.

"It's sure as hell a lot easier that way." He chuckled as he lifted his head, moving farther back until he let go of her wrists and released her from the sensual spell he had been weaving around her.

She should have been thankful.

Instead she wanted to whimper in disappointment.

"I just bet it is." She rolled her eyes, fighting to balance her equilibrium once again. "Are we finished in here, or was there something else you wanted to check out?"

She stooped down to retrieve the flashlight that had rolled against the wall before flipping it off and re-securing it on her utility belt. Right beside the wicked submachine pistol she had pulled from her closet and holstered there that morning. She'd be damned if she ever carried another Wounder.

"Oh, there are many things I would like to check out." The heavy-lidded stare had her stomach tightening, her pussy spasming.

"I bet there are." She hid the spurt of laughter that was building in her chest. "But if we're finished with these damned caverns I'd really like to head back to town. I do still have some sort of life here. Living it brings me some satisfaction, you know. And I'm getting rather hungry."

For food, she chastised her aching clit. Just food. No sex. Sex with a Breed was not a good idea. It involved all sorts of complications. Possessiveness, arrogance, and other adjectives she really couldn't seem to pull out of her head right now. She was certain they weren't good ones though.

"Hmmm," he murmured. The rumbling sound wasn't comforting. "We'll check the other cave just to be certain before heading out. If they left the schedule here, they could have left something else across the gully."

"Fine." Another climb. Just what she needed. This time he was going first. She was *not* getting downwind of him with that sensitive nose he had. She was so wet she was certain she smelled of nothing but lust. Wild, hot lust.

She was so fucked. And if she wasn't careful, it was going to be in a too-good way.

◆   ◆   ◆

She fascinated him.

Braden admitted he could be in some very deep trouble where Megan Fields and her various mysteries were concerned.

It wasn't just the arousal that concerned him. He had been aroused before, but never had he been this hungry, this intent on one woman outside the drug induced "tests" the scientists had conducted in the labs.

Megan did more than just make him hungry. She made him yearn, and that could be a very dangerous thing. But she also made him curious.

Curiosity killed the cat, he thought mockingly as he searched the next cave, attempting to ignore the sweet heat that flowed from her.

He ached so desperately to taste her that the small, almost unnoticed glands beneath his tongue felt swollen. The scientists had labeled them as advanced taste buds, another of the anomalies of their human/animal genetics. There were quite a few of those.

But the glands had never become inflamed, swollen. And they sure as hell had never spilled the subtle taste of spice into his mouth. And now they were. The very thought of tasting Megan, of pushing his tongue into her mouth and feeling her soft lips surround it, made them throb harder.

Not to mention what the thought did to his cock. The head was pounding like a toothache that refused to ease. He could jack off, but he had learned last night that it brought even less satisfaction than it ever had. He just wasn't the "jack off" type, he guessed. He liked sex. He loved women. The taste, the sound, the softness, all the unique qualities that made women what they were.

The feel of their nails piercing his shoulders in climax, or the sweet explosion of earthy lust on his tongue as he licked their cream from between their thighs. Women were softness in a world gone mad. But Megan was making him mad, insane, so desperate for the taste of her that he was on the verge of taking her to the cave floor and covering her like the animal he was.

"There's nothing here, Braden." It wasn't the first time she had made the comment. "No fissures, no tunnels, no hidden little ledges."

Yeah, he had figured that one out five minutes ago. But *she* was here, the smell of her trapped between the stone walls, stroking his senses and filling him with a peculiar lust that he needed time to understand. To figure out how to control.

If they left the cave, the winds would dissipate much of the scent, and the surrounding land would diffuse it. He would have no time to revel in it.

In his memory, no woman had ever been so naturally hot for his touch. It was almost humbling. Fuck that, it was arousing as hell. He couldn't get enough of it, and if she wasn't careful, he would soon be tasting it.

"Keep looking." He bent along the wall he was searching, exploring a fissure that ran diagonally across the stone. It was thin, barely wide enough for the tips of his fingers, but enough to pretend interest in.

"Keep looking!" she exclaimed before breathing out in exaggerated patience. "You're too bossy."

"And you're too argumentative, but you don't see me pointing that out." She made him smile. It had been a long damned time since anyone had genuinely made him smile. He loved sparring with her, loved to listen to her snap at him and defy him. She was a challenge, both physically and mentally, and she kept him on his toes. And if he hadn't been mistaken, a definite smile had been edging her lips earlier and echoing in her voice.

"Don't I?" She was smiling for sure now. She might have her back to him, but he could hear the smile in her voice.

Unobtrusively he shifted the hard length of his cock beneath his jeans, hoping for some relief. The damned thing only seemed to swell further as he closed his eyes and drew the scent of her deeper into his head.

"Whichever one waited in this cavern couldn't have been here long," she finally said. "It doesn't stink like the other one did."

He had noticed that himself.

"I suspect they both spent some time in the other one." He shrugged. "Coyotes work better in teams. They challenge each other in their viciousness. It makes them more merciless."

He watched as she finished checking a shadowed corner and turned back to face him. Her face was flushed, her nipples pressing against her T-shirt as she snapped the flashlight off and clipped it to her belt. "I assume we're done here?"

"For now." He glanced around one last time. "Hopefully by this evening Jonas will have some information for us as well as the pictures of the Breeds who were murdered. I want you to look at them closely, see if you recognize them."

Even their trainers wouldn't have recognized them the day before.

"That sounds fine." She nodded. "Since I'm stuck with you at the house, I have to do some grocery shopping though. I bet you eat a lot, don't you?"

Her gaze roved over him. He knew the minute she spotted his erection and almost laughed out loud as her eyes widened in surprise.

"I have very strong appetites." He was almost choking on his laughter as heat enveloped her face.

She cleared her throat, a nervous little sound—part arousal, part amusement. "I just bet you do," she muttered, heading for the entrance of the cave. "Wouldn't surprise me a bit."

Damn, she was cute. Tough as hell, with a mouth as mockingly sarcastic as anyone he had ever met, and with more secrets than any woman should have. But she made him laugh and kept him on his toes. A major accomplishment.

"You might want to look into stocking up on plenty of proteins for yourself too." He kept his voice controlled, no sign of amusement or hidden meanings. "You'll need your strength."

She turned back to him, a retort on her lips until she met the deliberately innocent expression he kept on his face.

She narrowed her eyes as she propped her hands on her hips, drawing attention to the ripe curves that had the blood pounding furiously between his thighs.

"You're not fooling me, Arness." She arched that perfect little brow as she pursed her lips thoughtfully. "You think you are. You want to." Then she did smile. A sexy slow curve of her lips that had him gritting his teeth to hold back his groan. "Maybe you're the one who's going to need all that energy. I could be too much for you to handle, you know."

She turned then, and with a twitch of her pretty ass she stepped over the ledge to the first foothold that would lead her back to the floor of the gully.

Too much for him to handle? Doubtful. Not impossible. But very, very doubtful.

✦ CHAPTER 6 ✦

Megan doubted it as well. As they searched through the remaining caverns, she fought to keep her senses alert, using her ability to draw from Braden's shield to hold back the less desired effects of the Empathy and to use her talents to search for answers instead.

She wasn't adept at it. She had never had the opportunity to work in such a way, but she found herself intrigued by the opportunity now. And by the warmth and the subtle information she drew on the man as well. There were dark places inside him, but he kept them hidden; he didn't let them affect him. There was violence, yes. But it was tempered, softened with compassion.

There was also dominance, a dominance that edged at the shields she was borrowing—shields he was controlling. She probed at it, feeling the amusement, the lust, a hunger that was only growing.

She tried to ignore that, focusing instead on the remnants of emotions and actions that still lingered within the caverns. Not that there was much to latch on to. The Coyotes had come here to kill. They had followed the Breed couple from Broken Butte, but how had they known to start there?

They were there to kill the couple, then to wait on Megan. She sensed that; it had been uppermost in their minds. A clean sweep, but of what? What were they attempting to hide?

"There's nothing here." Braden finally sighed as they went through the last cavern, standing at the ledge and staring below with narrowed eyes. He gave his head a brief, firm shake. "Let's get back to the Raider and head out. I'll see if Jonas has come up with anything further in his interrogation of the Coyote he took back with him."

He swung from the ledge to the narrow path that led back into the gully as Megan followed.

Megan pushed back the stray strands of hair that had escaped from her braid as she began trudging toward the Raider. She was ready to get the hell out of the desert, to head into town for dinner then home to her soft, comfortable bed.

Bruises from the past week throbbed painfully, as did some new ones collected climbing the cliff faces. Her ear burned and her pussy had developed an erotic, sensual ache that tormented her with the knowledge that she was fighting something she knew Braden wanted just as much as she did. Well, she wanted it pretty damned bad; she could be in worse shape than he was.

"What did you really expect to find here, Braden?" She watched him curiously, still not certain what he was after.

"Anything. Everything. Nothing." She could hear the shrug in his lazy tone and gritted her teeth in irritation.

"Two out of three ain't bad." She mocked their dubious success with a roll of her eyes. "We found everything this gorge could have contained and nothing we needed to answer our question. You're on a roll, Braden." She jerked the driver's-side door open, sliding into the cool comfort of the vehicle with a sigh of relief.

"You do sarcasm very well, Megan." He turned to her as he slid into the passenger seat, leaning back comfortably as he smiled with a slow, too-sexy curve of his lips. That fuller lower curve made her nipples ache. It was bad when something as simple as a man's smile made your nipples ache, made them long for the feel of those sensual curves surrounding them.

"I try." She cleared her throat nervously, quickly turning away from the temptation of him as he emitted a completely male grunt of exasperation.

That shouldn't have turned her on. It was insulting, not in any way erotic. But the sound had her thighs tightening and her core aching. Dammit.

Maybe it was time for the Pocket Rocket, the little clitoral stimulator that came in so handy. Pocket Rockets were nice. Or her vibrator. It had been a while since the need for sexual release had been so imperative. Maybe it had never been this imperative, she thought. Nor had it ever had this ability to make her want to be closer to a man; to make her *need* to be.

And he knew what he was doing to her. She could see it in his eyes, in the way he lifted his head, his nostrils flaring. He could smell her, smell her heat and her arousal. And there was no way to hide it.

On the heels of that thought came another. She knew the Breeds' senses were more advanced than those without the altered DNA. But she wondered, how much more advanced were they?

She glanced at him from the corner of her eye and cleared her throat before asking, "How's your hearing?"

"My hearing?" he asked, his voice filled with lazy amusement and just a hint of curiosity.

She glanced over at him fully, widening her eyes inno-
cently. "Your hearing. You know, your ears? Can you hear
things better than other people?"

She fought the flush that threatened to build beneath the
skin of her cheeks as she turned her eyes back to the track
ahead.

"Better than non-Breeds, you mean?" he asked with interest.

She didn't trust that look of male innocence for a
minute, but the pretense had her fighting to hide her smile.

"Yeah." She nodded shortly. "That's what I mean."

"I don't know." Cool amusement filled his voice. "How
good is your hearing?"

Well, she wouldn't be able to hear him jacking off, but it
wasn't like his hand buzzed either . . .

"Normal." She shrugged.

"What would you classify as normal? What can you not
hear that you think I could?" Was he teasing her?

She spared him a quick look, frowning at the curious
expression. Was that laughter lurking in his eyes? Surely
he couldn't guess why she wanted to know?

She probed at the shields he used, but could detect nothing but the amusement.

"I don't know." She gripped the steering wheel harder
as she tried to appear casual and merely interested in his
unique Breed abilities. "If I were in the kitchen and you
were in the living room of my house, I wouldn't know it
if you were to use . . . oh, say . . . a pair of hair clippers."
That seemed like a good contrast. A small, even vibration
of sound, not too harsh, not too easy to hear.

"Hair clippers?" he asked hesitantly.

"Yeah." She nodded in all seriousness. "Hair clippers."

He tensed, clearing his throat as he shifted in his seat.
"Are you trying to find out if I'll hear you using a vibrator,
Megan?"

She lost her breath, her face flaming with mortification

as her head swung around, catching the narrow-eyed suspicion on his face before she jerked back to stare at the track.

"No," she exclaimed, shocked. How had he known?

"Because if you are, I will tell you now: I would know. I would smell the sweet scent of your pussy as you found your release, and I would hear even the quietest vibrator. And I would be very, very displeased. I might even have to spank you."

She swallowed tightly, certain her ass wasn't tingling in anticipation, but rather in trepidation. She glanced at his hand as it lay casually on his knee. It was broad, strong . . . She shifted in her seat.

"That wasn't what I meant," she muttered. "And what business would it be of yours?"

He was going too far. He had pushed every sexual hot button she had and was now attempting to deny her a release that would allow the dissipation of the tension those buttons were causing within her body. There were lines no man should cross, and as far as Megan was concerned, that was one of them.

"I can smell your feminine heat, Megan." His voice lowered, his words sending a flush of heat beneath her cheek. "And I know I cause it. You need satisfaction; you can find it with me, or you can suffer with me. It's your choice."

She narrowed her eyes as her independence flared within her.

"You don't command me, Braden." She sniffed disdainfully. "Not now, not ever, and especially not in this. Don't force me to prove it."

"Don't force me to lose what little control I have to not test the barriers you are throwing between us," he responded, his voice calm, warning. "Remember the beast you're dealing with here, Megan. I'm not a man you can tempt in the ways you would others, nor am I one you can tease in this area. For both our sakes, exercise due caution unless you want to experience the consequences."

His voice held a dark, warning rumble that sent shivers racing up her spine, and small fingers of lightning-fast sensation streaked through her nervous system.

Flattening her lips, Megan drew the Raider to a stop before engaging the parking system and turning to him slowly. He was leaning against the door, one arm lying along the armrest below, the other braced on the padded center console between them. He was relaxed but watchful, and aroused. She could feel the arousal reaching out to her.

"Being a Breed doesn't make you exempt from the normal laws of decency and privacy." She breathed in deeply as she stared back at him. "That's my home, Braden. My bedroom. When the door is closed, it means you are not welcome to invade that room, no matter the circumstances, barring physical danger. Don't think that just because you're bigger and more primal than I am that it changes the rules."

"Unfortunately it does." He growled, the hard rumble shattering the edge of calm she tried to force around herself. "It shouldn't, and I regret the need. But I find that my control in your presence isn't what it should be. Right or wrong doesn't come into it. Using the vibrator within my hearing would be tantamount to parading naked in front of another man, Megan. Don't make that mistake unless you're willing to carry through with the invitation."

Her chin jutted forward, anger spiking in her veins at the warning.

"No means no, Braden."

"Don't push this, Megan." She could feel it now, the edge of his control slipping.

She drew back, jerking to attention at the awareness that he was more primal, possibly more dangerous than she had imagined he could be where she was concerned.

"Megan." The hand that had been braced between the two seats lifted, his fingers moving for the strands of hair that had slipped from her braid. He smoothed them back as she watched him warily, her breathing rough, ragged, as his unusual gold eyes glittered with hunger and an edge of humor. "You make me yearn for things that I'm certain I shouldn't want. Things I'm certain you don't want. I'm man enough to understand my limits here, and to make certain you understand them as well." His fingers caressed a path of fire from her cheek to her neck. "Knowing you are hot enough, needing me enough to attempt to find your own release may be more than the animal inside me can bear. I wouldn't take what was not given willingly, but neither would I continue to straddle the line I now walk along. I would seduce you rather than allowing you the choice of coming to me. I don't want to do that, baby." His hand dropped from her, returning to the console. "Don't push me to that. I wouldn't like myself much for it, and I'm certain you would come to regret it. So in the interest of maintaining both our boundaries, use caution."

He was serious. She stared back at him with a hint of incredulity and wariness.

"Why?" she finally whispered. "Why do you care how you get what you want?" No other man she had ever known had cared.

His lips tilted with a hint of gentleness and a sensuality that sent flares of response racing through her.

"Because that beautiful body isn't all I want, baby," he answered cryptically. "Not by a long shot. I want everything. Think about that before you push the wrong buttons and tempt something you have no chance of controlling."

◆ CHAPTER 7 ◆

Megan moved down the staircase that evening after her shower. Everything felt off balance. Her emotions were in chaos, her physical responses confusing. Her reactions to Braden Arness had thrown her so off kilter that she wasn't certain what to feel at the moment.

After the Academy, and the disastrous results of training exercises, she had shut herself off, retreated to the desert and put aside the dream of making a difference within the world.

She had spent five years training to work in law enforcement, the first two in pre-Selection where candidates were put through rigorous classes involving legal code. The last three had been spent in the Academy after the selection process, the final year in real-situation training exercises.

The last training mission had been a hostage situation. The emotions pouring from the young woman being held by her drug-dealer husband had nearly incapacitated her, and caused an officer to be wounded. Her inability to focus on the perpetrator and his victim, rather than the emotions and the pain pouring through her, had nearly been fatal.

The Empathic abilities had shown up in her late teens. Her inability to form the barriers that others began building as children had been her downfall. She had stubbornly refused to give up her dream though. Forcing herself through pre-Selection and the Academy, right to the very moment that she knew without a doubt that the dream was over.

Megan moved into the kitchen, heading for the coffeepot despite the lateness of the hour, and tried to ignore Braden as he sat at the table with his laptop. He had been working there for hours, low growls coming from his chest as his irritation seemed to build.

The arousal was only growing as well. Unfortunately, finding release on her own was something she wasn't ready to tempt. Braden had been tenser since their confrontation in the Raider earlier; edgier, more aroused. That hunger was something she wasn't quite ready to confront.

"About time you came back down," he muttered as his fingers moved over the keyboard. "It's time we get to work."

She turned away from him, lifting a cup from the cabinet before pouring the dark coffee into it.

"What do you call what we were doing all day?" Every muscle in her body was protesting the workout. She could have sworn that rock climbing and cavern investigating was work. But hell, what did she know?

"Come here and sit down." He moved from the chair, making room for her as she moved around the table. "I pulled up the Breed database. Every Breed the Lab had information on, and some they didn't, is listed here. I have Mark and Aimee's files pulled along with their pictures. Go over them, see if you recognize them, or if you can recall any point that you may have been in contact with them."

She sat down in his chair hesitantly, her gaze flickering to the file pulled up on the screen.

"These pictures were taken while Mark and Aimee were still in the Labs," she whispered, seeing the nudity of Aimee's upper-body shot, as well as her disinterest in herself and her surroundings. "I've seen a few of the Breed files at the Academy. They didn't allow them to wear clothing." She looked up, watching as Braden pulled sandwiches from the refrigerator and poured himself another cup of coffee.

"We weren't human, so why did we need clothing," he grunted as he moved around the kitchen, fixing more coffee as he snacked on the food. He ate a lot; dinner had been finished an hour before and she was sure he had eaten enough for three grown men.

She turned her attention back to the laptop and the two files he had pulled up for her.

Breathing out wearily, she pushed her hair back from her face, wishing now that she had taken the time to braid it before coming down from her shower.

The thick mass never failed to slip over her shoulder. It also had the effect of making her feel softer, more feminine, when it was loose and unbound. It was a weakness she couldn't afford right now. The attraction burning between them wasn't dimming; it was only growing stronger. She needed something to douse it, not strengthen her inability to run from it.

"Mark and Aimee were created in France." He sat across from her. "To the best of my knowledge, they had never been in the States until a year ago, when they were rescued and relocated to the Breed Compound in Virginia. There are no records of any overseas missions. Just as there are no records of any trips you could have made out of the States."

There was a definite question in his voice.

Megan lifted her gaze from the computer screen and met his evenly.

"I've never been out of the States, Braden." She let a smile of amusement tug at her lips. It was obviously not the answer he wanted to hear. "And to my knowledge, I've never met these Breeds."

But they were familiar.

She turned back to the photos, wanting to frown at the odd prickling of recognition, but aware of how closely he was watching her.

"Why did you come back here after training at the Academy?"

"Didn't we go over this earlier?" she protested, swallowing past the lump of nervousness in her throat.

"You had excellent marks until your final training mission where your instructor was injured. After that you resigned, packed up and came home, despite several very lucrative offers from both public and private sectors."

She leaned back in her chair, refusing to look at him as she felt the demand filling the air. He deserved the truth. He was working with her and that put him in danger. He needed to know that.

"It's complicated," she finally sighed.

"I'm a smart guy." He seemed to bite the words out. "I'm sure I'll follow along just fine."

She looked at him then, catching the glittering suspicion in his eyes as he watched her.

"It has nothing to do with these Breeds," she finally answered, flicking the fingers of one hand toward the laptop. "It's a personal issue, Braden."

"Not any longer, Megan." He sat his cup down, leaning forward as he braced his hands on the top of the table and crowded over her. "My people are dying in this desert. Mark and Aimee left Sanctuary and drove straight here, into a trap, in a section of the desert patrolled by you. A search of their computer files showed that they had done a search on you before leaving. They were coming here to find you. Somehow the Council learned of it and sent those Coyotes to kill them and you, using their bodies to draw you in. Why?"

Guilt slammed through her. She jumped from her chair, facing him squarely now. She fisted her hands to keep them from shaking as she blinked back the moisture in her eyes. She didn't want him to see her for the failure she was. Unable to control her own abilities, a liability to anyone who fought beside her.

"Answer me, Megan." He caught her again, this time his grip tight enough on her upper arm to ensure she wasn't going anywhere, while careful to leave no marks.

The Academy had been five years of hell. She excelled because the strenuous work required complete focus. During training, she had gained some relief from the stress, the fears and the often volatile personalities who had come together in one area. It had amazed her, the number of the recruits who were there simply to act out the violence that raged inside them.

"Tell me why you're hiding. What did you see, Megan? Why are you cowering in this damned desert like a child afraid of the dark?"

"Because I am scared of the dark." She raged, her control breaking.

Tears filled her eyes as she stared up at him, trembling, terrified that he could be right. That she had possibly seen something, felt or sensed something that she was unaware of. Or worse, that she had ignored something that had caused those deaths, that somehow she could have prevented the violence.

"Let me go." She pulled out of his grip, refusing to meet his gaze as she turned her back on him and swiped at the tear that escaped her control and fell from her eyes.

"I'm an Empath, Braden." She fought the pain welling inside her, the dreams she had run from in the face of reality. "I hide in this fucking desert because it's quiet. Because there's no one around me for miles; no emotions, no fears or rage to batter at my damned head. Because I can function here." Her throat tightened at the admission.

Megan pushed her fingers in her hair, clenching at the strands as she fought for control amid the chaotic emotions raging inside her now. These were her emotions, her fears, and they were just as debilitating as the talent that allowed her to feel others.

"Empath?" His voice was thoughtful now, the anger of moments ago now throttled.

"I can't stand crowds, period. I can barely function here, in the town I've lived in all my life. Until you, I've never been around another human being I could tolerate for longer than a few hours at a time." She turned back to him, her own anger tightening her body as she fought demons she knew she could never win against. "I was in my late teens before it began developing; I couldn't hide it. Most Empaths develop sooner, at a time when it's possible for their brains to create the necessary shields to protect them. It didn't happen that way for me. I'm helpless against the influx of emotions and latent violence most human beings harbor. I can't protect myself from it. I thought I could make it in the Academy." She shook her head wearily, the guilt eating her alive. "It was my dream and I was determined to have it until I was nearly the cause of my instructor's death during our last training exercise. After that . . ." She breathed in harshly, wrapping her arms around herself and fighting back the pain. "After that, I just came home. Lance gave me a job with the sheriff's department and I tried to content myself with it."

Megan turned away from him, unable to risk staring into his eyes, perhaps seeing the condemnation she always felt she deserved.

"Then why join the Law Enforcement Academy to begin with?" he asked quietly.

"Because I was stupid." Her laugh was filled with bitter mockery. "I was stubborn, so stubborn, and too young to understand what I was getting myself into. That was my dream, and in my selfishness, I was determined to have it.

My barriers were strong enough to protect me if others were careful to tone down their emotions, which my friends and family had always done. The real world . . ." She breathed out heavily as she pushed her fingers through her hair, feeling once again the guilt she had never forgotten. "I found out how ill prepared I really was."

"But it's absent with me?" She felt him move closer. "Why?"

"The hell if I know." She turned back, surprised to find his chest no more than a few inches from her. God, how she wanted to lean against him. "There's a calm around you, some sort of natural barrier that, if I'm close enough, I can draw from." She shook her head in confusion.

He was silent, watching her intently. His eyes darkened to the color of old gold and began to glitter with heat.

"I'm not scared," she bit out, the bitterness that lived inside rising like a demon intent on destroying her. "I want to live. I want to fight, and by God I want to kick ass as much as anyone I've ever known. I dreamed of being part of the Breed rescues and had to back out of the program when recruits were chosen for the task force. I could be working anywhere, everywhere. But I'm a danger; not just to myself but also to anyone working with me. I can't take that risk."

"Megan, you can't live like this." When he touched her, she flinched.

Despite the gentleness of his hands, the soft rumble of his voice, she could feel the sense of failure inside her. She had failed herself, and she was failing him.

"I don't have a choice." She shook her head, attempting to pull away from him, to put some distance between them.

Didn't he know what his touch did to her? What it made her ache for? He could touch her and she wasn't seeing the deaths he had been part of, she wasn't feeling the brutality of his past or the violent anger she knew he felt toward the Coyotes. She felt the heat of his body, the calloused warmth of his hands; she felt a hunger that she knew was her own and it terrified her. Because she knew, once he was gone, she would never have it again.

"We all have choices." The dark baritone was a caress itself as his other hand landed on her hip, holding her in place each time she attempted to move away from him. "Stay still, Megan. You said you're calm when I'm near. That my emotions don't batter you; they don't bring you pain. Why?"

"I don't know." Her hands lay against his chest, and she knew she should be pushing him away. But she couldn't. He warmed her, took away the cold and replaced it with heat. "And I don't need to be babied by you. Do you think I want to get used to it, Braden? That I want to let myself use someone else's defenses for my own?"

Her fists clenched at the thought as she forced herself to push away from him, to leave the shelter he provided. "God, I don't need you to protect me any more than I need my family doing it."

"What you need is your ass paddled for attempting to fight this alone." He growled, his frustration apparent in his voice.

"Keep threatening to paddle me, Braden, and I'm going to make you regret it." Her eyes narrowed on him. This was the second threat.

"Or I'll make you enjoy it," he snapped back. "There are natural barriers to protect you from this, Megan. Why haven't you found them?"

"Do you think I haven't looked?" Why did men always think it was just a matter of finding something? "I've got a library of self-help books, Braden. I've watched every documentary and tried every fucking yin and yang psychological trick I can come up with. They don't work."

He was too calm now, too calculating.

"Did you suspect?" She felt tension fanning inside her as the suspicion began to grow in her mind.

"Of course I suspected." His eyes were narrowed on her

as he crossed his arms over his chest. "I didn't realize how debilitating it was, but I suspected you possessed the gift. I watched you in that canyon, Megan. You knew before the Coyotes fired. You sensed the danger and the death before you ever stepped foot from that Raider. It was only logical to assume you were Empathic."

She blinked back at him in shock. "And you never said anything?"

"What was there to say?" He shrugged negligently, his eyes still narrowed on her, his gaze considering. "All the signs were there."

"Is that why we've spent the day going over the murder scenes?" She kept her voice low, her fury contained. "You did it deliberately?"

His brow arched in challenge. "Of course. You have the ability to find the answers. I don't."

She breathed in roughly.

"And now?"

"And now, we'll go back." His voice hardened. "We'll work on your shields when this is over. When you're safe. But now, you need the edge to stay alive. We'll go back and you will work at figuring it out."

"No." The snarl was one of fury, betrayal. He was fucking using her. "I'll be damned if I will. I can't figure it out, Braden. Do you think I haven't tried?"

"That's exactly what I think." His voice hardened. "I think you've grown so used to hiding that it's become automatic. That the trauma of the gift coming so late, the inability to produce an adequate barrier against it, has resulted in an ineffective barrier. The pain gets in, the emotions and the shock of the intensity of the violence throw up just enough of a shield to keep the truth out, while allowing the pain to build. We'll work on that, too."

She stared back at him in horror. "You're serious."

"Of course I'm serious." His expression was completely

confident. "You can't afford to hide, Megan. These gifts . . ."

"It's a curse. At least call it what it is," she snapped out furiously. "And I'll be damned if I'll go back to the murder scene. There's nothing there. I tried."

"You didn't try. You hid. No more hiding."

Incredulity filled her.

"Fuck you!" She snarled.

"We'll get around to that, too." His answer had her gasping for breath, grasping for control. If she had had a gun in her hand she would have shot him.

"You used me," she threw back at him, becoming more enraged by the second. "The trips to the crime scenes, the tender little touches, the flirting. You've been using me. Nothing more."

"Don't kid yourself, cupcake." He snorted, a derisive little smile curling his lips as his gaze raked over her heaving breasts. "My dick's so hard and ready to show you otherwise that I wouldn't advise pushing this little boundary if I were you." The growl in his voice impaled her and sent lightning whipping over her nerve endings, tightening her clit. Arousal and lust, pulsing, red-hot and destructive, seared her womb.

Her juices gathered, flowed, moistening the outer lips, preparing her as the rage and lust seemed to feed from one to the other until every cell in her body and overly sensitive mind began to sizzle.

"You'll show me nothing," she cried out raggedly, betrayal slicing at her chest at the realization that while she was fighting to survive, he was determined to destroy her by making her experience the nightmares awaiting her in that gully. "You will pack up now and get the hell out of my house." She drew herself upright sharply. "I'd rather face the Coyotes than deal with your lies."

"My lies?" He stepped closer, stalking her, his head

lowered. His leonine mane flowed around the savage features of his face as the golden eyes glittered warningly. "I told no lies, Megan. I held nothing back. I've asked you for the truth for days, and *you* have lied."

"I didn't know anything. I don't know anything."

"And you don't want to know." Before she could stop him, before she could run, his arm snaked around her back, jerking her to him as his head lowered farther, his gaze locking with hers. "Well, baby, you might be able to hide from the rest but I'll be damned if I'll let you hide from this any longer."

His intent was instantly apparent. Megan's eyes widened, her fingers forming fists as she pressed against his wide shoulders, her feet fighting to find traction to jerk away from him. To escape the inescapable as his lips covered hers.

Time stood still. Nothing existed; nothing moved or breathed except Braden. His parted lips stole her breath. His tongue pushed past hers, sinking into the surprised depths of her mouth as a sudden taste of spice and heat exploded against her taste buds. The dark, rich taste had her lips moving, clasping the intruder as he licked, stroked. She met his tongue with her own, dancing around it as she attempted to draw more of the blistering taste into her mouth.

She had to fill herself with it, sate her senses with its unique heat as she fought to define the exact taste whipping through her mouth. There was no description. It was lightning and a summer storm. It was cinnamon and saffron, honey and sugar. And it was accompanied by the most incredibly pleasurable kiss she could have imagined.

As usual, Braden asked for nothing. He swept in and conquered. Claimed. She could feel the claiming in the hard hands that pulled her closer to his body, in the length of the erection pressing against her lower stomach, and gloried in it.

She was doing some claiming of her own.

Her hands sank into his hair, her fingertips glorying in the feel of the thick, coarse strands that fell well below his wide shoulders. Her hips arched as his hands moved to the rounded curves of her rear, lifting her, notching her thighs into his as his cock pressed against her swollen sex.

She needed to breathe, to scream out in pleasure, but the need for his kiss was stronger. The taste that filled her captivated her, just as he had captivated her since the moment she first saw him.

His tongue nudged against hers imperiously. She tangled with it, stroked it as a warning growl sounded in his chest. She could feel the hard, swollen glands beneath his tongue, knew the taste was spilling from them, and craved more. She needed more.

"Now." He growled as he drew back, nipping at her lips as she tilted her head, slanting against her mouth and fighting to pull his tongue back. "Suck it. Ease me, Megan."

His tongue speared into her mouth and her lips closed on it, drawing him in deeper as she began a hesitant suckling motion. He began to thrust in and out of her lips. The erotic action had them both moaning as the blood began to boil in Megan's body, burning along her nerve endings, searing her mind.

White-hot pleasure was whipping through her now. She shook in his grip, trembling as the ache in her pussy became deeper, sharper. God, she needed him. Hungered for him.

A hot, dark moan echoed in his chest as her whimpers grew in volume and the kiss became rapacious, his tongue thrusting in and out of her hot grip as she writhed against him. She had known it would be like this. Lightning hot, destructive. The pleasure was so intense, so deep, she wondered how she would survive when he left.

"Come here." She moaned as he lifted his head then dipped again for another kiss.

He pulled back again, ignoring her needy little moan, the demand that he return to the kiss. That he return the unique flavor to her mouth, to allow her to relish it, to sate herself on it.

Her head fell back as his lips traveled over her neck, his tongue licking at her flesh, sending riotous impulses zigzagging through her nervous system at the faintest hint of the roughness of his tongue. It was perfect. Not sandpapery; not smooth.

"Braden, God, I can't think." She gasped as his head lifted, the incredible taste of him still lingering on her lips, the feel of his tongue echoing on her flesh.

"Don't think." He growled, his lips at the swell of her breast, his tongue stroking the flesh there in long, slow licks. "Damn, you taste good, Megan. Sweet and hot, like sin itself."

"Enough!" She struggled against him, her fists pressing against his chest as his hand moved to her thigh, his fingers coming too close to the blazing center of her body.

God, she needed his touch. Had needed it for days. And now it was so close, satisfaction so near that she could taste it. It tasted of cinnamon and brown sugar. Of nutmeg and male heat. Pure male heat.

"Enough?" He grunted the word, the rough growl in his voice sending shudders quaking through her body as the animalistic sound seemed to echo around her.

"This won't solve anything." She tore from his grip, very well aware that he had let her go, and that it had nothing to do with her own strength, which had completely deserted her now. Even her damned knees were still shaking.

"It will solve many things." His gaze was heavy-lidded, his expression possessive, lustful. "You're mine, Megan. You know it as well as I do. You've sensed it from the very beginning. You know it."

Her head lifted as she fought the need pulsing heavily through her veins. It was mixed with fury. She hadn't asked him to do this to her. She hadn't asked him to interfere in her life, to attempt to use her. And he was trying to use her.

The curse he was so insistent that she court was one that would destroy her. She had seen the destruction years ago in her nightmares.

"Stop. I can't do this."

He lifted his brow. Megan felt her teeth gritting as anger surged hot and heavy inside her veins, mixing with the lust to create a cauldron of heat that blazed through the center of her body.

The lust wasn't so bad. Actually, she kind of liked that part, she had to admit. But his heavy-handed, know-it-all male stuff was going to get on her nerves fast.

He shook his head slowly as he crossed his arms over his chest and stared around the room.

"Why? So you can continue to hide, Megan? What is so frightening about knowing the truth?"

"The truth?" She pushed her fingers through her hair as bitterness welled inside her. "And how do you know the truth, Braden? I don't sense truth; I sense whatever was felt at the time. That doesn't necessarily mean it's the truth." Another painful piece of knowledge that the curse had taught her.

"In this case, it could bring you the truth," he pointed out softly. "The Council wants you dead, Megan, and they won't stop until you are. Unless you stop them first. Will you die for them?"

Will you die for them? She didn't want to die. She wanted to live. She wanted to fight as she was meant to fight, to know adventure, life. Love. She wanted all those things she had dreamed of as a child. Before she had begun feeling the remnants of broken lives and broken dreams. Before she had realized the danger she could become to anyone she worked with, anyone she was around.

"You don't know that." She shook her head fiercely. "You can't be certain."

His laughter was rife with knowledge, dark and brutal. His expression was a grimace of savage, remorseless truth.

Of course they could kill her. He was proof that they could and would tamper in ways nature had never intended.

"I can be certain." He tilted his head as he watched her. "And you know it's the truth. You know it, Megan, just as well as I do."

She flinched at his words. The news was still filled with stories of new horrors discovered within the Breed Labs, and the records found. The experiments, so horrible, so demonic that even now, years after the first Breed had come forward, the world could only look on in shock.

"Aimee was one year out of the Labs," he reminded her then. "If you read the files that were confiscated when the Lab fell you would know that before her rescue she was a toy. She hadn't grown in strength, in effectiveness, so she was turned over to the Council Trainers and guards for their pleasure."

"Stop." She didn't want to hear this.

"They raped her. Day after day, night after night. They allowed her to run; they let her fight and they laughed at her weakness as they raped her. Over and over again, Megan. Because she wasn't human. She was a creature. A toy. Without worth."

She wanted to cover her ears, to block out the remnants of memory, the muted screams she had heard as she stood beside the SUV. Knowledge. She had been able to block it for the small amount of time she had been there. She had kept a careful distance, hadn't touched the bodies, hadn't touched the vehicles. Had refused to open her senses enough to feel the pain screaming through Aimee's body.

But enough of it had slipped past the barrier she had slammed up that she knew of the betrayal.

"I can't tell you why they were killed." She clenched her fists as she crossed her arms over her chest, fighting to hold back the chill moving through her. "It doesn't work that way."

"How do you know it doesn't?" He continued to watch her intently. Too intently. His gaze sliced through her defenses. "You've never tried."

"And I can't start now." Once she released the fragile barrier between her and the world, she knew it wouldn't end. The pain would go on forever.

"Yes, you can. And you will." His voice was hard. Determined.

Megan found herself stepping back as his arms uncrossed, the power and strength in the hard muscles of his chest, his biceps, drawing her gaze. They rippled as he moved, much like the huge lions his DNA came from.

"I can't do what you want." She forced the words past her lips, seeing the steely determination in his eyes. "I'm sorry, Braden. I can't be what you need."

She turned and left the room, moving quickly toward the stairs, her only clear thought to escape him, to escape herself. She felt too much when she was around him. She had fought for too many years for the measure of peace she had found in her life, only to learn that all the planning, all the hiding, had been in vain. A curious sense of failure swept over her.

As she raced up the stairs, she was instinctively aware of Braden behind her, coming for her. He had no intention of letting her escape so easily.

As she reached the second-floor landing, his hard arm latched around her waist, pulling her against him a second before she found herself against the wall. A gasp left her lips as his hand slid between her thighs, cupping her, holding her heat captive in his palm.

"You are more than I ever dreamed I would find in this desert," he growled. "But that doesn't mean you'll control me, Megan. It doesn't mean you can run from me or that I will allow you to hide from yourself."

His fingers pressed closer, adding a heat and pressure to

her swollen clit that had her gasping in surprise. Her juices eased from her vagina, dampening her further as she felt the muscles swelling, pulsing erratically for his touch.

The taste of cinnamon and brown sugar lingered on her tongue, reminding her of his taste, the heat of his kiss.

"This isn't going to solve anything." She struggled against him, biting back her moan as he held her firm, his other hand moving beneath her shirt, his fingertips skimming her stomach before flattening just below her breast.

"I'm not here to solve anything except the danger stalking you," he reminded her, his voice a dark, deep male purr. The sound of it excited, terrified. "This"—he pressed closer to her back as his fingers began a gentle rubbing motion between her thighs—"isn't meant to solve. It isn't meant to be comfortable, or a place to hide. Starting here . . ." She whimpered as he pressed harder against her clit, rubbing more firmly as she went to her tiptoes to escape the extreme reactions racing through her body. "This is to show you. To tempt you . . ." A smile filled his voice a second before his teeth grazed her neck. "To remind you . . . I'm the boss, baby. You will do it because I say you will. You will learn how to use your gift, you will learn how to fight, because the alternative is death, and that is unacceptable. And you can do it one of two ways . . ." His voice deepened. "The easy way . . ." His hand smoothed over her stomach. "Or the hard way." His fingers pressed, stroked, rotated.

Megan's eyes widened as wildfire skipped through her veins and pleasure popped through her womb.

It wasn't an explosion. It wasn't an orgasm meant to destroy her senses or bring her to her knees in submission. It was meant to tease, a taste of ecstasy, a deliberately seductive, erotically diabolical surge of pleasure that would ensure she could never forget. Never forget who gave it, or where the ultimate pleasure could be found.

"Remember that cupcake." He growled before turning

and stalking to his room, anger radiating from him in waves as she watched him disappear.

She was still trembling, shuddering from the excessive pleasure and her inability to control it. She couldn't control the need, herself or him. Oh boy, she was in so much trouble now.

⋄ CHAPTER 8 ⋄

She wasn't in the best of moods the next morning. She had tossed and turned in bed, aroused, furious, and scared. Scared of the sensations she felt when Braden touched her, of her own reaction to him, and the bonding she could feel tying them together. The last was the crux of the matter. She had never bonded with anyone outside her family, especially not a man as hard and as formidable as Braden.

She knew what he wanted from her, knew he wasn't going to let her hide or ignore the very things she had fought to ignore for so many years. It would have been easily avoided if she could convince herself it wasn't something she wanted; but she knew it was. She wanted to learn how to control her talents, how to separate herself from her abilities and sift through the echoes of emotions to the knowledge beneath. She had never succeeded on her own, and though she feared the failure of trying again, she knew she would. She would, because the opportunity was there; because she knew it could well be her last chance.

With the emotions churning so restlessly inside her, it was no surprise that when Lance called, ordering her into the office for a meeting, it irritated her.

"Broken Butte isn't a large town," Megan lectured Braden as they drove past the city limit sign just before noon. "We're a very close-knit community. We don't mind outsiders, but we don't like governmental types." She sneaked a look from the corner of her eye as he slouched in his seat, his Stetson pulled low to shade his eyes.

Damn, he looked good in that hat. And she didn't want to remember how good he looked; didn't want to acknowledge it. She was still burning from his touch the night before, so desperate to be taken it was a wonder she hadn't gone to his bed last night.

"I promise I'm housebroken, Megan," he drawled.

"Only because it suits you at the moment." She grunted, shifting in her seat as she entered the outer edges of town.

She was aware of the long look he directed at her. It was impossible not to be aware of it. Her body was so highly sensitive now that she swore she could feel his gaze raking over her.

"Megan, sweetheart," he chastised her, his voice deepening to an outrageously sensual purr. "I promise to behave myself. Jonas assures me I passed Civility 101 with flying colors."

He had been like this all morning. Gently sardonic, watching her, his gaze patient as he seemed to wait on something. He could wait until hell froze over. It didn't matter what he wanted, she was determined to deny him.

Of course, she knew exactly what *she* wanted. Or rather, what her body wanted.

No way, no how. Whatever the hell was wrong with her, she was not giving in to it. She clenched her thighs together tighter, very well aware of Braden's carefully drawn breath. He could smell her arousal and that was just pissing her off.

"Would you stop it," she hissed as she pulled into the parking lot of the sheriff's office. "You start walking around sniffing the damned air and everyone is going to know exactly what you are. And for God's sake, keep those damned teeth hidden. One flash of that vampire smile of yours and little children will run screaming."

He smiled slowly. "Actually, most seem rather interested in it. I believe that fake Breed teeth even went on sale at the malls this year. I hear the Breed Pride is making a mint from the sales."

Megan pulled into the first available parking spot before laying her head on the steering wheel and shaking it in defeat.

"It's okay, baby." She started when his hand stroked slowly down her back. "I'll make it all better when we get home."

Her head snapped up. "You are certifiably insane." She groaned, shaking off his touch as he chuckled devilishly. "Keep your damned paws to yourself."

His grin was rakish as he tipped his hat back a bare inch, his eyes filled with mirth.

Megan shivered at the look. She would have moaned but she'd be damned if she would give him the satisfaction.

"Let's go." She released her seat belt before pushing open the door and stepping out. "Lance is already pissed off enough at me. I don't need to be late for this meeting to make it worse."

"Remind me to find a less confrontational partner the next time." He sighed as she frowned at him darkly. "You, Megan, are becoming downright hostile. For a woman who smells so sweet and warm, your attitude leaves much to be desired."

She just bet it did. If he kept this up she was going to show him the working end of her pistol and let him see just how confrontational she could really get.

"You know," he said, "I bet if you try real hard, you could stand right here and figure out just what this mysterious meeting is all about." Braden stopped several feet from the steps that led to the double doors.

She stared back at him in horror before glancing around to make certain no one heard his blasphemous words.

"Would you shut up," she snapped.

His brows arched questioningly. "Come on, Megan. It would be easy. Just give it a little try."

With a sneer she brushed past him and headed up the steps. She heard his sigh a second before a small, amused grunt of laughter preceded him up the steps.

"Well, you could have at least tried." He managed to grab the door handle before she did, pulling it open with a flourish as she rolled her eyes in exasperation.

Deputy Jenson's fury slapped at her as she passed his office. It was always present—the dark violence, the thirst for blood. He wasn't one of the good guys, but until he broke the right rule, Lance couldn't get rid of him. That edge of violence nagged at her until Braden moved closer, distracting her with his clean male scent and aura of male arousal that whipped around her senses.

Megan breathed in deeply, ducking her head as she gritted her teeth and moved purposefully to Lance's office at the end of the building. Separated from the main offices by the visiting rooms, it leant a less emotionally chaotic feel. Lance was a calm person, not given to violence, though with a ragged edge of bitterness that saddened Megan. He was still one of the easiest people to be around.

She knocked on his door.

"In," Lance snapped.

Megan cast Braden a frowning glance as she gripped the doorknob, feeling Lance's anger seeping through the panel.

"What did you do?" she hissed, not in the least taken in by his innocent look.

"Me?" He arched his brow, his eyes glinting with amusement. "I've been a good Leo, darlin'. What did you do?"

She snorted at his reply before pushing the door open and stepping into the room.

She was aware of the tension that snapped around her the minute she entered the room. Though she had been unaware of the other inhabitant standing across the room. And she bet he was a Breed. Dangerous, powerful, and not in the best of moods.

His eyes narrowed the instant she walked in, and heat flooded her face as he raised his head and inhaled quickly. Son of a bitch. What did they do, go around sniffing every woman in the world like a potential meal? So she was horny. Hadn't they ever smelled a horny woman before? Or was she somehow different?

The ridiculous thought caused her to turn and glare at Braden. He closed the door behind him and stared at the room's other occupant with a faintly questioning look. Evidently, he was just as surprised as she was.

"Jonas." His voice was cautious as Megan stepped to the side, closer to Lance's desk.

"Braden." The other man inclined his head slowly, his odd, silver eyes shifting to Megan then to Braden once again.

He was an imposing figure. As tall as Braden; muscular, savage. But this one—Jonas—could easily be a killer. Megan could feel the darkness that surrounded him, the emotions that clashed within him like lightning in the middle of a thunderhead. Rage, dark and barely contained, fought for freedom. But she could also sense honor, pain, regret. The regret was nearly as thick as the rage. All the emotions were subdued though, barely noticeable as an aura of control and determination held them back.

"Is there a problem, Lance?" She looked to her cousin.

"Megan, meet Jonas Wyatt. You saw him the night the

Coyotes were picked up at your house," Lance reminded her with a cold edge to his voice.

Megan nodded.

"What's going on?" Braden didn't seem inclined to beat around the bush. He moved in front of her, facing Jonas.

She moved to go around him, only to raise her brows as he shifted in front of her, blocking her once again.

Jonas's irritable growl as she pushed Braden out of the way had her eyes narrowing on him.

"Lance?" She turned to her cousin, growing tired of the disapproving frown Jonas Wyatt had leveled on her.

"Ask him." He waved his hand toward the Breed. "He called the meeting with a demand for secrecy. I just live to serve."

Megan winced. Evidently he had received an order from very high up to serve, otherwise he wouldn't be nearly as pissed.

Jonas flicked Lance a cool look. "I do apologize, Mr. Jacobs. The need for secrecy was high. The report I received from Braden concerning the printout found in that cavern was disturbing. The information coming in from other sources even more so. I needed to assess the situation myself."

"What was wrong with meeting at the house?" Braden was too close. He stayed on her ass, hovering over her like a dark shadow.

"The printout is being investigated," Lance snapped. "I will find out who accessed and printed it. It's just a matter of time."

"What's taking so long?" She shook her head in confusion. "The computers automatically log those passwords."

The voice that answered sent chills racing over Megan's flesh. "The password used was Sheriff Jacobs's."

Lance stared at her. She could feel the pain radiating from him, but also the protectiveness. Lance would never hurt her. She knew that just as she knew the sun would rise in the morning and night would come later.

"We have a problem then." She turned and looked at Jonas. She was seriously starting to dislike this one. "Someone has obviously managed to steal passwords."

"The sheriff assures us he doesn't write his password down or share it. He changes it weekly and uses strict privacy protocols on his computer."

Megan watched Jonas for long moments.

Lance was still, quiet. And that wasn't a good sign. An explosion was brewing and it was one Megan didn't want to witness.

"Tell him to stop, Braden." She stared into the savage silver eyes as she spoke to the man behind her. "Now."

"I'd like to hear an explanation myself, Megan."

She turned to Braden carefully. "I said *now*," she reminded him, keeping her voice soft, her fury throttled.

She didn't know the game Jonas Wyatt was playing, but she knew he was playing one, and he was using Lance to do it.

"I don't need your protection, Megan," Lance snapped then. "I'll find out . . ."

"If you're still in this office." Jonas's voice was condescending. "Such mistakes are not just criminal, they are also incriminating, Sheriff Jacobs."

"You son of a bitch . . ." Lance was out of his chair and halfway around the desk before Megan could step in front of him, placing her hand on his chest. But she jerked it back quickly.

She stared down at her hand, feeling the sharp sensation of distaste at the touch before staring back up at Lance.

"Fuck 'im." She kept her voice soft as she let a small smile assure him of her trust. "We both know better, Lance. And I know you'll find the proof. Don't let him get to you."

"Dammit, Meg . . ." He reached out, his hands gripping her shoulders, sending pulses of a painlike sensation that

attacked her nerve endings. She flinched back a second before Braden's surprising snarl filled the room and he pulled
her away from her cousin.

"What the hell?" Lance stared at her in shock. "Meg,
are you okay?"

He reached for her again, only to have Braden pull her
quickly behind him, ignoring her struggles as he did so.

"Dammit, Braden . . ."

"What the fuck is going on?" Lance's voice was filled
with confusion. Anger. "Is she hurt?"

Megan forced her way back in front of Braden, her elbow stabbing into his hard stomach as he tried to stop her.
"Don't push me back behind you again." She stared up at
him furiously. "When I need you standing in front of me,
I'll let you know."

The rumbled growl that came from his chest might have
intimidated someone less pissed off, Megan thought. But it
did little to impress her.

Jonas shifted impatiently, drawing her gaze back to him.

"He won't allow another male to touch you, Miss
Fields," Jonas snapped furiously. "Test him and you might
get more than you've bargained for."

"I didn't ask you." She turned on him, enraged, aware of
Lance watching her in surprise. "So you can just shut the
hell up."

"You didn't have to ask." His tight smile was cold and
dangerous. "I was being nice by offering the information."

"Jonas, you're not exactly making sense," Braden
pointed out, his voice not as lazy as before, but no less confused than Lance's had been. "And accusing Jacobs of betraying his cousin wasn't your brightest move." There was
a question in his voice as he obviously chose to ignore the
earlier statement regarding his possessiveness toward her.

"The evidence is there," Jonas pointed out. "The schedule comes from this office alone; no one else should have
had access to it. The information we've managed to extract

from the Coyote you captured indicates someone working from the inside. Jacobs is on the inside."

Lance's fists bunched, his expression contorting into lines of fury as he turned on the Breed. "I've had my fill of your accusations, Jonas."

Megan struggled to fend off the whiplash of emotions slamming into her. She moved closer to Braden and threw up every shield she could force in front of them, but nothing helped. Lance's anger was white-hot, his voice pain-filled, edging into violence as Jonas's silver eyes darkened dangerously. She shook her head, staring at him, fighting the stirring cauldron of sensations as they swirled around her.

She couldn't run. She couldn't escape the emotions.

"I've had my fill of your incompetence," Jonas sneered. "Tell me, Jacobs. Are you the one who directed Mark and Aimee into that desert? Did you play liaison to the Genetics Council and their Coyotes?" His anger was like wildfire, engulfing everything in its path.

"Like hell." Lance moved for the other man, his muscles bunching as Megan felt the whip of another emotion. Deceit. A lie. A carefully constructed game.

"No. Lance, he's playing you." She jumped in front of him again. "Don't give him the satisfaction of a fight."

"Playing what?" he snapped, attempting to pull away from her. "I'll be damned if I'll let him stand in my office and accuse me of trying to kill you, Megan."

"Stop." She shook his arm, ignoring the discomfort, staring back at him fiercely. "Listen to me." Her fingers tightened despite the building fire beneath her skin, the harsh reaction to touching someone else that made no sense. "He's playing with you, Lance. He knows you didn't do a damned thing. This is no more than a game."

She barely realized she was shuddering. She could feel Lance's rage beating within him, beating within her, demanding action. She couldn't let him fight; wouldn't let him fight. It was all a game, carefully constructed, for what reason she wasn't certain.

"Megan, let him go." Braden seemed to tower over her, his hand covering hers. His touch was cool, comforting where the touch of Lance's flesh filled her with pain. "He's hurting you. I can feel the pain pouring from you. Let him go."

She was shaking, fighting the sensations, staring up at the cousin who had been one of the mainstays in her life for as long as she could remember. The pain made no sense; the sharp discomfort in her hands streaked through the rest of her body, cramping her muscles, searing her skin.

"Hurting her?" Lance's frown was bewildered. "Meg, what the hell is going on?"

Lance moved back, pulling his arm gently from her grip as he retreated, his concern washing over her as some dark sizzle of satisfaction speared through the room. She turned slowly to Jonas Wyatt.

"I don't like you," she informed him, gritting her teeth in anger. "You are a sick son of a bitch."

He knew. She could feel it. He was aware of her abilities, testing them, pushing them all. His lips curved sardonically.

"Perhaps." He tilted his head in acknowledgment of the insult as she stared back at him in confusion.

"Why did you do this?" she asked quietly.

"Because it needed to be done." Jonas arched his brow. "You see, Miss Fields, we have a spy somewhere in this little setup. If not here in this office, then elsewhere. Possibly both. I'll find out who it is, one way or the other. Thank you very much for assuring me that in this case I was wrong. Sheriff Jacobs is innocent."

Her lips parted in shock.

"It's all a game," she whispered. "You knew I was empathic. You used me to try to trap my cousin," she accused him, the anger growing in her voice as she twisted her head to stare up at Braden. "You told him."

It made sense now. Somehow he had learned of the empathic abilities and turned them against her by confronting Lance in front of her and then watching her reaction.

"You bastard!" She struggled against Braden's grip. "You cold-blooded, unfeeling son of a bitch."

"Megan. Stay still." Braden's arms surrounded her as she tried to slam her elbow into his abdomen, jerking against his grip. "You don't want to do this alone. Not right now. Too many emotions are whipping through you. Settle down and think first."

His voice was at her ear, slicing through the chaotic din of the blood thundering in her ears, of the emotions and sensations that attacked her brain. Fury. Anger. It was her weakness. She couldn't manage even the simplest shield against them on her own.

Lance was trying to pull his own emotions back, to spare her the pain of his fury; but it was still there, whipping through the room as though it were a separate entity.

She could feel herself shuddering in Braden's grip. She was breathing harshly, her mind soaking up the psychic waves rolling through the room. So many emotions. But over them all, satisfaction. Satisfaction, as well as anger, that poured from Jonas Wyatt.

Her gaze rose to his as she grabbed hold of the fragile barrier she could feel surrounding her, the calm that flowed from Braden and encompassed her in its protection.

"Get the hell out of this office, Jonas," Lance snapped. "Now. And don't bother coming back here."

"Sorry Sheriff." Jonas's smile was flat, tight with his own anger now. "Unfortunately, we're not quite finished yet. I came to find a spy; instead I find out that my best Enforcer has now mated your cousin. Quite an interesting little development, I must say."

Braden froze behind her as Megan blinked back at the Breed.

"What are you talking about?" she snapped.

Suddenly, the air in the room felt too thick, too tension-filled to allow her to breathe. Jonas glanced behind her at Braden.

Jonas's smile was cold. "The Mating isn't going to do her much good unless you carry it through, Braden. Hurry and knock her up before she loses her mind."

None of this was making sense. Jonas wasn't making sense.

"You're pushing me too far, Jonas." Braden's growl was savage, animalistic. "Insult her again and I'll kill you."

Jonas's brow arched, his gaze locked with hers.

"Did I insult her?" he murmured. "I stated a fact, Braden. You have mated this woman. It's a little-known phenomenon that began with Callan Lyons, the Pride's leader, and his woman. You are both in the middle of Mating Heat. You marked her, kissed her, infected her with that hormone in your tongue that is more binding than marriage. And there's only one cure." His lips curled coldly. "Well, perhaps not a cure exactly, but one of the few hopes of easing the arousal that will become so painful, so debilitating that she'll risk every area of your life. Congratulations, buddy." The last remark lacked any sincerity whatsoever. Not that it mattered.

Shock now filled the room. It slammed into her, ripped through her brain as she turned slowly to meet Braden's gaze and felt the absolute, complete horror that raced from him and struck her mind, blinding her to every other emotion.

His denial was so strong, so fierce, it slapped her like an open-handed blow, pushing her back, reaching into the depths of her soul and withering a hope she hadn't known had bloomed within her.

In that moment, she cursed her abilities with everything

she had, just as fiercely as she cursed the men staring back at her.

"I didn't want you either," she finally whispered as something in her soul flamed in agonizing pain, forcing the lie past her lips as she turned and moved jerkily away from him. "What I do want are explanations." She turned to Jonas, blinking back the tears that were gathering in her eyes as she met his flinty look. "Now."

◆ C H A P T E R 9 ◆

Mating Heat. Megan listened in silent shock as Jonas explained the physical symptoms, the need, the arousal and what had caused it. He was very clinical about it. She was thankful that he had asked Lance to leave before explaining more fully.

It began with a certain touch. A kiss, a nip, any caress that allowed the Breed saliva—infused with the hormone that caused the glands at sides of their tongues to swell—into a body's system.

The nip on her ear would have done it, perhaps. She remembered the sensitivity of her earlobe after the confrontation, the slow-rising arousal, the clash of emotions that kept her so off balance.

It hadn't exactly begun there. She remembered following Braden through the tunnels, intrigued by his scent, by the air of danger and excitement that flowed around him. She would have wanted him anyway, but would she have wanted him with the strength she did now? That quickly?

She risked a quick glance at him and admitted she would have. He had drawn her to him, fascinated her, became a conspirator in adventure within the first half hour of their meeting. And she knew, despite the conflicting emotions raging within her, that the little nip he had given her had little to do with that.

That didn't make his rejection of her easier. Her chest was tight with the tears she was holding back. She assured herself she wasn't going to cry. Not yet. Though maintaining control on her emotions became harder by the second as Jonas's explanations whipped through her head.

"We've watched the phenomenon advance," Jonas explained as he sat on the edge of the desk, his mocking gaze touching on both of them. "Some of the females it affects with greater strength than others. From the smell of the heat pouring from her, I'd say your woman is one of the strongest."

Now there was one pissed-off Lion Breed. Her eyes followed Braden for long minutes, taking in the emotionless expression, the flat chill in his eyes and the strength of the barriers he had slammed between her and his own emotions.

And perhaps that was for the best. The rejection had sliced through her with a pain in her chest that she hadn't expected. Forcing the hurt back was next to impossible as she listened to Jonas explain the Mating Heat and its implications.

"Mating Heat means forever, boys and girls," he announced sarcastically.

Megan crossed her arms over her breasts and stared back at Jonas defiantly.

"I can tell you're just thrilled over it too," she mocked him coldly, ignoring the odd little glint of amusement that flickered in those icy gray eyes. "What happened Mr. Wyatt, did you suspect this before you came out here and set up this little meeting?" She waved her hand to encompass the three of them. "You knew Lance didn't print out that damned schedule, just as you knew that Braden would discover the fact that I'm an Empath. You came here to be certain that the Mating you suspected had actually happened."

His brow arched. A slow upward tilt that conveyed a sarcastic response more clearly than words.

"I suspected," he admitted with a slow incline of his head as he glanced at Braden and grimaced. "I was hoping that this time my suspicions would be wrong."

His gaze when it returned to her was condemning.

"I'm certain his hopes agree with yours," she snapped as she flipped her hand toward Braden's silent form, covering her hurt with anger. "So find a cure."

She ignored the rumbled growl that came from Braden.

Jonas chuckled. There was no mirth to the sound, only mocking knowledge.

"The Breeds have been searching for a cure for more than five years," he said. "There's a ban on this information, Miss Fields. Breaking that ban could and would endanger more lives than just yours or Braden's. It also comes with a rather stiff penalty."

"Oh yeah, I'm just going to run right out and call a press conference," she bit out. "Can the orders, Mr. Wyatt, I'm not in the mood for them."

His eyes narrowed. "For a woman whose abilities cause her to be too frightened to join the real world, you can be rather confrontational, Miss Fields." There was nothing kind about the tight smile that shaped his thin lips.

"Enough, Jonas." Braden's voice was a hard rumble as he shifted from his position against the far wall and stood straight, tense.

He didn't want her, so why protest if another man dared to speak sharply to her? Why protest anything about her period?

"Did I ask for your help?" she snapped before Jonas could speak. She ignored the frown that lowered his brows and had his gold eyes glittering in warning.

"You don't have to ask," Braden growled, as though he had rights. As though she were some sort of responsibility now.

"Oh yeah, that's right." She wrinkled her nose sarcastically. "You're my big bad mate now." She gave an exaggerated shiver. "I should be all grateful or something, shouldn't I?"

"Or something," he muttered, eyeing her warily.

"Yeah, especially considering just how enthusiastic you were once Mr. Wyatt here let us in on the secret of that great kiss you're packing. Gee, maybe we should bottle that stuff, Braden. It would sell better than the plastic Breed teeth."

She was aware of Jonas watching the confrontation with interest. If she hadn't disliked him on sight, she would have certainly disliked him now. That, added to the anger rising inside her, wasn't helping her attitude in the least.

"Your mate has a smart mouth, Braden," Jonas commented softly. "You should work on correcting that."

"Yeah, why don't I just do that for you." Braden grunted as he watched her carefully.

"Excuse me boys, I'm still in the room here." She waved her hand at them as she spoke. "The little woman doesn't need to be spoken over. This Mating Heat or whatever the hell you want to call it hasn't fried my brain in the least."

Braden and Jonas both directed fierce frowns toward her. It could have been cute, if she weren't so pissed off.

"You know, I think I pretty much have the basic information now." She smiled tightly. "He wants me because his hormones are all jacked up, that's all. Hey, no biggie. Nature sucks, right?" She smiled brightly, holding the pain back. "Well, tell you what, Mr. Director of Breed Affairs. Just load your little golden boy right back up in one of those fancy little helicopters I hear you boys fly around in and transport him right back to your nice, secure little compound and see if you can't cure him of it. I'll do just fine on my own. Just like I always have."

She was furious. She wasn't a damned hormone magnet, and she couldn't care less whether Braden liked the effects of some chemical reaction that was all his fault anyway. She hadn't asked him to mess with her life, and she would be damned if she would ask him to continue to be a part of it.

"Just like you always have?" Braden snapped back then, his own voice heating. "Hiding. Aren't you tired of hiding, Megan?"

"Actually, I think I am." She inhaled roughly, facing the two men as she tilted her chin and glared back at them. "But there's one thing you did teach me, Braden. That little shield of yours is right handy. Given enough time, I'm sure I can copy it. I'm nothing if not adaptable when I have to be. And I can adapt without you."

He stared back at her as he crossed his arms over his chest, his eyes slowly narrowing as a hint of predatory calculation entered them.

"Don't dare me, sweetheart," he warned her, his voice soft.

"Dare you?" She shook her head as she retained the tight, sarcastic smile she had adopted. "I'm not daring you, *sweetheart*. I'm telling you. I didn't need you before you began this funky hormone stuff, and I sure don't need you now."

"May I point out that the Mating Heat is harder on females than males." Jonas spoke up at that point, his voice curiously bland. "You may want to rethink that."

"Did I ask for your opinion?" She turned and stomped toward the door. "If the two of you will excuse me now, I'll go see if I can repair some of the damage your inept humor has caused in this office." She gripped the doorknob, turning back to scowl at Jonas. "One of these days, someone is going to play this game better than you do, Mr. Wyatt. And when it happens, I want a ringside seat."

His lips tightened further as he glanced at Braden.

"Your mate has a mean mouth." He growled. "It could get her into trouble."

"I believe it already has," she retorted in turn before jerking the door open and stalking into the hall. The hard reverberation of the slam of the door was an all-too-brief, satisfying sound as wood cracked against wood. And a muttered Breed curse was heard from the other side.

Let them curse. As far as she was concerned, she'd had enough.

◆　◆　◆

Braden stared at the door, his head tilted, eyes narrowed. She was pissed and hurt, and he couldn't blame her a bit. His thoughts and emotions had been too chaotic to allow her past his shields after that first instant rejection. He couldn't risk it; not yet.

"The hormonal surges inside her will only make her worse." Jonas sighed, his tone more relaxed now.

Braden snorted. "Thanks for the warning. Just what I wanted, my woman ready to skin me alive. Thanks, Jonas."

"I'm really hoping this Mating shit doesn't become a habit," Jonas said. "This makes two damned good Enforcers I've lost to it. Tarek Jordan didn't resign due to injuries as his file states. The son of a bitch mated his neighbor. Can you believe that? Send a man on a mission and the next thing you know, he's Mating the little sexpot next door. Now this." He shook his head with an edge of irritation.

"Worry more about why I shouldn't kick your ass for pissing her off," Braden growled, pushing his fingers through his hair as he breathed out roughly. "Damn, you could have at least tried a little tact here."

Braden could only shake his head at that point. The

Director of Breed Affairs was known for his manipulations and carefully calculated games. He wasn't known for his mercy or his compassion.

"Fine. You made sure my life was a little harder for the next few days. Surely that wasn't the only reason you came out here today?" He shrugged his shoulders restlessly, trying to forget the implication that sex could be coming. He was dying to touch Megan, to claim her, to mark her. Mating Heat be damned. She was his woman; he had just hoped to ease her into that fact.

"Not hardly." Jonas moved to the desk, sitting on the edge of it casually as he crossed his arms over his chest. "The printout definitely came from here; our little Coyote buddy assured us of that. He's alive, by the way."

Braden arched his brow. He hadn't expected that.

"It's not easy but that boy talks when it matters. I'll let him live until he's not talking anymore."

"Do you know who printed the schedule?" Braden was determined that the bastard who had betrayed Megan would pay.

"I have it narrowed down. Unfortunately, Sheriff Jacobs was on the short list. The other two were Lenny Blanchard and Deputy Jose Jensen. I'm having a tail put on them; we'll have answers soon."

"Blanchard doesn't seem the sort." Braden shook his head slowly, thinking of the friendly desk sergeant.

"Those are usually the ones that make me the most nervous," Jonas growled. "Watch your ass. I can't spare a team out here yet, Braden, or I'd have one covering you, you know that. But I'm working on something, so hopefully, I'll have a team soon. In the meantime, I'll get an investigation started on the two deputies and see what I can find out."

Braden nodded at that.

"And now for the biggie." Jonas smiled with too much enjoyment. "You and the missus have tests to undergo. Think we can talk her into cooperating?"

Braden dropped his head. Cooperation? Megan? Now?

"One of these days, one of your Enforcers will end up killing you, Jonas." He snarled as he lifted his head and dropped his arms. "And I'll be damned if I'm not there to see it."

Jonas chuckled at the sentiment. "Hold that thought, buddy." He smiled with all appearances of looking forward to it. "It's been a while since I've had a good fight; I think I'd enjoy the challenge."

And there lay the problem. Jonas was rarely challenged. He played where he could, never in a manner that endangered his Enforcers, but in ways that made them willing to kill him. At the moment, Braden understood the sentiment and he was certain Megan did as well.

She was hurting. He had felt it when she stormed out of the office, and as much as that worried him, it also sent a surge of satisfaction thrumming through his senses. The key to Megan was in touching her emotions, her heart. She was fiercely independent, determined to make a difference, even if it was only in her own little corner of the world. She was a fighter, one of the finest alpha females he had ever laid his eyes on. With a bit more training, and the right shields, she would make a hell of an Enforcer. He turned his gaze to Jonas, wondering how his commander would take having a non-Breed on the payroll.

Jonas scowled back at him. "What?"

"She would make a hell of an Enforcer." He kept his voice low; God help him if Megan heard him plotting her life out. "You don't have to lose an Enforcer, Jonas, you can gain one instead."

Jonas's eyes narrowed. "She's not a Breed."

"She's an Empath. And her gun collection is better than mine." He snorted at the description. Unfortunately, he knew there was a risk. Her weapons collection rocked. "But even more than that, even if she weren't my mate, she's still my woman. I won't leave her behind." And he couldn't give up the fight. Bringing down the remnants of the Council and the Pure-Blood societies was too important.

"You're not fighting the Mating." Jonas settled himself more comfortably on the desk's edge as Braden watched him carefully. "She didn't seem pleased."

Braden sighed wearily. "I don't like having decisions taken away from me, Jonas, even by nature. I knew she was mine, but I hadn't decided how to convince her yet. This complicated things. She felt the rejection of the idea of the Mating and now she's pissed. But she'll get over it." She wouldn't have a choice.

Braden stood still as Jonas continued to stare back at him. He had that habit, as though he could see into a man's soul and gauge his worth. For most it was disconcerting; for those who worked with him and fought beside him on a daily basis it was a comfort.

"Okay." He nodded sharply. "Build her defenses and her shields. And training her is your responsibility. I'll leave it to you."

Now, he just had to convince Megan.

As a silence descended between them, the door snapped open and Lance Jacobs stalked back into his office.

"Get the hell out of here," Lance snapped when he spied Jonas sitting on his desk. He then turned to Braden. "Megan is in her office, but if you're not careful you'll be hoofing it back to the house tonight." There was no compassion in his voice whatsoever.

"I know where your mate gets her streak of mean from now," Jonas grunted to Braden as he slowly straightened from the desk. "It's hereditary."

"You just keep believing that," Lance muttered as he moved behind his desk and took his seat. Slouching back in the chair, he watched both men with calculated interest.

"She's going to fight you every breath," he informed them after several moments passed. "And you can put a ban on whatever the hell you want to, Jonas, that's my damned cousin your messing with. She's close enough to be a sister. Don't think because she lives in that desert alone that her family won't back her. Every damned one of us."

"Right down to the Special Forces uncles?" Jonas arched his brow as Braden smothered a sigh.

"Especially those." Lance's smile was tight, merciless. "Remember that. And while you're at it, get your asses out of my department; I'm damned sick of dealing with Breeds."

That seemed to be the general consensus of anyone dealing with Jonas.

Braden stayed silent, watchful, measuring the sheriff as he scowled back at Jonas. The man had an unusual air about him, at once old and young. He had seen pain, he had known death, and he had come back, wary, bitter. Braden knew his past, knew his file down to the last detail, but sometimes one could read much more in eyes that stared back from a weary expression.

"I'll head back to Sanctuary." Jonas nodded abruptly, drawing Braden's attention from the sheriff. "Let me know when you're ready for me to return with Elyiana."

The tests. The very same ones he suspected Megan would fight like a rabid wild cat.

"I should know something soon." Braden nodded before heading to the door.

As he stepped into the hall, he clearly heard Jonas's last warning comment to the sheriff. "We'll be talking again soon, Jacobs. Very soon." And Braden wondered just what the hell the Director of Breed Affairs had up his sleeve now.

• CHAPTER 10 •

Megan stalked into the house and up the stairs more than an hour later. She heard the back door open behind her. She had known Braden would be coming in soon, knew she had to face him eventually. But not yet. She couldn't force herself to stay, to face the rejection she felt in Lance's office. To see in his eyes the anger that surged through him at the knowledge that they were bound together in ways she could have never imagined.

She had left the office without him, sneaking from the building and rushing to her Raider. She hadn't expected to be greeted by the sleek black heli-jet Jonas had flown in on, or to see Braden as he lounged against the side of the house waiting on her.

Mating Heat. Adrenaline rushed through her at the thought, sending her heart racing and, unfortunately, her womb clenching. Whatever it was, it had bound her to him. She had felt it from that first moment they met, the aura that surrounded her, calmed her. The arousal that tormented her.

The kiss that left her weak, hungry for his taste. Cinnamon and brown sugar.

She could almost taste it on her lips, her tongue. Craved it, had been craving it since he had kissed her the night before. The heat that filled her sex was driving her crazy. She clenched her thighs against it, determined to hold back that particular need. She had never just rolled willy-nilly into bed with any man and she would be damned if she was going to start with Braden.

At least, not right at this moment.

She slammed her bedroom door closed before stalking to the wide window at the end of her bed. She swiped at the tears that dampened her cheeks. The drive from the sheriff's office had left her alone just long enough for her to lose control of her emotions.

She knew she needed to be stronger than this. But it hurt. For the first time since her talents had shown themselves she had been able to be close to a man. She could feel his arms around her and had known only his heat and hardness, not his nightmares or his fears.

She had begun to hope that it meant something.

How stupid. A cynical, weary breath accompanied the thought. She should have known better. Life didn't work like that. And now she was bound to a man who had rejected the bond that she had felt growing between them. It had a name. Mating Heat. It wasn't natural, or so Jonas claimed; but her heart had other ideas. And the blow to her emotions that Braden's rejection had caused had shredded her control.

She flinched as her door opened, her breath hitching, another tear falling as she felt him enter the room.

"Megan." His voice was soft, regretful. "I know what you felt at the office. It wasn't you. It wasn't a denial of you. You have to understand that."

She hated the fact that she had given away her pain, revealed how much that single impression had affected her.

How much she had hoped the feelings building between them were more than just lust. For her they were, and that hurt the most, knowing they hadn't been for him.

"It doesn't matter, Braden." She fought to swallow past the emotion blocking her throat and kept her back to him, her tears hidden. "I understand."

His life was a battle, day to day. Why would he want or need someone who couldn't fight her own battles, let alone stand beside him in his?

"Do you, Megan? I don't think you do, but you will. Very soon."

"Stop." Her voice broke as she shook her head.

She could feel him moving closer, could glimpse the image of him in the glass of the window. "Please Braden, I need time . . ." Her shoulders shook as she fought the sobs that built in her chest. "I'm sorry. Please . . ."

"So you can continue to hide?" His tone grated at her already shredded nerves.

"Yes!" She whirled around, staring back at him with a look that mingled fury and pain. "So I can hide. So it doesn't have to hurt so fucking bad."

Anything else she would have said locked in her throat the second she saw his eyes. They glowed. Amber lights flickered in the deep gold color as his tight, hungry expression gave his face a savage cast. He looked like a conquering warrior. A man intent on possession.

She stepped back quickly.

"Now there's a fine idea," he drawled as he stepped closer. "Keep a bit of distance between us, darlin', because the closer you get, the sweeter that soft little pussy smells and the harder my dick gets. You really don't want to make it harder. Any harder and I'm going to have to do away with these jeans and see just how deep I can push between those pretty thighs and how loud I can make you scream as you come around me."

The explicit words sent heat flaming through her body

as invisible fingers of lightning began to course from nerve ending to nerve ending, sensitizing her, stoking the fires inside her hotter. She felt the wet heat dampening her panties further.

"Why?" she cried out then. "You don't want me. You don't want this . . ." She waved her hand between them to indicate the Mating Heat. "Why do you care?"

"You like fooling yourself, don't you, baby." He stepped closer. Megan retreated. Now was not a good time to get within touching distance. "Now see, that's where you are entirely wrong. I wasn't rejecting you, Megan. I was rejecting what nature had done, not you. There is no reason for your anger."

She lifted her chin defensively. "I have a right to be angry with you. You were using me in those cliffs, using my Empathy to find the answers you needed just as you let Jonas use me to try to trap my cousin. Just as you used what I . . ." Felt. She wouldn't say the words, wouldn't address the pain of his rejection.

His gaze flickered with regret; the emotion washed over her, clenching her chest as another tear slipped free.

He shook his head slowly, his hand reaching out to touch her cheek, his fingertips rasping over her flesh with heated pleasure.

"I would never use you." His voice throbbed with the vow. "I have been alone so long, Megan. Alone within myself, knowing, feeling that nothing in this world was ever meant to be mine. Then suddenly something was mine. You were mine." The possessive tone had her blinking back at him in surprise. Both his hands framed her face, holding her still as his thumbs smoothed over her damp cheeks. "Mine. Everything inside me locked down in fear because suddenly I had something to lose. And so did you. And the thought of that was unbearable. I've lost too much already."

Her lips parted as her heart began to race, not in lust

or excitement or adventure, but in hope. She had found someone who matched her, a warrior and a shield. A man she could respect; one she could argue with and enjoy. She hadn't wanted to lose that. Hadn't wanted to be alone again.

"No . . ."

"Yes." He snarled, emotion thickening his voice. "Do you not understand yet, Megan? This Mating is not just a physical phenomenon. It is not merely chemicals gone haywire. Look inside yourself. If you could love any type of man, lean on any other person, who would this person be? Who is the lover that haunts your dreams? What fight boils in your blood? We would have been two parts of a whole, no matter who we were or where we met. You know this. Just as I know this."

She clenched her teeth, fighting the surging emotion of the realization he was right, but also recalling the denial she knew he had felt earlier. She had something to lose.

"See?" He latched onto the emotion she couldn't hide, his fingers pressing against her scalp as his taut features became more primitive, more exotic for the emotions he was fighting to contain. "Feel it, Megan. Feel what I knew. My soul would die without yours to fill it. Without you to hold me close in the darkness of night; without your laughter to bring the light into the darkness that has filled every fucking day of my life for as long as I have drawn breath. For the first time in thirty-four years I am alive. I live because of you, and the thought of going back to the desolation of being alone scares me to death."

His emotions slammed into her, filling her, heating her.

"Feel me." He groaned, his voice rough, tormented. "I know your gifts, for mine are their companions. When we battle, I feel you reaching out, connecting to me as nothing else ever has, feeding me what you know even as you draw on my strength to brace yourself against the pain. You are the Empath, I am the shield. Two parts of the whole, Megan." He released her then, stepping back to stare at her with such an excess of emotion that she could barely breathe, let alone speak. "This was what I tried to deny, to reject, even knowing that if I lost you, no matter how, my soul would be as dead as the Coyotes who search only for blood and for death."

He released her, only to pull out of his shirt pocket a small plastic pack that held several pills. His gaze probed her expression as she lifted her eyes questioningly.

"And that is?"

"This," he glanced to his palm then to her before his lips twisted with an edge of bitterness, "is a nifty little drug designed to ease the worst of the symptoms of the Mating Heat. The pain if you don't get fucked often enough, as well as the forced conception caused by the hormones secreted from my body, can become . . . harmful. Unfortunately, mating a Breed isn't always pleasant. Unless you want to get knocked up, you take the little contraceptive."

"A birth control pill?" How insane.

"After a fashion." He shrugged, inhaling deeply in a gesture that reinforced the excess of emotions that were filling them both. "Though the hormones in it are radically different than those once used on the drug market. These are more to block the hormone released from me, rather than those of your body."

"So why aren't you taking it?" She glared at him furiously.

"Because, darling, I'm not the one who will suffer if you don't conceive. You are. The Mating Heat builds until conception occurs. The hormone continues to grow within your body, overriding everything else but the need to have sex and to procreate. This will ease the symptoms as well prevent ovulation. So make your choice."

"Will it make it go away?" She continued to stare at the innocuous little pill. Was it the cure she had so rashly demanded?

"Nothing will make it go away." He didn't sound

displeased. "Ever. But it will give us a chance to figure the rest out, Megan. We were well on the road to where this is going anyway."

She raised her gaze, staring back at him for long, silent moments.

"You would have rode off into the sunset the moment your job here was finished."

He gripped her hand and laid the small container in her palm. "No Megan, I would not have left you. For even a day. Now take the little pill, baby, and then we'll talk more. Eventually."

He was going to take her to bed first. She knew it. Just as she knew her next breath would be filled with the scent of him, she knew that the moment that pill passed her lips he would make his move.

"Braden." She licked her lips trying to still her nerves. "It's been a very, very long time for me."

To be honest, she hadn't attempted sex in years.

"Take the fucking pill," he growled then. "I've tortured myself with the thought of touching you, of feeling you hot and tight around me. It's all I've thought about since the moment I saw your courage in that damned cavern. I don't know if I can wait much longer."

Evidently, she wasn't the only one the Mating Heat was driving insane.

She snapped open the container, her breathing becoming harsh, rough.

"I still don't like this," she informed him as she lifted the small blue pill. Though she knew different. She hated the situation, hated the confusion filling her, but she knew her feelings for Braden were something that went much deeper, flowed much stronger than anything even resembling "liking" him.

He growled in response.

"This is not the smartest thing I've ever done." She opened her lips as she lifted her hand closer to her mouth.

His eyes flared with sensual promise as she laid the small pill on her tongue, closed her mouth, and swallowed. It went down easy, without the aid of liquid, no doubt helped along by the intense watering of her mouth.

The growl rumbled in his chest again. Feline. Dangerous. It was a sound that had her pussy clenching in spasmodic convulsions. She gasped at the intensity.

"How long does it take to help?" She watched him, knowing there was no fighting the hunger as he stepped closer.

She retreated again. And again. Until her back came flush to the wall, his broad chest trapping her against it.

"Hell if I know," he muttered. "Hell if I care, as long as I can do this."

She expected a kiss. What she didn't expect was the abrupt lowering of his head until his lips were at her neck, his teeth scraping over the flesh as his tongue stroked it in a sensual caress. She went to her tiptoes; the sensations were so intense, so filled with pleasure.

Shudders raced down her spine, spread between her thighs and seared her to the very core. She felt the syrupy dampness wetting her further, felt her clit pulse and throb with the need for his touch as her nipples tightened beneath her blouse. God, how she needed his touch. Everywhere, all over. She craved it. Ached for it.

Her head fell back against the wall; her hands gripped his forearms as his fingers curved at her hips, arching her against him as he bent to press the hard wedge of his cock against the soft pad of her pussy.

She jerked at the friction, a whimpering moan escaping her lips as her nerve endings seemed to sear with the flames of building passion. She couldn't get enough air. Hell, she didn't need to breathe. If he would just kiss her, touch her, still the ache growing in every cell of her body, then she might have a chance of surviving.

"Damn, you taste good." His voice was filled with

wonder as he caught the lobe of her ear between his lips for a brief nip. "Sweet and hot. You make me wonder if I'll keep my sanity once I push inside you."

Her sanity wasn't going to last that long.

✦ CHAPTER II ✦

"You're so soft, Megan." The sound of his voice, the rough growl that whispered over her senses made her lose control. His hand moved from her hip to rest just beneath the swell of her breast. The subtle stroking of his fingers there had her breathing faster, her nerve endings sensitizing, reaching out for his heat. Sensations whipped through her body, tendrils of electricity flickered over her, holding her entranced as his fingers curled in the fabric of her shirt and began dragging it upward.

She stared up at him, fighting past her dazed senses and the need for his kiss as she felt cool air meet the bare flesh of her stomach. He was taking her shirt off, lifting it slowly as his tongue stroked her lips, the taste of cinnamon and brown sugar tempting her.

"Braden." She was shaking, her breasts so swollen, so sensitive that the thought of him touching them stole her breath.

Never had arousal been so intense or pleasure so fiery.

"Yes, baby?" The hungry growl weakened her knees as she felt the shirt lift slowly over the material of her bra.

"Kiss me." Her hands still gripped his forearms, even as they rose, his hands lifting her arms before whisking the material of her shirt over her head.

"I will." He nipped at her lips. "I promise. But not yet. I want you to feel this first. I want you to know it. To know you need it, hunger for it, before I kiss you."

"You kissed me last night." She panted roughly as he caught her hands and lifted them, holding her wrists in one hand and stretching them above her head as the other flipped open the latch of her bra. "Braden." She fought to breathe as she felt the material part, the lace scraping against her sensitive nipples. He stared down at her with narrowed eyes.

"One kiss." He growled, his head lowering. "That was just one kiss."

He smoothed the material from the swollen mounds, making certain to rasp it over the burning tips of her nipples as she cried out at the sensation. Wicked forks of fire shot from the heated tips to her womb, stealing her breath, her mind, as she trembled at the caress.

Her eyes closed, her body jerking in sensory overload as she felt his breath whisper over the tips.

"So pretty," His voice was like dark, midnight-velvet, rough and sensual. "The softest pink in the world. Innocent pink. Are you a virgin, Megan?"

She shook her head desperately.

"Thank God for that." His voice echoed with relief, with an erotic hunger that stole her breath. "Because I don't know if I would have the control to take you as you deserved if you were that innocent. And God knows it would kill me to hurt you."

His tongue licked over her nipple with just a hint of roughness. It was enough to have her arching against him, her pussy convulsing as heated liquid flowed from it. She twisted in his grip, desperate to get closer, to feel the moist caress just one more time.

When it came she nearly screamed. His lips covered the tender peak, drawing it into the furnace of his mouth as he began to suckle her. His tongue flickered over it like a wild flame as a hungry growl echoed around her. Heat raged around her, through her, ripped through her womb and exploded through her body as he sucked at her breast, nipped at her nipple, and tortured her with a pleasure she could not have imagined existed.

"Braden . . ." Her hips arched against the wedge of his cock as his knees bent and he thrust against her jeans-covered mound.

She could feel him, thick, hard. Between layers of clothing he burned her, stole reason and pushed her closer to a mindless abyss of pleasure. His tongue flickered over her straining nipple as he bent to her, suckling at her with a slow, easy rhythm.

"I can smell you." His voice was almost reverent, his lips drawing her gaze, the swollen curves heavy, sensual. "As sweet as a spring rain, as hot as fire. I want to taste you, Megan."

She swallowed, certain she wouldn't survive the overload of pleasure. She stood still, staring back at him, trembling as he released the snap of her jeans and lowered the zipper slowly.

"Kick your shoes off."

Megan moved to toe the sneakers from her feet, forcing her legs to obey the simple commands as his head lowered, his lips caressing her collarbone, his teeth scraping it.

"Good girl," he crooned when the shoes were pushed aside.

Slowly he lowered her arms, releasing her wrists as he placed her hands against his lower stomach. He gripped the T-shirt he wore and jerked it over his head, staring back at her intently.

"Undo my jeans." He growled.

"Braden." Her hands trembled as the heat of his flesh soaked through her palms. "I can't think." She shook her head weakly, fighting to make sense of the needs tearing through her, the lust so unfamiliar, so much stronger than anything else she had ever known.

"Then don't think, baby." His hands cupped her face before moving to her hair, pulling at the length of her braid. "You undo the pants, I'll release the braid. Such soft, pretty hair. I want to feel it brushing over me, Megan, caressing me."

Her fingers gripped the snap of his jeans. God, she had never even done this before. It came loose easily, sliding from its mooring as his abdomen flexed with a convulsive shudder.

"The zipper now." The nylon band that held her hair came free.

The feel of his fingers unwinding the thick ropes of hair made her eyes close, her fingers moving to the zipper. Beneath it, his cock throbbed, thick and warm; it waited beneath the material for freedom. Pulsed in eagerness.

She gripped the tab of the zipper, lowering it, easing it over the straining length of his erection. Her thighs clenched against the ravenous need, the hunger burning her alive.

"There you go." Her hair was free and so was his cock.

Thick, hard, the material of his jeans parted over the straining length as his hands moved to her jeans, pushing at the material and quickly moving it over her hips to her knees.

"Lift." He gripped her thigh, forcing her to lift her leg from the material before repeating it on the other.

All that protected her now were her panties. Wet, sodden silk that clung to her flesh as her knees weakened dangerously. Gasping, her hands gripped Braden's shoulders as he bent and lifted her into his arms. She could feel the

strength in his powerful arms, feel the need that held him
in its grip as firmly as it held her.

His expression was tight, his eyes gleaming with hunger.
But even more, she felt tenderness despite the obvious savage need ripping through him. She felt his determination to
hold her, to gentle her, felt his fear of hurting her. The wash
of emotions was intense, all consuming. The ability to feel
what her lover felt during sex was one of the reasons she
had abstained for so long. The powerful mix of lust, triumph
and self-satisfaction had turned the act into something to
be avoided rather than experienced.

With Braden it was different. As his tongue twined with
hers, she could feel the incredible control he was exerting
over himself. Just as she could feel his needs. The images
flickered through her mind, explicit, erotic. She moaned,
her own hunger increasing as he laid her back on the bed.

He bent and removed his boots quickly, then straightened to push his jeans over long, powerful thighs. His body
appeared completely hairless. Even the heavy sac beneath
the length of his erection looked smooth, impossibly sexy.

As he stood before her, staring down at her, she could
feel the blood pumping through her body, adrenaline and
lust flaming beneath her flesh.

"It hurts." Her womb flexed as the muscles tightened in
her vagina. "It's not supposed to hurt, Braden."

Fear mixed with desire as the implications of what was
happening began to hit her. Uncontrolled hunger beat at
her like the wings of a frightened bird as she felt her pussy
spasming with a greedy lust she couldn't control.

"Not for much longer," he promised sensually as he lay
on his side next to her. He leaned over her as he eased her
into his embrace, one hand stroking her thigh. "I promise it
won't hurt much longer.

His lips slanted over hers as she felt his hand moving
closer to the soaked material of the panties. Felt his fingers
caress the damp material as he growled fiercely. She was

flaming, burning. Her thighs parted for him as her hips lifted, pushing closer, needing more.

Suddenly the fierce control that held him back snapped. She felt it, gloried in it even as she feared it. The sound of the panties ripping from her body was accompanied by her own desperate moan as his fingers touched her, parted the swollen lips and slid through the thick cream that covered them.

Her hips bucked, a moan tearing from her throat as his finger circled the tender opening, caressing her, teasing her with his touch a second before he began to enter her. She felt the rasp of his calloused finger as she writhed in his grip. Her vaginal muscles tightened around it, begging for more.

Within seconds there was more. Another finger joined the first, working in slowly, stretching her, preparing her for more. Her hands were buried in his hair as she drank in his kiss, his taste. The sweet taste of the destructive hormone blazed within her, sending her senses careening with a pleasure she could never have imagined possible.

Her thighs parted farther, her hips moving against his hand as her clit grazed against his palm, sending fireworks blazing through her nerve endings. She was close. Oh God, she was so close.

"Not yet." The fierce growl came as he tore his lips from hers and slid his fingers from the tight, wet clasp of her body.

"Don't . . . don't you dare stop." She reached for him, fighting against the powerful hand that once again gripped her wrists as he began to move from her.

"Stay still, Megan." His voice was a whiplash of demand and furious lust. "For God's sake, don't start fighting me now."

He pushed her legs apart as he held her still, moving between them before shockingly lowering his head to the slick, swollen folds of her sex.

His tongue swiped through her tender flesh as a growl of pleasure tore from his throat and her hips drove upwards involuntarily. He released her wrists, only to grip her hips and hold her still as his tongue circled her clit before moving lower to lap at the liquid heat flowing from her body.

So close. Her thighs tightened as the wicked tongue moved over her flesh, his destructive lips sucking her clit between them. He flicked at it with his tongue before moving lower, lifting her, and then driving inside the greedy depths of her body and triggering an explosion that had her screaming in release. Her body tightened, arched further as her head fell back, her lips opening as cries tore from her throat.

As though he had been waiting just for that, Braden came quickly to his knees, lifted her closer then tucked the head of his cock at the suckling mouth of her vagina before beginning to move inside.

Megan shuddered beneath him as she felt him begin to stretch her. Felt each slow thrust and retreat as he began to work his erection into the convulsing sheath. It was too much sensation. Violent flares of pleasure tore through her body with each inch pressed into her. She stared up at his face in dazed fascination.

His lips were pulled back from his teeth, his head thrown back as the muscles of his neck flexed powerfully. His hair flowed around him as perspiration gleamed over his body. His hips worked slowly, pushing forward, drawing back, stealing her breath as another inch of her pussy was conquered with each forward motion. Desperately, her hands clenched in the blankets beneath her as her whimpers again turned to cries and muttered, senseless pleas.

Fireworks were exploding inside her, searing each nerve ending, burning tender flesh as he worked deeper inside her.

"More." She was gasping for breath as she made the order, her body demanding that he hurry. "Please, Braden. It's not enough. More."

His snarl filled the heavy, lust-filled air of the room as his hips rolled, pushing him further inside her. Yet it wasn't enough. Hungry greed echoed in her clenching vagina, which spasmed with sensation as her juices spilled around his flesh.

"Dammit, if you're going to fuck me then do it," she cried. "Stop teasing me to death . . ."

She cried out a second later as he drove home, burying the hard length of his cock inside her.

Control was a thing of the past. There was nothing now but the drive to release, the need to still the burning hunger raging through her. Her hips lifted with no urging from his hands. Her cunt milked at the driving flesh, tightening around him, flexing, pulsing as each stroke drove her higher, sent her flying until her orgasm slammed through her. It jerked her shoulders from the bed as her hands gripped his arms, her eyes staring into his as he drove home again. Harder. Deeper. A tight, almost painful grimace twisted his expression as she felt the head of his cock throb, swell further, then . . .

Horror swept across his face as she felt the change. The swelling of the already thick crest, the extension reaching out, locking into the back of the pulsing muscles that gripped him, feathering inside her, pressing firmly into a spot that sent sensation crashing through her mind.

The new orgasm it triggered was too much to bear. She could only convulse. She slammed back to the bed, her body jerking, her cries pleading whimpers of insensible words as she heard his roar, felt the hard, hot blasts of semen spewing inside her and the hot kiss of the flesh locking him to her.

Megan stared up at him, her eyes wide, her gaze locked with Braden's glittering, golden depths as she felt the odd pressure pressing into the too-sensitive flesh high in her pussy. Emotions whipped from him into her. Distant, scattered thoughts that slipped into her now-open mind as she felt her strange connection with him become deeper. Stronger.

Barb.

Bonded.

Locked together.

Possession. Raging, intense, soul-jarring possession.

He stared back at her in tortured disbelief.

Animal.

The thought was filled with pain and self-disgust. And it wasn't her thought. It came from him. From the deepest, darkest reaches of his soul.

She felt her lips curve, her smile weak, though tinted with the small shred of amusement that began to fill her.

"I like your animal . . ." she whispered, her voice strained as another shudder of orgasmic pleasure tore through her body. "My animal . . ."

· CHAPTER 12 ·

There was nothing like the morning after. Braden stood on the back porch watching the sun come up, a mug of coffee steaming in his hand as he stared at the mountains in the distance. He could feel the eyes watching the house. Friendly and enemy alike. He knew there was at least one team of Felines watching over them, but he was certain there was a Coyote in the midst somewhere.

He closed his eyes for a moment, letting the fresh air of a new day wash over him, through him. The tint of malevolence wasn't strong. There was just a hint of the danger, of the evil stalking them. Not close enough to matter, but out there all the same.

As he sipped from the coffee mug and scanned the area searching for the most likely spot in the ridged hills surrounding them for the Coyotes to hide themselves. Jonas had the maps and aerial shots of the land through the secure satellite connection the laptop used. The most likely spots had been marked, though the team scouring the cliffs and hidden caverns had yet to find any sign of the Coyotes. There were just too many damned places to hide.

At the moment, he almost wished he were sitting in one of them.

He could hear Megan in the kitchen, muttering to herself as she went over the files. Again. The laptop sat on the kitchen table, the database of Felines and available information open to her. There would be no keeping her out of it now. As his mate, she would have to adapt, to learn how to live the often violent, rarely secure lives they led.

His mate. His body had certainly reinforced that sentiment. The memory of the pleasure and the shock of the barb emerging from his cock the night before still had him grasping for understanding. For acceptance.

He pushed his fingers through his hair restlessly, fighting to ignore the throb of his erection behind the material of his jeans. It refused to ease. And he'd be damned if he would take her again without her asking. Without some sign that she wasn't sickened by what had happened the night before.

Not that she had appeared sickened by it. But a woman on the edge of unconsciousness couldn't very well be trusted to be truthful. She had given in to exhaustion moments later, her body relaxing in his arms even as her tight heat held him captive within her.

"Braden, what the hell is an A Force?" she called out in frustration. "You really need a directory here."

He winced at the question. He was a part of A Force.

"Assassin, Megan." He kept his voice tempered, hiding the irritability feeding him now.

Silence filled the air as his lips twisted in knowing mockery. He turned and stared through the open door before stepping back into the house and securely closing the panel.

She was staring at the monitor, her hands lying gracefully on the keypad while she went through the thumbnail pictures displayed and the stats given.

"Fourteen marks, three waste points," she recited the statistics. "What does that mean?"

"Fourteen kills, three of which were innocent marks I was unable to save." He no longer tormented himself over the three he had been unable to maneuver out of the line of fire.

"Three." Her voice was raspy, uncertain. And who the hell could blame her? This wasn't exactly a woman's dream of happily-ever-after.

"Three." He nodded as he moved back to the coffeepot. "The files are there, Megan. If you have questions, read them."

Maybe the fact of who he was would distract her from what he was.

He was careful to keep his senses open, to catch any hint of condemnation that could come from her. He felt none. He felt confusion, anger, but no accusation. Finally he turned to her, watching her curiously.

Her emotions were as easy to read on her face as they were in the air around her. She would be easy for the Coyotes to find if she were caught in a situation that required her to hide not just her physical self, but her mental self as well. The animal senses were rapier-sharp in all Breeds. Picking up on emotions was nearly as easy as using scent to guide them. How she had managed to surprise them the day they attacked her home, he had no idea.

She was confused, aroused, and hurting. Surprisingly enough, the hurt seemed to be *for* him, not because of him.

"You didn't write the reports." Her eyes were moving over the page as she clicked on the details.

He tilted his head, watching her intently. "How do you know?"

She shrugged. "I can tell. It's too graphic. Too focused on the fact that you didn't kill savagely enough." She lifted her eyes, the blue orbs dark with pain.

His lips twisted at her last words. His Trainer had written the reports, and in each, Braden knew the emphasis on his apparent mercy had been notated. Braden would have been canceled eventually, and he knew it, simply because he could not force an illusion of satisfaction in killing.

"I regret their deaths, not my actions," he assured her. "I did what I had to do to protect others. To protect myself. Those of us who survived realized early on that we would only do so by being smarter than those who created and attempted to train us."

"The three innocents?" He watched her swallow tightly, saw the compassion in her gaze. It soothed him, even when he felt he deserved no ease for those deaths.

"A scientist who attempted to break away from the Council. He escaped with a newly born Breed babe and attempted to reach someone within the media. He was killed, though the child was never recovered. Also, an Interpol agent investigating one of the European scientists, as well as his contact, the young son of one of the Council members." He kept his voice cool, his manner distant. He had done what he had to in his battle to survive. "If I hadn't killed them, if I hadn't performed as ordered, others would have died. If a Breed failed, then his closest littermates died as well. If he didn't return, then every Breed within his assigned Lab was murdered and the facility shut down." He clenched his jaw as he remembered the bonds of loyalty and the fight to survive that had tethered them during those times.

"Loyalty," she whispered.

Braden inclined his head slowly. "Foolish perhaps, but the majority of us were born with a sense of bonding, of loyalty to those we considered littermates. There was no breaking it."

"Did you try?" He saw the shimmer of tears in her eyes and felt his heart clench at the emotion reaching out to him. There was no pity, but there was pain. For him. For those he had fought to protect.

"I tried." He nodded slowly. "Each mission. I had a plan in place; I could have escaped. I could have found safety for myself." He grimaced at the thought. "The others wouldn't have died easily, and I knew it. I couldn't be the reason for it. My own death would have been preferable. As long as we lived, there was always a chance of survival, of finding a way to save the others as well."

"I thought the Council frowned upon loyalty and friendship between the Breeds?" He could feel her searching for clarification, for understanding.

"They punished us severely for it." He pushed his hands into the pockets of his jeans as he leaned against the wall, his lips tilting mockingly. "We were created to murder, to revel in any blood we could spill. We were their disposable soldiers, their robots if you will. Animals who could pose as humans and could strike with deadly force.

We weren't created for loyalty, but the scientists and trainers knew it existed. There was no way for us to hide it entirely."

Tears shimmered in her eyes before she turned away from him, the compassion that filled them clenched his heart. She had forced herself to be so strong, enduring alone for so many years. But he could feel her now, reaching out to him, a warmth that eased into his soul and relieved the bleak chill of his memories.

She moved from the table quickly, hitting the power button on the laptop to abruptly disconnect the pages she had pulled up. Her face was pale, her body tight with tension.

"It doesn't do any good to run from it, Megan. You knew our lives weren't exactly happy hour," he pointed out calmly when he wanted nothing more than to smash something, anything. Preferably the computer that held the incriminating information.

He ached for her. For himself. How horrifying it must be to be bound to a man you knew could kill you with one thrust into your body. To know he could stare into your eyes, whisper your greatest fantasy, and murder you a second later. But it was information she had to have. Secrets she had to know.

She was his mate. He refused to hide anything from her.

The air thickened with tension, fear and pain whipped around him. Not through him; his natural blocks were too strong for that. But he felt it, knew it for what it was.

She turned back to him slowly.

"Do you think I blame you for any of that?" she snapped as she flicked her fingers to the laptop. "That I would ever believe you had done anything other than you had to?" Bitterness twisted her lips. "You might be as arrogant as hell, Braden, but you're not a murderer."

He stared back at her silently, watching as her expression softened, the militant light of battle slowly fading from her eyes.

"I wish I could ease the memories, the pain." Her whispered admission surprised him. "I would take the nightmares if I could, Braden."

Shock tore through him as he read the truth in her eyes. His little Empath, who had hid from the world and from other's nightmares, was willing to take his in order to ease his pain and accept it as her own.

"Then you're insane." He growled, feeling his erection swell in his jeans as he watched her, saw the emotion that filled her gaze and felt it swirling around him.

Her gaze flickered to it. The scent of her pussy drifted to him, her arousal growing as adrenaline began surging through her body.

"Yeah, that remark resembles me sometimes." She flashed him a cocky smile that had his heart aching.

"Don't romanticize me, Megan." He growled then. She had to know the truth of the man she was bound to now.

"I'm not a hero, and I'm sure as hell not Superman. I kill, and sometimes I even enjoy the blood I spill." Council Trainers, their soldiers . . . And one day, he swore, when the main Council members were found, he would exact his own vengeance.

"No, you're not Superman." She rolled her eyes at him as she propped her hands on her hips and confronted him with a frown. "But neither are you a monster. If you want to put distance between us, find another way to do it."

"Wouldn't you like that," he snapped. "You've been trying to throw me out since the beginning."

Her eyes widened at the anger he displayed.

"What's with you?" She lifted her chin and narrowed her eyes in challenge. "You've been fighting to get into my bed and override my defenses against you since you first met me. Fine, you had me, you bit me, you mated me. And now dumb little Megan cares one way or the other if you die. Feeling a little trapped now, are we?"

Braden glowered back at her. He didn't feel trapped, he felt . . . off balance. Women feared him; even those who came to his bed were wary of tempting his anger. But Megan accepted him, defended him even when he couldn't defend his actions himself. She terrified him with her courage and her ability to accept not just the Mating, but him.

He finally sighed wearily. "I don't feel trapped, Megan." He felt like snarling at his own helplessness to see her safe from the threat against her. "You have to know the truth about me. Dealing with this situation requires that you know who and what I am. Otherwise, you cannot make the choices you will have to rationally."

"I have a feeling few people deal with you in any kind of rational manner." She crossed her arms over her breast, the loose T-shirt she wore riding up the hem of her shorts to flash a tempting strip of flesh. He wanted to lick it.

"This is possible." He dragged his attention from the

bare flesh to reply to her comment. "I was never considered one of the tamer specimens."

"Why did you pull that up for me to read?" Her lips thinned in annoyance and suspicion.

"It's a part of me, Megan." He shrugged. "Part of who I am. If you don't learn it now, you may have to later. And controlled conditions are always best."

"You think you're fooling me. You're not so cold, Braden."

"I'm not?" Actually, there had been times when he had been forced to be worse.

"You're trying to piss me off," she accused him heatedly. "Trying to make me think you're nothing but a cold-blooded killer."

"That's exactly what I am, Megan." There was no sense in hiding the truth. "Accept that now. You read the reports; you saw the truth of me. I kill. I track down my prey, and I use whatever means necessary to kill them quickly and effectively. They have no worth in my eyes. Understand this now. It's a life you will have to share with me. One you will have to learn to live within. You are my mate. My fight has now become yours."

Surprise burned in her expression, just as excitement flowed from her.

"This Mating crap has rotted your brain, Braden." She deliberately provoked him. He noticed she attempted to do that a lot. One day, he would have to cure her of that habit. Maybe. "I don't *have* to do anything. I do as I please. What's between us won't change that."

She stared back at him defiantly. That defiance made him want to take her down. To show her exactly who was the stronger, who controlled. She belonged to him and she damned well better get used to it.

"You will follow, Megan. I lead." That description was beginning to grate on his nerves and it was time to put a halt to it.

"Sorry Lion Man, but that's not exactly how it works."
She snarled, her chin lifting defiantly as she stood before
him like a spitting little tabby cat. "This Mating Heat stuff
doesn't change that. And while we're on that subject, just
how many different women can you do this to, anyway?"

Braden tensed. He hadn't expected this one, and evidently she had just thought of it herself. Her eyes widened
then narrowed as her lips tightened in suspicion.

"As far as I know, Breeds mate only once. For life." At
least that was the information he had received. "Just as true
lions are known to."

"Real lions have a freakin' harem," she spat out, her eyes
glinting suspiciously. "One male, up to a dozen females."

"They mate only one," he assured her arrogantly. "And
pray to Heaven I follow their example because if I had to
deal with another woman even similar to you, I would go
ahead and walk into a den of Coyotes for the relief. You,
Megan, are threatening to destroy any control I have managed to learn over the years."

"It better be a one-time deal," she muttered, frustration
thick in her voice as she paced the room once again. "Because I don't share."

Seconds later she stopped, turned to him, and narrowed
her eyes. "If you're such a big-shot assassin, why haven't you
tracked down the people who murdered the Breeds here?"

"First, I need to know who I'm tracking." He grunted.
"You keep killing the suspects, Megan. You can't question
what isn't breathing. Out of four Coyotes sent after you,
you've left only one alive. Give me something to work with
here, baby."

She crossed her arms over her breasts. Nice, plump little breasts that fit his hands exactly. Hard nipples spiked
beneath the cloth of her T-shirt and the scent of her need
whipped through his senses like wildfire burning out of
control.

"It's kind of hard to be nice when those assholes are

trying to kill me." She finally shrugged. He had a feeling she had intended to say something far different.

"Once I learn who is behind it, then I'll go hunting." He kept his relaxed pose, leaning against the counter, ignoring the almost hidden glances she made toward the erection straining against his jeans. At this rate, his cock would end up bursting the zipper before the day was out.

"Yeah, you do that," she finally muttered, turning away from him to pace back to the table.

She stood behind the chair, leaning against it as she stared down at the computer once again. The information there was not what was on her mind. He could feel her nervousness now, knew what had been coming. Her subtle glance at the erection straining beneath his jeans warned him that her attention had now shifted from his killing expertise to other matters. Those matters weighed heavily on his own mind, and were the very ones he had wanted to avoid.

"It's called a barb," he informed her coolly, knowing that putting it off wouldn't make it easier. "But I have a feeling you already knew that."

A deep flush filled her face then, and he swore her nipples tightened further. They poked against the shirt with the same insistence of his cock pressed against his jeans.

"Did I ask?" she snapped, jerking back as she straightened fully and glared at him.

His shoulders lifted negligently. "I could see it on your face, Megan. You're so nervous you're about to jump out of your own skin. There's no sense beating around the bush or ignoring what happened."

"I could be a little put out that I seem to be stuck with an arrogant know-it-all assassin intent on pissing me off this morning," she pointed out, managing to project cool disdain despite her embarrassment. "That would throw any girl off track, don't you think?"

"Some, perhaps." He tilted his head in acknowledgment

as a smile tugged at his lips. "I think it excites you more than anything else. Your nipples are hard. Would they get harder if I told you about all the cool weapons you could play with?"

She breathed in deeply, her expression becoming mutinous as she stared back at him.

"Oh yeah, blood and guts really just turn me on." She snorted sarcastically. "I bet yours would do wonders for me."

"It's not my blood you want right now, Megan." He tensed as her gaze dropped once again, her breathing becoming heavier as her eyes flickered over his crotch before jerking up once again. "It's a little late for pretense, baby. That barb might have you nervous as hell, but you want it. I can smell it."

"I'm going to cut your nose off." She rubbed at her arms before a light shiver shook her slender frame. It was building in her, just as Jonas had said it would. The need to mate, to conceive. For three days to a week the overwhelming need would be near impossible to deny. After that, the arousal would be easy to tempt, though the reactions closer to normal. Nothing would make the barbing disappear. Thank God. It was the most pleasure he had ever known with a woman. More pleasure than he had ever given one, even under the influence of the scientist's drugs.

"I thought your little pill was supposed to fix this." Her voice was huskier, filled with her heat as it began to climb within her.

"It only eases the harsher effects of the Mating Heat. There will be no pain if you don't deny the arousal." She might not be in pain, but it was killing him.

She swallowed tightly as she stared back at him, her gaze mischievous, hungry. Her high cheekbones blazed with heat as she dampened her pouty lips with the flick of her pink tongue once again. He wanted to feel that tongue. Licking him, stroking him.

This was his woman; his scent covered her, his seed filled

her. His teeth clenched with his need to mark her. He had denied himself the growing desire to give her that sensual bite to her neck the night before. Had fought the impulse with every straining inch of control he possessed. Today, he would not deny himself.

She licked her lips again, slowly, weighing her options, he thought in amusement. The woman was definitely attempting to side with caution this morning. He wondered which would win out, the need for caution or the need to fuck. He knew which one he hoped would win.

As he watched, he felt a frisson of unease skirt down his back as her expression suddenly cleared of nervousness and indecision. It was replaced with pure feminine sensuality. It was enough to make a grown man wary.

A second later her eyes darkened to near black and the flush on her face deepened. Hunger filled her. He could smell it on the air around her, taste it in the spicy hormone that suddenly flirted on his taste buds as the glands beneath his tongue began to throb in demand.

He tensed as she moved, walking slowly around the table with her eyes narrowed on him. He almost smiled. It was more than obvious that the little minx was out to prove something. He just wasn't certain what.

"You are starting to irk me, Braden," she told him as she rounded the table, gliding forward as the scent of her arousal began to cloud his mind, and his judgment. Damn, he wanted nothing more than to throw her to the table and fuck her until she screamed for mercy. Or for more.

"I do seem to be rather good at that." He contained his laughter. Hell, he was fighting for breath as her hand flattened against the tight muscles of his abdomen, the silken warmth sinking into his flesh as her nails pressed into the skin.

He uncrossed his arms, one hand reaching out to thread through her long hair as her lashes fluttered.

"Be certain, Megan," he growled out. "I'm riding a

very thin edge of control right now. I cannot promise you gentleness."

She opened her eyes, the dark depths reflecting so many emotions they took his breath. He could feel her fears swirling around him, the fear of the bond between them, her wariness of it. She had been alone so long. Too damned long. Forced to forget she was a woman with needs. Forced to hide herself and her gifts in her quest to protect those she loved. Her dedication to her family, her obvious love and sacrifice for them touched him. How much more loyal would she be to a lover, or to one who held her heart?

His patience was a fragile thing right now. Despite his best efforts, he could feel his normal calm eroding further as the animal impatient to mate surged to the surface. He grimaced as her nails scraped his abdomen, scratching along his flesh until they stopped at the waistband of his jeans. She smoothed her hand over the waistband, her fingers pausing at the snap, delicate, graceful fingers that trembled.

Braden trailed his hands down her arms, curiously watching the small shivers that raced over her flesh. He was certain her responsiveness was due to the Mating Heat. But she was his mate. What did it matter why?

"You are as soft as the finest silk." He sighed, losing himself in her passion.

"I need you." Her voice trembled with emotion. "I'm not used to needing someone else like this Braden. It terrifies me."

He could feel that fear pouring from her. The aching knowledge that she was bound to him, that for the first time in her life she couldn't run. She couldn't protect herself, or him, from the changes rapidly taking over her life. Megan had built her life around protecting others. And doing it alone.

"I like your need for me." He caressed her waist, pushing beneath the T-shirt to touch warm, soft skin. "Feeling it wrap around me, binding me. You are a miracle, Megan," he told her softly. "My miracle."

The zipper lowered slowly, easing over the erection throbbing painfully beneath the material. God help him, he wouldn't last long at this rate. Lust already burned inside him, prickling over his flesh, demanding that he touch her, taste her . . . possess her.

His.

A low, tortured growl left his throat as she slowly freed him from his jeans.

Uncertainty and fear were rapidly losing way beneath her hunger. He felt it pouring from her, sinking into him, heightening the sensations ripping through his body.

Control.

He slammed the barriers down within his mind instinctively. He couldn't lose control at this point. The desires rising between them were too fragile, and would be too easily damaged if he pushed at the wrong time. He needed to let her feel instead. To let her sense his needs, his passion, his pleasure.

He leaned back against the counter, giving her the opportunity to do as she pleased. To touch him, to guide the passion rising so rapidly between them. To investigate her own hungers. That was important, he knew, to allow her the freedom to touch, to accept him.

"I've never touched another man like this." Her nervous admission broke his heart. She was a woman of strength, of passion; to have denied herself to the point that she rarely touched, or allowed herself to be touched, must have been agonizing for her.

"That's okay, baby." He groaned. "You are doing exceptionally well."

Her fingers traveled the length of him, stroking from balls to tip as she tortured him with her touch. Leaning forward, her lips touched his chest, her tongue peeking out to lick at his flesh tentatively.

Sweet merciful God . . . His thighs bunched as pleasure slammed through him, rocking him as her fingers smoothed just beneath the head of his cock, where the barb had emerged and locked his cock into the tight depths of her vagina the night before.

"You can feel it." Her voice was reverent, filled with pleasure, a pleasure that was killing him as she probed at the ultrasensitive flesh where the barb would emerge later. "Just beneath the skin. It throbs."

His whole body throbbed. Ached. Screamed out for her touch as her breath caressed his skin. Her lips moved over the hard muscle, her tongue licking, spreading fire across the flesh as her head dipped, her teeth raking the hard, flat nipple that rose to her touch. And all the while her fingers stole his breath as they stroked his cock.

"Baby, this is a very dangerous game you're playing." He fought to hold back, to allow her the freedom she needed. Yet she also needed to understand that a very thin edge of control separated the man from the animal.

"I like living dangerously. Remember?" He felt her smile a second before she began to move lower, lips and tongue raking across his skin as she moved closer to the straining length of his cock.

That fickle flesh jerked in rising anticipation, eager for her kiss, the liquid warmth of her mouth. His mouth filled with the taste of the hormone spilling from the glands beneath his tongue. He swallowed slowly, his teeth gritting as his lust rose higher, hotter. Sweet God, he was burning alive.

"This is insane." He growled as her tongue painted a trail of electric sensation down his abdomen.

His hands moved from her waist, reaching for her head, for the soft weight of her hair as she drew steadily closer to the trembling, eager flesh throbbing in her hand.

He prayed for patience, for control. She needed this, perhaps even more than he did. Needed to touch and taste where before she had never been able to, never dared to.

And God knew he wanted it more than he wanted his next breath.

"Hmm, it's hot." She was going to kill him with pleasure. "Hot and sexy. You make me feel sexy, Braden." Wonder filled her voice, pierced the savage haze spreading through his mind.

"God help us both, Megan. You are so fucking sexy you burn me alive." Her tongue licked teasingly at his navel as his hips jerked in reaction, driving his cock closer to her hot little mouth. "But so help me, if you tease me much further you may have little choice in this game you're playing."

◆ CHAPTER 13 ◆

She could feel his desire, his hunger. It raged around her, inside her, whipping through her mind, her body, until the lust that filled her overwhelmed her caution, her reserve. She knew what he wanted, what he ached to feel.

Her fingers gripped the width of his straining erection as her mouth watered to taste his flesh. The desire was like a beast raging inside her until she lowered her head to the silken crest.

She licked the desperate flesh rather than consuming it as she knew he wanted. Her tongue slid over the damp head, licking at the small drop of pre-come that beaded from the slit. He jerked in her grip.

The taste of heated male, salty and wild, filled her with an addictive hunger that she knew had little to do with the arousal she could feel pouring from him. Her hunger, her need, tore through her unlike anything she had known before. There were none of the conflicting emotions she had felt years before when she had attempted any intimacy with a man. None of the selfishness or sense of triumph. It was pure, undiluted need, pleasure, the desire to give as well as receive.

"Megan, teasing can be a bad thing at this point." Amusement lay beneath the rough need in his voice as his hips jerked against her flirty licks. "I would advise caution in your play, sweetheart."

His control was tenuous; she could feel his struggle to hold back.

"Hmm, you don't like it?" she murmured against the straining flesh. The brief thought that they were in the kitchen, still mostly dressed, and playing such erotic games sent a thrill of excitement racing through her.

"Maybe I like it too much." He seemed to be speaking through gritted teeth as her tongue moved lower, probing beneath the flared cap at the pulsing point where she knew the barb lay hidden.

"Teasing can be fun." She licked the straining head a second before she let her lips cover the point, suckling at it timidly as her tongue raked over it once again.

His hips jerked as his cock seemed to swell in her grip. Lust, rich and hot, swirled around her, in her, meeting her own, driving the heat tormenting her higher. Every cell in her body seemed sensitized, ready to explode in climax.

"Teasing can be dangerous." His voice was rougher now, more primal.

She licked at him again before lifting her lips, raking over the hard flesh before her mouth opened and slowly—so slowly she could feel the savage hunger growing, deepening, pouring over her—she consumed the hard crest.

"Sweet Jesus . . ." Braden felt his control slipping.

He could feel the point where the barb emerged growing hotter, a pinpoint of pleasure that tortured and tormented as her lips began to rake over it, just as the sensitive area on the other side pounded with the need for release.

Her lips tightened around his cock, drawing out the pleasure as she learned the shape of him, her curiosity and her pleasure wrapping around him. Feminine hunger slammed into his senses as her suckling mouth began to move with more confidence, with greater intensity.

Son of a bitch, it was killing him. Never, even when trying, when attempting to feel the hunger that drove his partner, had he been able to feel this. Sweet, pure female need wrapping around him, driving his lust higher.

He gripped her hair, holding her to him as her mouth tightened on him, sucking him with a voracious hunger that consumed him.

"Sweet mercy." He growled, his fingers tightening in her silken strands. "That's it, baby, suck it harder. Your mouth is so fucking hot you're burning me alive."

Her tongue flickered beneath the crest, a hum of pleasure vibrating against the already violently sensitized flesh.

His hands cupped the back of her head as he began thrusting, unable to halt the movement of his hips, pushing into her mouth, retreating. His teeth gritted at the ecstasy consuming him. He was going to have to stop her soon. Saints alive, he didn't know if he could hold on to his control to keep from hurting her, to keep the beast raging inside him from taking her with a force he knew could destroy them both.

She hummed against him again, sweet moans of rising desire that tore at his determination to hold back. Her fingers caressed him, stroked the throbbing shaft, curled around the taut spheres below and sent his senses spinning.

"Good girl," he crooned almost mindlessly now. "Sweet baby, there you go. Suck my cock, Megan . . ." He gritted his teeth as his head fell back. His hips moved in short, digging strokes, filling her mouth as the vibrations of her moans, the scent of her arousal, stole his sanity.

"Enough . . ." The barb was throbbing beneath the head, pressing out as he felt his balls tighten with the need to come. "Enough, Megan . . ." He pulled at her hair, desperate to tear her away from him before he lost all semblance of control.

Her nails nipped at his thighs as her teeth raked his flesh warningly, the small bite of pain sending his senses exploding with heat.

"Fuck . . . Megan." His hands dug into her scalp as he tried to hold her still, fought the climax that surged through his body. Electric trails of sensation raced up his spine, tightened his scrotum. His sanity and control receded beneath her suckling mouth.

He felt the barb press outward, extending as her tongue began to flicker desperately over it. Her mouth drew tighter around him as rapture erupted through his body. His seed filled her mouth, explosive jets of semen shooting inside the moist depths as her tongue fought to lick at the hard extension, extending his climax, sending bolt after bolt of sensation racing through his cock.

Megan was lost in the primitive taste and response filling her. Braden did nothing to hide either his mental or physical pleasure. Both filled her, empowered her, and stripped away any caution, any reserve she could have mustered from him.

She drew back from the still-hard, pulsing erection, staring in dazed fascination at the thumbtip-sized extension pulsing beneath the head of his cock. Its position would allow it to be anchored in the most sensitive portion of a woman's vagina. High, behind the hard clutch of muscles that would have gripped him had he been buried in her pussy.

As she watched it slowly receded, sinking back into the flesh as though it had never been there.

"It's amazing." She smoothed her fingers over the area, a smile tugging at her lips as his hips jerked in response and his hands pulled at her hair.

"It's damned strange." He growled, pulling her up, forcing

her to straighten against him as he stared down at her with his dark gold eyes, his long honey- and earth-streaked hair falling around his face. "But right now, it's the least of my concerns."

The primal throb of power and lust in his voice sent chills racing through her body, followed by a wave of heat that nearly buckled her knees. His eyes glittered with his lust, the planes of his face savage, intent on possession.

"What does concern you then?" She meant to sound teasing, flirtatious. The words came out as a plea instead.

The smile that shaped his lips stole her breath. Arrogant, assured, a confident male animal.

"This concerns me." His hand moved from her hair to her thighs, his palm sliding between them as he cupped the saturated curves of her sex, grinding against her clit and sending fire racing through her nerve endings.

She arched in his hold, aware of his arm tightening around her back as her knees weakened with the extreme pleasure. She ground herself against him, a gasping cry escaping her throat as liquid fire seemed to consume her.

"I can't . . ." She lost the strength to finish the cry as she felt him tear at the material of her shorts, dragging the soft cotton out of the way as she trembled against him.

"Control it?" His rumbled growl was filled with satisfaction. "Hell no. You can't, Megan, and I wouldn't stand for it if you could. I want you out of control, baby. Burning with me. Feel. Feel how good it is."

She jerked against him, her legs straightening until she stood on her tiptoes, her eyes widening, dazing as his finger pressed against the tender opening before sinking inside her.

She felt the slide of moisture rushing from her, easing his way as he filled the sensitive depths of her pussy. His finger moved wickedly, stroking her, rasping against the delicate nerve endings as she shuddered in pleasure.

Oh God, it was so good. Too good. She could feel him

inside her, the calloused pad of his finger creating a friction intended to drive her crazy.

"You're pussy is hot, Megan." He growled in her ear as his teeth scraped the lobe. "Hot and sweet, like the finest cream. As tight as a fist. Taking you is more pleasure than I ever imagined existed."

There was no subterfuge, no lies. She could feel his pleasure whipping around her, sinking into her, mixing with her own to create an intoxicating sense of rapture. Her hands roved over his shoulders, the feel of the tiny silken hairs covering his flesh prickling her palms. She wanted to feel him fully against her, feel that satiny pelt rubbing over her, stroking her flesh with a lazy eroticism that stole her mind.

She mewled in rising hunger as his finger moved inside her, thrusting with diabolically slow strokes as she teetered on the edge of orgasm.

"Are you going to tease me all morning?" She finally gasped as she felt him change the angle of his hand, felt another finger joining the first. A ragged, tormented moan was her only recourse as he stretched her further, filling her, stealing her breath.

"I want to lay you down and lick at all that sweet cream pouring out of you," he drawled in her ear, his voice a seductive growl of primal hunger. "I want to fill you with my tongue, Megan, and consume every sweet drop of cream I can force from your body."

She shuddered, moving against his hand, helpless in the grip of the overpowering need to have him do just that. To feel him licking her, eating her inch by inch.

"Now." She groaned helplessly. "God, do something before I die."

The words had no more than left her lips when his fingers slid from her pussy, giving one last caress to the spasming flesh before he bent and pulled her quickly into his arms. Her hands gripped his shoulders, her head falling against his chest as her lips moved to the hard muscle, opening over it then sinking against the tough male flesh helplessly. She wanted to mark him. To taste him. To fill him with the same pleasure he sent racing through her body.

If the tight, hoarse snarl was any indication, she had succeeded.

Within minutes she was naked, lying in her bed and watching as he jerked his pants from his powerful thighs.

Before she could do more than marvel at the powerful male creature intent on possessing her, he was moving over her, his lips catching hers as his chest raked erotically over her already tingling nipples. Wildfire filled her as his tongue pushed between her lips, sweeping into her mouth as he nudged against her tongue, demanding she take him as she had the hard erection earlier.

She arched against him, accepting the riotous demand as the spicy taste filled her senses. Their moans echoed around her, his animalistic, hers beseeching. Pleasure raked through her as he held himself above her, his hands framing her swollen breasts as his fingers began to pluck and plump them. She had never considered her breasts a particularly erotic area, until Braden touched them. Until his hoarse growl filled her mouth a second before he broke the kiss, his lips moving purposely across her jaw and down her neck. He licked at her, nipped at her skin and raked his teeth over the sensitive area before moving inexorably toward the thrusting, hard-tipped mounds.

When he reached them he paused, his eyelids lifting languorously as he glanced up at her, his full, strong lips swollen from their kiss.

"Mine." The harsh, gravelly pitch of his voice had her trembling in anticipation as his warm breath wafted over her straining nipples.

Resistance was futile, she thought with a spurt of amusement. He was claiming her; she could feel it in every cell of her oversensitive brain.

"Am I?" she challenged him then, smiling up at him with deliberate mystery as she arched into his grip. "Prove it."

She loved challenging him, loved making his eyes darken, his cheekbones flush with lust.

His fingers tightened on her nipples, sending an electric surge of pleasure tearing through her womb. She gasped, her head falling back weakly, nearly begging at that point for him to fuck her.

"You are," he promised her, more than satisfied with her response if the tone of his voice was anything to go by.

"Says who?" She was dying for him to prove it. Aching for it.

He chuckled at the deliberate challenge, his thumbs raking sensually over her nipples with a rasping pleasure that had her gritting her teeth to keep from begging him to consume her.

"Oh, I will prove it, baby." His voice was low, intent. "In ways you could never imagine."

She tensed at the husky murmur, anticipation and trepidation sliding through her at the misty images that filled her mind. Him behind her, covering her, taking her . . .

"I don't think so . . ." Her gasping laughter surprised her as her eyes opened, meeting his gaze with amused defiance.

She shouldn't be amused. He was deliberately allowing her to sense his emotions, as well as the desires filling him. And there were many, many desires. They had her blushing from her toes to her hairline, a fiery heat filling her at the thought of them.

"Never say never, baby," he warned, his eyes sparkling with his own amusement as his head lowered, his tongue licking over the top of her breast. "There are so many different ways I could claim you. You have no idea."

Oh yes, she did. The pervert! Those ideas of his were whipping through her head now, thoughts, pleasures she could have never imagined. And they were stealing her will, stealing any resistance she might have thought to make. Well, for the most part.

Any thoughts of resisting, surrendering or chastising him for deliberately playing with her mind were washed away beneath the moist, rough warmth of his tongue as it curled over her nipple. The sensitive tip screamed out in pleasure, causing her to jerk at the sensations as a strangled moan left her lips.

She twisted beneath him as he covered the taut point, suckling it into his mouth, rasping against it with his tongue as liquid fire shot through her pussy. Oh hell, she liked that. She liked that so damned much. It was incredible. Hot and tempestuous, and so exciting she almost screamed with the pleasure. Except he stole her breath. Stole her breath, then stole any thoughts she could have made as he moved to the next mound, repeating the action.

He stroked, nibbled, licked and rubbed. His tongue just a bit rasping, just enough to titillate and make her crazy for more. And the way it stroked over her nipple as he sucked at it firmly was definitely making her crazy.

Her hands tangled in his long hair, holding him to her as his fingers plucked and tormented the peak his mouth wasn't covering. Sharp sensation surged from her nipples to her pussy and stole her breath with the sharp spasms that surged through her womb.

He wasn't content to linger there, no matter how desperately she pulled at his hair as he began to move lower.

"Stop teasing me . . ." She was panting. Panting was so juvenile. But there she was, panting for breath as he licked his way down her stomach, nipping and kissing and generally driving her crazy.

"Hmm, teasing is good," he reminded her as his hands moved to spread her thighs. Wide.

She shuddered as his teeth raked at the inside of her thigh, her muscles clenching, fighting to close against his head despite the broad hands wrapped around her knees, holding her open.

"You smell so sweet." He placed a nipping little kiss in the crease between her thigh and her desperately aching cunt. The pressure pounding in her clit had her trying to arch closer, to force his mouth where she needed it. And oh, did she need it.

"Braden, I didn't tease you like this." Oh hell, that wasn't a whimper. It really wasn't. And she wasn't begging, she assured herself. She just couldn't breathe enough to make her voice firmer.

"You mean like this?"

She screeched as his tongue swiped through her aching slit, from the entrance to her hungry pussy to the swollen nub of her clit.

Harsh tremors shook her body as she reached for release, only to hear his heated chuckle as he sent a breath of air to tantalize her aching flesh.

"You're evil." She panted, straining to get closer.

"That wasn't evil," he growled. "This is evil."

His tongue flickered over her clit, the touch so whisper-light that the taunting strokes only pushed her arousal higher without allowing her to explode.

Her hands clenched in his hair, pulling at it, her ragged moans demanding relief. A sharp nip to her thigh had her stilling for a second. Only a second. The eroticism of the small bite caused her to shudder as her head whipped back and forth on the mattress.

"Stay still, minx," he ordered, his voice growing darker, hotter as she strained against him. "Let me do this."

His head moved lower, his tongue reaching out to rim the flooded entrance of her pussy.

"Mmm, delicious." He lapped at her, licking with such sensual destruction that she swore she was going to go up in flames and disintegrate into ashes before he ever gave her relief.

She moaned, a low, pitifully desperate sound that she knew she was going to blush over later. But for now, the pleasure was sweeping through her, rocketing through her bloodstream and building in intensity.

"Like that, baby?" His hands slid from her knees to her inner thighs, his thumbs catching at the plumped flesh of her pussy to open her further.

She nearly wept as his tongue began to tease at the opening, flickering, licking, lapping at the juices easing from her. The vibration of his growling moans was another caress streaking through her.

"I hate you." She moaned with a spurt of laughter as his teasing threatened to steal her mind. He was killing her.

He laughed, a low wicked sound that sent shivers racing over her flesh.

"That's okay, baby," he crooned. "I like the way you hate."

His tongue sank inside her, parting the clenching muscles, licking at the sensitive flesh and sending her exploding as her hips arched and the breath rushed from her lungs.

One thrust. That was all it had taken. One deep, powerful thrust of his wicked tongue and she was exploding around him, melting, burning beneath the erotic lash of each caress.

She was barely aware of him moving, able to do no more than gasp as he flipped her to her stomach before pushing her knees up, forcing her to hold her hips from the bed. In that position, she was open to him, completely defenseless as she felt him rub the head of his cock against her quaking pussy.

"So pretty, Megan." The growl in his voice was deeper now, more primal. "So wet and hot."

He pressed against her, the wide crest opening her, stretching her with unbelievable pleasure.

"There, baby." He came over her, covering her as he

began to work his cock into the gripping muscles of her pussy.

God, it was killing her. He was hot and thick, spreading her open, caressing nerve endings she had never known existed until he possessed her.

Megan whimpered as her fists clenched in the blankets beneath her, her eyes closed, aware of nothing but Braden taking her, holding her beneath his powerful body, his tongue caressing her shoulder, his teeth raking it as he thrust slow and easy inside her.

She shuddered, clenching around him as she pushed back, eager to take every inch, to experience once again the amazing pleasure she knew she would only ever find with Braden.

"There, baby," he crooned at her shoulder, placing stinging little kisses there as he began to move inside her. "See how sweet and tight you are? Like a snug little glove created just for my cock."

His explicit words had her moaning in excitement, the gravelly, growling sound of his voice piercing her womb as his erection tunneled through her pussy with increasingly hard strokes.

The air around her began to pulse with hunger. His. Hers. The smell of hot sex, sweat-soaked bodies and lust filled the room. Braden's growling moans, her desperate cries echoing around her. The sensations weren't just pleasure—they were desperate, grinding, furious sex.

Braden braced himself over her, his teeth opening over her shoulder as his hips moved faster, pounding his cock inside her with sharp, jackhammering thrusts that had her screaming. She tilted her hips and rocked back into him as she felt wildfire twisting through her pussy, her spasming womb, climbing higher, hotter.

He snarled at her neck, and as though the trigger had been released, she exploded. Her back arched, white-hot heat whipped through her body as her orgasm ripped through her nerve endings at the exact moment she felt Braden's teeth sink into her shoulder.

Pain, pleasure—both exploded through her, one driving the other higher until she didn't know where they began, where they ended or if reality would ever return.

The hard, erotic extension locked him inside her, heating her further, driving her climax harder. She felt Braden's cock jerk, felt the hard, jetting pulses of his seed shooting inside her as he growled again, a low, throaty sound of pleasure as his release rocked him as hard as hers tore through her.

Megan collapsed beneath him, feeling his lips lift from her shoulder, his tongue lapping at the wound she knew he must have made. It should have hurt like a son of a bitch; instead, she felt only a low, distant ache and a slight sting. And Braden.

"You bit me." She could barely push the words past her lips. "Told you not to bite me again."

He growled. The sound sent a pulse of pleasure raking over her nerve endings as she moaned in defeat. Hell, what was a little bite? She was sated and exhausted, more relaxed than she could ever remember being. She could handle a little bite or two. Maybe.

CHAPTER 14

"This biting stuff is going to have to stop." Megan surveyed the damage to her shoulder in the mirror over the sink as she frowned at the slight bruising. Talk about the hickey from hell.

Two small punctures pierced the flesh, reminding her of the gory vampire books she liked to read. She shivered at the thought.

"It's not that bad." His voice was quiet as he stood in the doorway watching her, his eyes dark gold, his expression carefully blank as he glanced at her shoulder.

She tried to sense what he was thinking and feeling, but he held it back, keeping it carefully behind the shields that seemed such a natural part of him.

"Wish I could do that," she muttered in exasperation before pulling on the soft cotton tank top she was going to be forced to wear beneath her blouse. This was definitely a no-bra day.

"You could, if you tried." Megan stilled. She could hear the determination now, carefully banked.

Lifting the cotton blouse from the hook on the wall beside her, she shrugged into it, buttoning the loose material as she ignored him and his comment.

"I need to go into the office this morning." She tucked the shirt into her jeans before snapping them and latching her belt. "I'm sure I have plenty of paperwork piled up and waiting. I may as well take care of it while we're waiting for whatever answers you're going to come up with for this."

Braden crossed his arms over his chest. She ignored the action.

"The paperwork can wait." Damn. His voice hadn't changed; neither had his expression. That wasn't a good sign.

"For what?" She turned and faced him squarely now. It was better to get it out in the open and fight over it before they left the house. She was evidently not going to like whatever he had to say or he would have said it already.

"We have a job to do, Megan," he reminded her. "We have to find out why those Breeds were murdered and what the Council wants with you. We're not going to do that in this house fucking ourselves to death, or in the office completing your paperwork."

"I didn't tell you to infect me with that funky hormone shit you have going on, Braden," she pointed out with a scowl. "So don't blame me for your own horniness."

He grunted at her declaration.

"Stop trying to change the subject." He straightened from the doorframe, pulling himself to his full sexy, broad height as he stared down that perfect nose of his. Well, maybe not so perfect. She looked closer, barely detecting where the flattened plane appeared to be misaligned by the smallest degree. Aha, an imperfection. She knew he had to have one somewhere.

"So tell me what the subject is." Unfortunately, she was

afraid she already knew. "I haven't heard you actually state anything, yet."

"We're heading back into the desert today," he informed her. "Area Six-fifteen, Section C. It's a small canyon we suspect Mark and Aimee may have gone to before heading to the gully where you found them."

Megan paused. "And you know this how?"

His lips quirked. "Jonas managed to pull another small bit of information out of that Coyote you let live. We're going to check the canyon because evidently the Coyotes hadn't made it there yet. That was their next stop. But we suspect Mark and Aimee might have stopped there."

"And you know this how?" she asked again.

"GPS tracking was turned off in their vehicle, but they kept a directional and mileage recorder on. Analysis of the electronics indicates they were in that canyon for as long as twelve hours. Alive."

She stared back at him silently. She knew what he wanted. He wanted her to use the Empathic abilities she possessed to find the answers the others couldn't.

"It won't work," she told him softly. "If it would work, I wouldn't have to run to this desert to hide. I would have gone to my superiors and let them help me find a way to make it work."

"I'm not your superior, Megan," he reminded her, his voice dangerously deep now. "And the situation has changed. Because, baby, I can do more than just mute the emotions flowing around you. I can amplify them. Today we will find answers."

"Hold on just a damned minute." She rushed through the bedroom, determined to catch up with him as he moved down the stairs, obviously ignoring her.

"Braden Arness, you hold it right there," she snapped, grabbing the rail and taking the steps two at a time as she rushed after him.

He stopped all right, turning just in time for her to slam against his chest. She grunted at the hard contact, silently cursing the hard muscles before pushing back from him fiercely.

"What the hell are you talking about? You can amplify them?"

He arched his brows.

"Get your boots on and I'll show you. It's time to find answers, Megan. It's obvious the Coyotes are not going to attack again any time soon and give me a chance to force the answers from them. And we can't stay here, hidden in the desert forever, waiting on them. We find our answers on our own now."

She stared back at him, fighting the fears rising inside her. She knew what it was like, the struggle to sift through the bleak emotions, the violence of lives forcibly taken. It was hell, slicing into her brain with torturous strength. She had never managed it before, had never found so much as a glimmer of hope that it could be done. Even her grandmother, with her experience in controlling her abilities, had never truly been able to do it.

"And if I can't?" she asked, hating the thought of failing him, of failing them both. "I've tried before, Braden."

"Not with me you haven't," he pointed out coolly. "There comes a time, Megan, when you have to stop hiding and start fighting. I can help you if you'll let me."

Or he could force her to do it his way, whatever it took. She saw it in his eyes, in the grim set of his mouth. She could feel her stomach twisting with nerves, her mind already rebelling against the coming pain. The emotions and horror attached to a violent death took years to recede from the area in which it occurred. It would be just as strong now as it had been when she first met him.

"Do you want to die like them?" he asked her then. "Do you let the Council win, Megan? Or do you fight back?"

She fought. The answer was instantaneous. She had never given anything up without a fight, she just didn't know how to fight this battle.

She moved around him carefully, stepping into the kitchen where her boots sat by the door, her holster and belt hanging on the coat rack on the wall.

She stared at the Glock strapped into its protective holster before picking up her boots and pulling them on quickly. The belt went around her hips, the velcro anchors around her thigh. Moving to the hall closet, she opened the hidden door and lifted several sheathed knives from the velvet-covered shelf as well as a powerful snub-nosed machine gun.

"You're expecting them to be there," she said. She could feel it. Not in any sense of emotion or thoughts coming from Braden, but with an inborn gut-deep knowledge she couldn't explain.

"They've been watching the house." The information didn't surprise her. "I suspect they haven't attacked because they're aware of the team of Felines watching from one of the points above us. They'll follow though. It's even possible they have a team in place."

"So how do you expect to get around them and into that canyon? And if we do, how am I supposed to figure anything out?" It seemed a recipe for disaster to her. "I can't function in those circumstances, Braden." The emotions would attack her if she abandoned the defenses she had built against them. Slight though they were, they allowed her to function for short amounts of time.

"You did fine in the gully the other day," he pointed out, his voice never deepening nor warming.

"You helped me." She knew that, realized it with an aching sense of failure. "I hid in that shield you have around yourself."

"Because I let you." His voice was lower, dangerous. "I've let you use the shields, because you needed them.

Your mind needed to learn how they worked, even if it did so subconsciously. As powerful as I suspect you are, you'll learn quickly how to create your own shields by using mine as a guide."

A bitter smile curved her lips. "And if it doesn't work?"

"Then we're both in a shitload of trouble." There was no doubt in his voice. "Do you want to risk that?"

Her lips trembled as she pressed them tightly together. Rather than speaking, she bent to strap one of the knives below her knee, the other to her thigh.

"I don't like the way you stack the odds. Have your buddies take out the team watching us here," she suggested.

He grunted. "If they can, they will. There's always the chance they can't. Now let's get moving. I want to get there before noon."

He turned and strode from the house, clearly expecting her to follow him. Damn. And she was going to do it, she knew she was. He smelled of danger, of adventure, of a way to conquer her demons and find the freedom she had longed for all these years.

And, in that moment, as hopeless as he made the mission seem, she knew he wouldn't carelessly drive them into the arms of their enemy. He had been doing this all his life, planning each move, each battle. He knew what he was doing.

That didn't mean she had to like it.

It didn't mean he wasn't going to tell her exactly what was going on. In that moment she knew beyond a shadow of a doubt that this was no more than a test. The decision to follow him, to trust him. And she would be damned if she wasn't going to pass it.

Braden kept his expression calm, his shields carefully in place as Megan opened the door to the Raider and jumped into her seat.

"GPS, pull up Area Six-fifteen, Section C, Casper's Pass." The windshield immediately became a cross-section of lines and map points as he backed the Raider into the turning area and pulled out.

"There's the canyon. Lance and I always called it Casper's Pass, though officially it has no name. We named it that for the sound the winds make at certain times of the day, like ghostly laughter weaving through the canyon. Here." She pointed to a section of marked range, hilly, appearing impassable if one used the GPS appearance. "There's a rarely used road that weaves through this range. It's pretty much hidden, even from the air, so satellite would have a hard time finding it. If we disconnect GPS and the locator beacon on the Raider, we could slip through here. It would bring us above the canyon and allow us to survey it from a point where damned near all the canyon is in full view. It could give us an advantage that the other routes won't."

Braden glanced at the screen, his brow furrowing as he stared at the direction she laid out by touching the points on the screen. As she had said, it was hidden, so well that even the Breed satellites had been unable to detect it.

"The Raider can traverse it?" The range looked remarkably rough.

"Lance and I went fishing up there last summer with Grandfather." She pointed to the blue area indicated no more than a mile from the observation point she suggested. "We took the range road with his Raider. It was rough, but definitely passable, and the area is also greener than the valley below, which cuts down on the dust trail. Without beacon, locators or dust points, the satellite imagery—if the Council is using it—can't pick us up here. They won't be expecting us if they're there."

Excitement. He could feel it building in her, along with fear. And arousal. He inhaled slowly, restraining the lust building within him.

"Stop sniffing." He almost grinned at the disgruntled

tone of her voice. "Leaving the house was your idea, not mine. I was perfectly happy bouncing in bed."

"You have a way of describing things that astounds me, Megan," he drawled. "Next time, we'll try the kitchen table and see what you come up with for that one."

"Ewww, I eat there," she retorted in mock distaste.

He glanced at her, allowing a smile to tilt his lips.

"I'll just make a meal out of you," he told her, not bothering to hide the hunger in his voice.

She flushed. He loved watching the color move beneath her skin, the way her eyes darkened and her breathing roughened.

"Pervert," she accused him, though her voice lacked heat. "I'll wait until we get closer to the area before I disable the GPS and locator beacon. Otherwise, anyone at the office can track us. I'll never believe Lance would betray me, but there are several people there I wouldn't trust as far as I can throw them."

There were several people he knew would sell her out in a second. Jonas had pulled profiles on each and every deputy on the force, as well as the sheriff. Their records weren't nearly as clean as the state investigators had listed them.

"I anticipated that." He nodded, pointing to a small area several miles from their present location. "I'll pull over here and disable. While I'm at it, I'll contact the team watching the house and see if they were able to take out the Coyotes there. We hadn't pinpointed their exact location yesterday, but I'm hoping that when we drive off, they'll begin moving. My team will be able to locate them if they do."

Silence filled the vehicle then. Braden was aware of Megan breathing in roughly before disengaging the GPS map and settling back in her seat.

She watched the road in front of them, her body tense, her emotions chaotic. He knew the step she had taken hadn't been an easy one.

"I could fail," she finally reminded him, fighting to

steady her breathing, her fears, as though frightened of giving the words strength by voicing them.

"And you could find freedom." He kept his hands tight around the steering wheel, refusing to reach out to her, to comfort her as every instinct inside him was demanding he do.

He was supposed to protect his mate. To fight her battles, to cherish her. And God knew he had grown to cherish her. Hell, he was so in love with her he was acting more like a callow youth than a fully grown Breed. She was his other half; the Mating would not let him deny it.

Taking her into danger wasn't sitting well with him. He knew the problems she would face as she learned to build the shields she needed. The pain she would endure in opening herself up to emotions that filled that damned canyon. She wasn't a Breed; she had none of the natural, instinctive blocks to protect her mind from the horror she would face. By letting it in, she would experience it, the same as Mark and Aimee had experienced it. She would know their pain, their horror, and their deaths. And with any luck, the secret of why they had made the fateful trip to Broken Butte in search of her would be revealed.

"Freedom would be nice." Her voice was reflective, thoughtful as she responded to his earlier comment. "It would be very nice."

What she wasn't saying, he could feel. Freedom was adventure. It was the warrior's soul given the chance to fight, to make the difference it had longed to make.

She would have no choice but to fight. Further training, if they survived this mission, would be a necessity. He was an assassin. He didn't capture the scientists and Trainers who had worked within the Council. As far as he was concerned, there was no redemption for the corruption that filled them. They were diseased animals. And like such creatures of the wild, the only peace the world would know was in their deaths.

He flexed his shoulders, feeling the scars crisscrossing his back that he had never allowed Megan to see. The whips used in the training centers and Labs were created to maim, to kill in the most painful ways. He had learned early on to avoid that punishment at all costs. But he had learned it at a painful price.

"We'll go slow." He made the promise against his better judgment. "We can observe the canyon from above, see what you can pick up from there."

"It's too far away," she said regretfully. "I drive through the canyon when on patrol, looking for tire tracks, or sensations of previous movement. I can't do that from a distance; I'll have to get into the canyon. Normally, GPS will pick up life signs, but something jammed it in the gully, so I'm hesitant to trust it now."

"Yeah, I noticed that. My Raider wasn't picking them up either. The jammers were gone when the team went through the canyon though."

"Unless it was being used from another point. Did we miss one of the Coyotes?" She turned to stare at him, a frown creasing her brow.

"We missed one." He nodded, certain himself that there had been a third Coyote. "That's why we won't rely on GPS this trip. We'll use what God gave us to survive, Megan." He couldn't let her do otherwise. "We don't have a choice. We find out now why they want you, and what my people were doing here. And then we take them out."

◆ C H A P T E R 1 5 ◆

The route they took to the canyon was longer than the others, but as Megan promised, the grassier terrain yielded no dust clouds and the sheltering hills and passes muted the sound of the motor as it made its way to the location.

It wasn't an easy drive, and one he was certain only the Raider or a terrain-eating motorbike could have traversed. The Raider sliced through several streams before squeezing through passes he was certain there was no way it could scrape through.

Before noon, they were pulling into a hidden copse of trees. Braden cut the motor before leaving the vehicle. The edge of the canyon was just ahead.

Braden pulled the binoculars from the backseat and began surveying the area while Megan looked around nervously. He could feel her fighting to lower the shields that were so much a part of her and search for any hidden enemies.

"What do you feel?" He kept scanning with the binoculars; the heat-seeking capabilities of the equipment couldn't be blocked. There was plenty of wildlife, but so far none of the two-legged variety.

"Fear." Her voice was flat, tight.

"How strong is it?" God, he hated this. He could feel her hesitancy, her instinctive rejection of the emotions trying to bombard her.

"Probably mine," she answered with resignation. "I'd rather face the Coyotes and bullets than try this."

"Let's move in closer. I can't detect any hidden life signs. If they're here, they're below."

The Coyotes wouldn't anticipate their arrival from above. They would expect them to take the same course into the canyon that Megan would have taken on patrol.

"There're several ways into the canyon from here." She kept her voice lowered as little by little she forced the mental blocks to recede.

It wasn't easy for her. He could feel the struggle she was waging to drop them, to allow her sensitive brain to pick up whatever emotions leaked from the canyon below. They were there; he could feel them, just as he could feel the presence of the Coyotes.

"We'll stay high for now." Bending low, they moved from the shelter of the thick trees, staying parallel to a mass of boulders that appeared to have been dropped like a child's marbles along the top of the canyon.

Megan moved along the edge of the thick pine growth, thankful for the cover of brush as she moved closer to the area where she would have been most vulnerable during patrol.

She couldn't feel the presence of the Coyotes. The dark malevolence that was so much a part of them, the thirst for blood, was absent. She knew them now, knew the feel of them, the smell of them.

She was aware of Braden moving behind her. The sense of calm, the shield that normally reached out to her wasn't there now. The absence of it sent her pulse racing; the knowledge that she was mentally on her own was almost frightening.

She couldn't feel the Coyotes but the tendrils of violence that reached out from the canyon floor had her chest tightening. Rage. Fear.

She breathed in roughly, fighting to allow it in, to sift past the rage and anger for the core of the emotion. There was always a core. A driving reason behind the pain. But at this distance it would be next to impossible to detect.

"Mark and Aimee had been here. They knew the Coyotes were following them," she said, her voice rough as she felt him behind her.

He was tense as he covered her. The shields he had allowed her to use before weren't available, but there was something else, a connection, a sense of energy pouring from him into her.

"Let's move back, work our way to the canyon floor and see if there's anything there. Maybe the distance between here and the entrance they used is still too much."

God, she could feel them already, distant though they were. The shadowy impressions of emotion clenched her chest as the overwhelming grief, the bottomless pit of rage and pain, sought her out. Why had those Breeds been here? What had they wanted from her?

They backtracked quietly. As they neared the upper edge of the cliffs, Megan pointed out the steep trail that led to the canyon floor. The weaving path led between boulders, scrub pine and a multitude of brush. It wasn't the safest route, but it was relatively secure.

"I'll go ahead of you." Braden paused at the top of the path, glancing back at her, his gaze darker, filled with concern. "Are you doing okay?"

She nodded stiffly. Dropping her barriers, ineffective though they were, was still hard. It wasn't something she was used to doing and her mind was rioting at the vulnerable position she was placing herself in.

"How did you learn to use your shields?" she asked.

"Most of it is natural instinct. Animals have the ability to sense emotion, to sense danger, while remaining unaffected by it. They know it's there. My abilities are stronger than many of the other Felines. I can drop my shields and sense emotion without feeling it, but I can't pick up specifics. I can pick up the fact that there was death, pain, rage or danger. But I can't sift through the emotions to reach the secrets."

"And what makes you think I can?" She tried to regulate her breathing, to hold back the fear that reached out to her and weaved through her consciousness.

"Observation." He paused at a particularly steep stretch of the path before moving to the left several feet in search of surer footing. "And the fact that I can feel you drawing on my shields. It stands to reason that you could also draw on my abilities and pick up more."

"To increase them." She paused as she stared back at him. "You're going to increase what's already there."

Breathe. In. Out.

She could handle it. She would kill him later, but for now, she could handle it. Do the job; that was the important part. The rest she could tackle later.

"I'll be here with you, Megan." He turned, his expression still, almost blank. "We'll work on it together. We'll balance each other. I promise."

Her lips flattened as she fought the bitterness that seemed to seep through her. Balance each other.

"You won't feel what I feel, Braden." The betrayal still stung. The sense of being used seared her soul. "That's not balance."

"You'll see." He turned and continued down the path. "Explaining it would make no sense, but you'll see what I mean."

The closer they moved to the floor of the canyon, the stronger the impressions came. At this point, it wasn't the rage or the death. She felt determination, a sense of purpose.

She paused at the wide entrance, fighting to still the tremors that passed through her body. One of the unfortunate side effects of her abilities was the fact that she felt not just the emotions of the event reaching out to her, but also the lives the victims had lived. Not clearly. Not enough to find answers or even completely understand the darkness that filled her mind—and would later fill her dreams. And the darkness within the two Breeds who had died here had been deep.

She paused just within the rising cliffs, closing her eyes and trying to focus. They hadn't been frightened. They had stopped here, staring into the canyon for long moments, aware of something . . . Danger.

"They were hunters." Braden's voice was soft. "Mark and Aimee were paired in the Labs because their abilities complemented each other. Mark was a perfect shot; Aimee was more in tune with the weapons—what would work best where—than he was. She had a feel for them. She was an excellent tracker; he was a strategist. We suspect they were mates, but they never came forward to verify it."

Megan sensed that the two had been close, though they had fought to hide it. The small distance she felt between them wasn't a result of that attempt to hide their bond. It was a result of betrayals. They had loved, but that love had been marred horribly.

"They were mates." She frowned as she sifted through the impressions. She could feel a bond, and it was strong. Strange, the information that could be found on the outskirts of violence. As though everything that had been felt had been saved, impressed upon the area like information to a hard drive.

Braden. He stood just behind her, his primal DNA a magnet to the psychic impressions.

"Concentrate." His voice was almost mesmerizing. "I'm

here, Megan. I know what's here with us. Trust me to help you."

She moved slowly into the canyon, one step at a time, feeling the presence of the two Breeds as she made her way between the sheer cliffs that rose above them.

Mark had been hard, fierce. He had believed implicitly in whatever they were there to do. Aimee had been less certain. She hadn't been frightened, but rather wary. She could sense things easier than her partner, her mate.

Megan inhaled sharply as she stopped. She hated this. Her insides clenched with pain, a physical sensation to match the mental excesses as she felt the spirit of the woman reach out to her.

She felt death.

"I can't . . ." She whimpered then, desperation rising inside her as her hands went to her own stomach.

"You're not a part of it, Megan." His voice was at her ear, his hands gripping her hips, holding her to her feet when she knew she would have fallen. "Feel around your mind, right now." His voice hardened. "Keep your eyes closed, baby. Remember. You are separate. Separate yourself."

Separate.

Her hands clenched at her stomach as she felt the pain rising in her soul.

"She was pregnant." She wanted to curl into a ball, to find a hole that would hide her, that would let her grieve. No. No. That was Aimee. Aimee had wanted to hide.

"She was pregnant." Braden's voice was low, aching with sadness. "Why was she here, Megan? Why did she want you? Go beyond Aimee. There's a place beyond the emotions, the pain, where the truth lies. What did she want?"

What did she want? There were so many emotions rolling over her, through her. Sift through them. Find the core. There was a core.

"Revenge."

Megan stiffened, gasping at the strength of the thought. Aimee wanted revenge.

"Keep your eyes closed." Braden growled as they flew open. "Close your eyes, Megan. Concentrate. Feel the strength I'm lending you, learn how to use it and keep looking. What is the core, baby?"

She was gasping for breath. She could feel the fine sheen of sweat that covered her face, her neck. It wasn't the heat, it was the shaking cold inside her.

Revenge. The word whispered through her mind again. But first, they needed proof. Here lay the proof. They would move to the other side of the curve and wait. GPS on Mark and Aimee's vehicle had been disabled, stealth had been enabled.

"Breed vehicles have stealth?" she asked, confused, thinking of the special electronics that blocked life signs by law enforcement vehicles.

He stiffened in surprise. "Not normally." His voice was grim now. "Sometimes, only when authorized."

She kept searching, desperate to find the answers here, now. She didn't know if she could go further, if she could force herself to pull in the shattered emotions that lingered here. Already her mind was screaming, demanding to be allowed to hide from emotions that weren't its own.

The emotions were stronger here than they had been in the gully where the couple had died. They had rested here within the shelter of this canyon. They had held each other, loved, and accepted that the battle they had taken on may not be successful.

Megan felt herself weakening. Her knees shook, her chest felt tight with a need for oxygen that should have been there. She was gasping for breath; surely she shouldn't feel so deprived?

Behind her closed eyes, sparks of light exploded before her gaze, shifting colors, sizzling heat. She felt a premonition of death, a race to make a call. Another call. Had they been betrayed? Aimee had felt the betrayal beating at her brain, the sense of danger, of death.

Then, through the building emotions, the knowledge of another's danger, another's death, came a sense of impending doom stronger than the impressions lying in wait. Her eyes flew open as she realized they were closer to the sharp bend that led further into the canyon than she had realized.

"Stop." She hissed, digging in her heels, staring at the curve, her muscles freezing, her mind screaming.

He stopped. Time stood still as she fought to get some sort of control, to separate herself.

"Someone is there." She could feel it. Knew they weren't alone.

"It's the strength of your abilities." He began to soothe her.

She shook her head desperately. "I feel them. They're there."

"I don't feel it." His voice was cold, analyzing. "What do you feel, Megan?"

Her hand fell to her holster as she loosened the clip that held the Glock in place and allowed it to drop into her palm. She was aware of Braden doing the same.

"Do you feel it?" she asked him.

Friend or foe? She couldn't be certain. It wasn't a Coyote, she knew that.

He jerked her to the side, moving to the base of the cliff, using the scrub and boulders that littered the area as a shield.

Megan fought to slam the barriers in her mind back in place, almost whimpering in pain as they refused to lower. As though once lifted, they would be forever out of reach.

"What is it?" she asked. She wanted to clasp her head in an attempt to hold back the sensations still rushing toward her. Whoever, whatever waited on the other side was cold, emotionless. She sensed nothing but their presence.

"Non-Breeds." Braden's voice carried no farther than her ear. "At least two."

"Moving or still?"

"Waiting. The scent hasn't changed. They know we're here. What do you feel?"

She shook her head. "No emotion. Just presence."

She felt more than heard his curse.

"We move back above the canyon." He growled in her ear. "Back to the Raider."

Backing up, Megan kept her gaze on the curve that led around to the other side of the canyon. Why wait there? What were they searching for?

Her mind was alive with twisting emotions that made no sense, that she had no time to sift through. But she could feel the answers there, just out of reach. Both Mark and Aimee's, as well as whoever lay in wait now.

They definitely weren't Coyote, she thought as Braden pushed her back up the path to the head of the canyon. She kept low, moving between the sheltering boulders and brush as they rushed up the steep slope.

Silence was imperative. She was aware of Braden's silent demand, of how he braced her when needed, keeping her from stepping in the softer areas and leading her along firmer ground.

From below, she could feel patience, silent watchfulness. Whoever was there knew that she and Braden were also, or at least suspected they would be rounding that curve. They were waiting on them.

She wanted to whimper as pain seared her mind. It took every ounce of strength she possessed to flee back up the path, to concentrate on climbing rather than lying down and moaning at the pain.

As they neared the top of the cliff, Braden pulled her to an abrupt stop. She felt it then. Just above them, waiting.

"You stay." He pushed her behind the boulder they were using as a shield, turning to stare at her, his eyes blazing gold with fury. "I'll be back for you."

She caught his arm, defiance filling her. She had come this far, she would be damned if she would let him shelter her now.

"I'll be behind you," she told him, careful to keep her voice low. "From here, we can break off, shimmying along the side. We can move to the top of the cliff with the smaller boulders and brush covering the entrance. We'll be hidden and on either side of them."

His lips flattened, an instant denial flashing in his eyes.

"It will work, Braden," she whispered. "We're not that far from the Raider. You can smell them, right?"

He nodded briefly.

"You'll know where they're at once we get to the top. You can signal to me and we can take him out. It's the only way."

She could feel it. Her brain was a morass of sensations and information she couldn't make sense of, but this made sense. Someone was waiting on them, possibly to stop them.

"We fight together or we don't fight at all," she told him fiercely. "I won't be coddled."

"You'll be dead if you don't do as I tell you." He growled. "Let me check it out first."

Megan stared back at him furiously.

"Go then," she said coldly, releasing his arm and settling back against the boulder as anger burned in her chest. "I'll just sit here like a good girl and wait on you."

"You do that." He grunted, nodding sharply. "Give me ten minutes. If you don't see me after that assume the worst and use this."

He pressed a small locator in her hand.

"And this is?"

"The signal goes straight to Jonas. He'll have help out here soon. Stay hidden and shoot anything that moves the wrong way. You're fairly secure right here." He touched her cheek before flashing her a wicked grin. "But I do intend to be back, baby."

He grabbed her by the back of the head, pressed a quick, hard kiss to her lips, then moved off.

Son of a bitch. He was trying to protect her. Playing the big bad Feline hero taking care of the weak little woman. She snorted at the thought. She did *not* think so.

One.

Two.

Three.

She watched him make his way to the left, using the craggy outcropping of the cliff to hide his presence. He was smooth, she had to give him credit for it. If she hadn't watched him move into the brush and boulders then she would have never known he was there. But that was okay, she wasn't too damned shabby there herself.

Four.

Five.

Six.

Now.

She moved away from the boulder, sliding to the right, careful to stay low as she began to shimmy up the side of the trail at the opposite angle.

Of course, he would know what she was doing; there wasn't a chance he wouldn't catch sight of her. But those below, and whoever the hell waited above, wouldn't have a clue. She knew this area like the back of her hand, had played here as a child, hunted as an adult. She and Lance had trained in this area with her father and grandfather as teachers. She knew how to stay hidden.

Staying on her belly, she used her knees and elbows to scuttle along the slope, staying low, moving between and around the brush and craggy outcroppings of rock. The paths worn into the steep slope made it hard to stay under cover, but her grandfather had taught her how to blend into the landscape around her and to use even the most insignificant cover effectively.

Within minutes she was edging over the bank, watching with her eyes, feeling with her mind as she kept the gun balanced in her hand. Braden was moving through the brush and tall grass several hundred yards across from her, working his way to the Raider.

She couldn't see him, but she could feel him. And boy was he pissed.

Now was the time to find their watchers.

She focused on the land around her, her eyes scanning as she felt for the odd, the unnatural . . . the evil. The Raider was parked beneath the pines in the distance, hidden from sight. They would be where they could watch the vehicle as well as any paths to it.

There.

Her gaze swung to the pines, lifting, narrowing as she fought to catch sight of anything unusual within the branches of the tree.

A tight smile curved her lips as she began to move quicker now, heading for a point between the Raider and that particular tree as she kept an eye on the unassuming little splotch of color that almost blended perfectly with the tree.

Almost. Once she knew where to look, picking out the different shade of green wasn't that difficult. Whoever it was, they were well trained.

As she moved into position behind one of the thick tree trunks between the Raider and the watcher, she searched behind her, around her. She could sense nothing, no eyes on her, no prickling awareness of a weapon aimed her way. There was more than one, but evidently not within sight of her.

Moving easily, she leveled her weapon at the watcher,

seeing just enough of his camouflaged body to know that if she had to shoot, she could take him out.

Now, where the hell was Braden?

◆   ◆   ◆

He was going to beat her ass.

Braden stifled the growl in his throat as he caught Megan inching her way from the safety of the boulders and working her way to the top of the canyon. There were at least two snipers hiding somewhere in the field, perhaps more farther ahead.

They weren't Breeds. This was military, or at least military trained. Cold and efficient, aware that any hint of emotion would give their positions away. He could sense them, but he couldn't follow the path of that knowledge to their location.

They were in the pines. He paused as he moved over the rim of the canyon, staring into the pines that hid the Raider from view. They would be in there, most likely in the trees rather than on the ground. The scent was too diluted, too hard to follow for them to be accessible. So that left no place to go but up.

As he snaked his way through the gently swaying grass, keeping close to the scattered boulders and thick vegetation, he watched the trees, narrowing his eyes as he sought any sign of movement.

They were good. They weren't moving.

He checked Megan's position and began to push himself closer. The watchers' vantage point from above gave them an edge on him. They could watch the Raider as well as the field and have a bird's-eye shot on anything that moved.

But that was okay. He could move pretty damned fast, and once the first shot went off, the watchers' position would be compromised. Tightening his lips in renewed fury, he watched as Megan quickly made her way toward the pine thicket. She was good. And fast. He could barely catch sight of her as she crawled the distance on her belly.

He moved in line with her, keeping an eye on her until she disappeared behind one thick tree trunk, then another. Once beneath the pines, she was marginally safer. But marginally didn't help his nerves much.

He moved quicker now that Megan was beneath the pines, drawing in the scents trapped within the clearing as he made his way to the area. The Raider was perhaps forty feet away, beneath the trees, to the east. That gave Megan an edge in getting to it if the whole deal went from sugar to shit.

Damn her, he was going to beat her ass for doing something so stupid. She wasn't trained to fight like this. Her mind was too sensitive right now to go against opponents who were better trained and determined to kill.

There he was. The first watcher was positioned on the lower limb of a tree just ahead. The sole of his boots gave him away as he shifted. A rifle barrel was tucked into the pine needles, its dark eye trained on the edge of the canyon behind Braden.

Excellent.

He moved in carefully, gauging the jump to the limb and how quickly he could raise an alarm. Braden knew he would have to be fast.

He slid the knife he carried on his leg free of its sheath, the metal making no sound as it cleared the leather that held it snugly in place.

Wickedly sharp, lethal. He paused as he came within distance of a throw. Wound or wipe? Damn, he hated not knowing, but any friendly took their own chances sneaking up on him.

Turning the weapon, he balanced the blade in his hand before pulling back for a throw.

"I don't think so, Breed."

Braden stilled as he felt the movement behind him then. Son of a bitch.

He raised his hands slowly, calculating the risk.

"Nice looking knife, Bree—" The voice was silenced as Braden flipped the blade with a hard twist of his wrist and went to the ground in a quick roll.

Turning, he jerked the powerful rifle from the gasping soldier before turning and shooting into the pine. Two down.

Bending low, he ran for the pines and Megan.

✦   ✦   ✦

The shot ricocheted around the clearing as the soldier fell from the pine headfirst to the unforgiving ground below. Adrenaline surged through Megan's body the second the shot was fired. The blood also began to race through her body, her senses heightening, the need for action rushing through her like a runaway train on a collision course with every dream she ever imagined.

Instinct kicked in, her mind opening, the sensations, impressions and instant information slamming into it and combining with the excitement that tore through her.

She knew the two fallen men weren't the only ones, but the others were far enough away to give her and Braden a chance. She sprinted from the trees, running hard and fast for the Raider, her feet pounding against the earth. Adrenaline gave her a burst of speed, a rush of strength she had only ever known the few times she had been in a truly dangerous situation.

She loved it. Craved it. This was living.

She slid against the Raider seconds later, jerking at the door handle as her fingerprints registered with the security and the door flew open.

Jumping into the seat, she started the motor and revved it hard as she slammed the door, her gaze scanning the area for Braden. A flash of golden brown ahead had a smile curving her lips as she pushed the gas to the floor. The heavily grooved tires bit into the dirt, rocketing her forward as she headed for Braden. Gunfire was pounding the back of the Raider as she swerved to allow the vehicle to intercept the hits.

Turning the wheel quickly, the Raider blew up dirt and debris as she reached over and flung the passenger-side door open just in time for Braden to throw himself inside, the bullets spraying around them barely missing him.

"How many?" She turned the wheel again, pressed the pedal to the floor and raced through the pines as she headed out of the clearing.

"Three." Jerking the mother of all automatic rifles from the backseat, he slapped an ammo cartridge into the underbelly before swinging the seat around to face the back.

"Hold on," she screamed, glimpsing the vehicles racing through the entrance toward them.

A heavily armed Desert Dragoon headed her way. Small, wide and compact, built for speed and handling in desert terrain, the Dragoon was easily the better vehicle. And besides, it had weapons. Lots of weapons. Two laser-guided rocket launchers with heat-seeking specs, an easily maneuverable machine gun mounted to the roof and operated from inside the specially secured interior.

And whoever was driving it knew what the hell they were doing. Following behind were two stripped down, weapon-ready motorcycles eating up the terrain.

"Bastards!" She jerked the wheel, spinning around as she instantly gauged the distance between them and the canyon. The Dragoon was good, damned good, but it didn't jump distance worth a damn. That was why Lance went for the Raiders instead. And to be safe, he had tinkered with both his and Megan's.

"Hang on," she yelled as Braden's curses sizzled the air.

"God dammit, how did they find us so fucking fast." He was snarling.

Megan laughed.

"I got your back, baby," she yelled, stomping the gas and heading for the canyon. "Hang on to your ass though."

The canyon was almost eight hundred yards away, plenty of room for gaining speed, especially with the special booster attached to the underbelly of the Raider. She flipped open the port between the seats as Braden flipped around.

"Fuck. Megan. What the hell are you doing?" The canyon was wide; she gave him credit for his concern.

"Desert Dragoons can't jump the cliff," she yelled back. "The cycles might follow us, but we'll lose those rockets the Dragoon is carrying."

"And you think Raiders can jump?" he shouted incredulously. "Holy shit. I'm beating your ass, Megan. I'm telling you. We live through this, and you've had it."

Her laughter met the threat as she began to count. She passed the halfway point. Four hundred feet to go. Her speed was rising fast, but not fast enough to jump without help. She fingered the accelerator switch, watching the speedometer as she held the gas to the floor.

"Laser guidance detected." The Raider's automatic defense system activated, the computer's modulated voice giving the warning. "Firing can commence within three feet."

Three more feet. If she didn't keep that Dragoon far enough behind her, then they were toast. She watched the rapidly approaching canyon, calculated the distance of landing and then the two seconds it would take to reach the cover of trees. Almost there.

Her finger itched to hit the accelerator as the canyon loomed closer.

Almost there.

"Laser guidance can commence in two feet."

The Dragoon was gaining fast, but it couldn't jump the distance. Easy maneuverability, but heavy on weapons from what she saw.

Almost.

"Laser guidance can commence in one foot."

She didn't bother to check rearview mirrors. Speed was hitting one hundred and twenty, almost, but not enough. Just another second. Another second.

One hundred feet. Fifty feet. Twenty. She aimed the Raider for the natural upsloped lip.

"Hang on." She hit the accelerator, her breath wheezing from her chest as the Raider shot the last few yards, hitting the dirt ramp and flying through the air.

"Hell yes, baby!" Braden yelled as the Raider cleared the canyon and slammed down on solid earth seconds later, bouncing them in their seats and activating the quick inflate on the seat belts that held them in their seats, preventing possible injury in the event of such a sudden drop.

"Rocket activation, no lock," the computer voiced as Megan sent the Raider speeding into the cover of the trees, twisting the wheel brutally to avoid the thick trunks as she headed down the sharp slope to the road below.

"Those motorcycles are on our ass. Their mini rockets will do some heavy damage." Braden flipped around again. "Security, disengage window, retain security field."

The wide back window dropped away as Braden began firing.

Megan activated the link to Control that Braden had programmed in days before.

"Lance. Lance, where are you?" She yelled out the question as she fought the wheel, bouncing over rocks and more than one deep water-weathered gully in her race to reach the flat land below.

"Control, this is Deputy Fields. I need a copter in the air ASAP. I repeat, I need a copter in the air, position Area Six-fifteen, Section A, heading to Twenty-four. Two cycles, enemy fire. Come back, Control," Megan yelled into the link as Braden fired behind them.

"Son of a fucking bitch, Megan." Lance was screaming

into the link in less than a second, the fury pounding through his voice bringing a smile to her face. "Copters lifting off in three secs, destination Six-fifteen, A. How many?"

"Two cycles, one Dragoon on the north side of Casper's Pass, approximate pass near twenty-four, R." She called out the road number she suspected the Dragoon would use to intercept them. "Cycles carrying automatic fire on board, Dragoon packing launchers."

"Get in range, you jackal-assed bastards." Braden was yelling as he fired, his voice feral, enraged.

"Copter's ETA to intercept three minutes," Lance yelled, the sound of his Raider whining through the link assuring her he was moving fast toward them. "I'm five minutes from your intercept point, copter B moving in ahead of me. Don't shoot the friendlies, God dammit."

"Not me, cuz," she yelled back, twisting the wheel as the hollow twang of bullets pelting close to the vulnerable outside security port warned her that they weren't playing with dummies. "Get these bastards off my back. They know my weakness here, Lance."

"Moving in, Megan. We're moving in. Copter B is closing in fast," John Briggins, the department's best pilot, reported in.

"Right!" Braden screamed out the new direction.

Megan threw the wheel to the right, cursing as the Raider jolted, slamming forward from the blast of the minirocket that exploded too damned close.

"Rocket fire. We have fire. Cycles equipped with short-range rockets, look out for the dust."

She twisted the wheel, holding down the gas as she and the Raider bounced from the sharp decline to flat terrain.

"Prepare for acceleration." She hit the button, praying for just a little more. Just enough speed to clear them from the short-range rockets.

"Head for pass two-zero-four," Briggins ordered briskly through the link. "We're seconds away. Hang on."

"Fuckers. Sons of bitches." Braden was cursing furiously as he sprayed gunfire from the back window. "Those cycles have security shields, Meg. Punch the gas. Punch the gas."

"Gas out," she yelled back. The accelerator was dead.

"Lay that foot to the fucking floor. We have one closing in, prepare for fire . . . Right. Right."

She flipped the wheel, curses raging as she felt the rocket fire. Too close. Too fucking close.

"Hang on . . ." The rocket cleared the vehicle, striking to the side, the resulting explosion throwing the Raider through the air, flipping it, then throwing it back to earth with a bone-jarring force that had Megan seeing stars.

Impact protocol kicked in, the padded levers that suddenly extended from the seats taking the force of the blow and holding them in their seats. But nothing could compensate for the violence, or the jolt.

The Raider landed on its side, tires spinning as she heard a roar. Furious, animal rage. The sound echoed in her head as time seemed to slow down, moving with a distant, ethereal quality that had her fighting to breathe.

She searched desperately for the release control to the seats, grunting as the inflated belt and padded grips released her and dumped her against the passenger side of the vehicle.

Gunfire still raged as she shook her head, fighting to clear it while feeling for her gun.

There. Her fingers curled around the grip as she began to crawl to the opened back window. Braden was no longer in his seat; the security belts had been torn loose of their moorings. She had to find Braden.

And who the hell was roaring?

She fell from the jeep window, her face slapping the ground as her senses fought to right themselves. One of the motorcycles lay on its side, the rider stretched bonelessly on the ground, his neck turned at an odd angle. No danger there.

Another roar split the air as the steady *whap whap whap* of the helicopter came in closer, swirling dust and dirt in the air as she finally found Braden.

Her eyes widened. He was bloody, his shirt torn from his back as he grappled with the other cyclist. Not that there was much fight there. As she watched in amazement, Braden jumped, twisting in midair as one arm came around the other man's neck, the opposite palm cupping the large head. A quick jerk, and the man was dead before Braden landed on his feet.

His head went back, his lips opening as another roar filled the air, his sharp incisors flashing in the sunlight.

She struggled to her feet as Braden's head lowered, his gaze finding her automatically. The golden color gleamed from his tanned face, the feral expression slicing through her consciousness as she stared back at him, watching as he began to stalk slowly toward her.

Dangerous. Primal. He strode to her, sweat, blood and dust gleaming across his naked chest, his hair flowing around him, his muscles bunched, tight.

When he reached her he didn't jerk her to him. His hands went to her shoulders, lightly, moving over her efficiently as she swayed before him. A second later, obviously reassured that she was in one piece, he then pulled her into his arms, lowered his head to her shoulder and bit her.

Son of a fucking bitch. This biting shit was going to have to stop.

She struggled in his arms, only barely aware of the buzz of loud voices behind her. Lance was yelling over her father, the first argument she had ever heard between them. There was growling in her ear, the sound rough and too primitive.

"Let me go, you growling, sharp-toothed, SOB." She snarled as he finally raised his head, a drop of blood—her blood—clinging to his lips.

Adrenaline was surging through her body, arousal in the

midst of triumph, success and overwhelming excitement. And he had to pull the alpha claim-his-mate crap. She didn't think so.

Before she was even aware of the thought her arm cocked back, fingers tightening in a fist and slamming toward his face. He jerked back, but not fast enough. Her fist connected with his eye, not as strong as it could have been—after all, she had just flipped a Range Raider, not exactly child's play there. But hard enough that she knew it was going to bruise.

"Neanderthal," she bit out as he stared back at her in surprise. "Keep those vampire teeth off my fucking neck before I have them extracted."

She jerked her shirt over her shoulder. To be fair, he had bit her there, not her neck. But she wasn't in the mood to be fair. She stared around, her frowning gaze settling on the two dead riders.

Propping her hands on her hips, she ignored the incredulous male expressions around her and snapped out furiously, "You couldn't even save me one, could you, Purr-boy? Just one. Was that too damned much to ask?"

He breathed in slowly, easily, then nodded.

"Yep, cupcake. In this instance, one would have been way too many. Count yourself lucky I let you drive. I promise, it will be the last time." If his expression was anything to go by, the ride had been as wild for him as it was for her. Exhilaration glittered in his eyes with the same strength that it throbbed in her veins.

She smiled, a slow, wide curve of her lips, before encompassing the silent men in her gaze.

"Today is a good day." She nodded with a laugh. "Yep. Damned fine. Now, where's that fucking Dragoon . . ."

She was like that damned bunny Braden had seen in the old vids they used to watch in the Labs. What was it called? The little pink froufrou thing with the drum? Something to do with a battery? An Energizer Bunny? Kept going and going and going . . . She was making him dizzy. Hell, that flip had damned near scrambled his brains, he didn't need a fist upside his head to help him along. And add to that the fact that until she disappeared into one of the bedrooms with the Breed doctor, Elyiana Morrey, she had been bouncing around like a Mexican jumping bean.

Not that he blamed her for hitting him. He still didn't understand that bite he had given her. The compulsion to do it had been so primitive, so overwhelming he hadn't even thought to ignore it. He had bitten her, then just as quickly began to lick the two small punctures he had made in her shoulder. He had marked her, and some primitive instinct had demanded that he force her to submit to him, in at least some small way.

Not that Megan would ever submit. She was as much an alpha personality as he was himself, which explained the fist she had used against him. She knew what that bite meant, every bit as much as he did. A claiming. An attempt to force some measure of control over her, if nothing else, in the certainty that she was still his. That the hormone that bound them together would continue to fill her system, and make her hunger for him just as much as she hungered for justice and for adventure.

Now midnight was rolling around and all he wanted to do was sleep away the pressure in his head. Right after he got rid of the pressure in his dick.

"Braden, we couldn't find the Dragoon." Jonas stepped out on the porch where Braden was nursing a cold beer and a pounding headache.

He pushed his fingers through his hair wearily as he sat perched on top of the hard rubber doghouse Megan's mutt had occupied when he first arrived at the house. The top of the roof was flat enough to sit on, the side of it slanted enough to brace his feet on. He bet the inside would hold him and Megan both, let alone that wolf-sized mutt she called her dog.

"Where the hell do you hide a Desert Dragoon?" Braden shook his head. He knew the technology the Breed community now possessed. They could find the proverbial needle in a haystack, but they couldn't find a heavily armed Dragoon in the middle of a fucking desert?

"It could be hidden in any one of hundreds of caves and caverns." Jonas stepped closer, his silver eyes looking damned odd in the dark. What the hell was he, anyway? He smelled like a lion, but Braden was damned if he acted like one.

"I don't like this, Jonas. Those weren't Coyotes, they were Special Forces–trained and some of the best I've gone up against. They had the weapons and the vehicles in place for an ambush with no idea when we'd be heading out there. They knew the route we'd take and Megan swears only her family could have known of it. And I can't believe Lance would try to hurt her. In any way."

"Jacobs isn't under suspicion." Jonas affirmed his own thoughts. "I agree with your earlier assessment though. There's something else going on here, but I'll be damned if I can figure it out."

Neither could he. Braden had gone over the information backward and forward and still hadn't found the answer.

It would have been easier to take Megan out in a hundred different ways. Why wait? Why attack at the canyon when it would have been much more efficient to do so on the way there? It was almost as though they were being tested. As though Megan was being tested. But for what?

"She needs to go to Sanctuary, Braden." Jonas's voice was quiet, firm. "She might not survive the next attack."

Braden propped his elbows on his knees and stared into the dark glass of the bottle he held. The heli-jet sat a short distance from the house, while several teams of Felines kept silent watch. He could sense them in the darkness, watching the house and those within it.

It was like that at Sanctuary. Callan and his people did their best to keep the mountain more of a haven than a compound, but the ready watchfulness of the Breeds on alert could be felt at any time of the day or night. No one slacked off, no one forgot the fact that the Genetics Council and the Purist societies working against them were just waiting for the slightest break in their defenses.

It wasn't a prison, but damn if he didn't feel just as hemmed in there. It would be worse for Megan. He saw her today. For the first time since she had run headlong into his life, he had really seen her. Her eyes shining, the fierce fire of battle blazing in them. She lived for adventure. Loved the fight, the racing adrenaline, the triumph. Just as he did.

And he had seen something else, something he had only realized in the past hours. Megan did have the proper barriers, those that kept out the harmful effects and allowed the information through. She had used them instinctively today, racing across that mountain like a daredevil from hell, instinctively turning the wheel, steering clear of the worst of the gunfire as well as the natural obstacles. With training she could learn to use those barriers as well as her talents with lethal effectiveness. She could be the perfect partner; she would be the perfect mate. But she would never survive Sanctuary.

He lifted the beer, finishing it off lazily before twirling the bottle between his fingers.

"She won't go," he finally said softly.

"Or you won't let her?" Jonas asked, his voice dark. "She'll die in this desert, Braden, and you'll go with her. Let her make the choice."

"Do you think I don't know her, Jonas?" He kept his voice low, pushed back the anger that the other man would question, and tried to remind himself that Jonas's job was to protect the Breed community as a whole. Megan was Braden's mate. Capable of birthing the future. That would definitely fall under the heading of protection.

"I think maybe you're not thinking this through," Jonas said carefully.

Braden felt a small spurt of amusement at the other man's comment. This wasn't the first time he had been accused of such a thing.

"I'll ask her." He owed her that.

He fingered the bruise at his eye. Damn, he was almost too scared not to give her the choice. Even when shaking on her feet that woman packed a wallop.

"Don't ask her, Braden." Jonas's voice hardened. "Pack her up and stick her ass and yours in the heli-jet. We'll figure this out another way. Keep her safe."

Braden rolled the bottle between his hands before turning his head and staring up at the other man. Was he being selfish? Was his own need to be free overriding the need to protect his mate? His woman?

"Braden, they will kill her." Jonas's voice was harder now, more determined.

"I said I'll ask her." He leaned back against the house, staring out into the night. "You don't just tell a woman like that to do much of anything, Jonas." He grunted. "She'd cut your balls off and throw them in your face."

He shook his head at the thought. She drove him crazy, made him so horny he thought he was going to die, and she warmed him. God help him, she warmed every corner of his soul and he hadn't even realized it until that fucking Raider had flipped and those bastard soldiers had opened fire on the defenseless vehicle.

He had thrown himself at the first rider, snapping his neck before jumping for the second. Rage had boiled in his blood, a red haze of fury unlike anything he had known sweeping through him.

As he killed the second, she had pulled herself out of that damned Raider, staring back at him, dazed, wobbling on her feet, but alive. And he had bit her.

He shook his head in confusion as he remembered the primal compulsion. It had surged from his gut, swept through his body and he had acted. Without thought, without remorse, his only instinct had been to lock his teeth into her vulnerable shoulder as the glands of his tongue spilled their rich hormone into the wound.

"What do you know about the Mating, Jonas?" He had to fight to stay calm, even though calm had always been easy to attain, no matter the situation. "Why the hell do I keep biting her?"

"Come to Sanctuary and we'll discuss it," Jonas suggested evenly.

The blatant blackmail had Braden staring back at him

coldly. Jonas was a manipulative bastard, there was no doubting that. But Braden had no intention of letting him manipulate Megan.

"We've never fought, Jonas," Braden mused softly. "We've butted heads a time or two, but never really been at odds. Don't put us there now."

Tension thickened between them. Jonas was his supervisor. For the most part, Braden did his job and was usually in agreement with Jonas on how it should be done. Until now.

"Tell me what's going on, man." The rumbling growl in his throat was something he seemed to be doing often. Something he had rarely done before. Megan was not a good influence on him. "And tell me now."

Jonas sighed roughly. "We're not sure yet, Braden. Too much is still unknown. The bite to the shoulder allows the hormone into the mate's body faster. We know that much. At the moment, that's all we know. But the Council scientists know this as well. They're dying to get their hands on a Breed mate. And they will, eventually."

They were testing them then. The soldiers that attacked them were Council based, Braden had no doubt of that. But now he was beginning to suspect that Megan's death wasn't all they wanted. They would suspect the Mating; it would be impossible not to if they were aware of the possibility. Attempting to see if mates were more effective, if Megan's abilities were stronger in his presence, if she could be used against him or vice versa. It was the way the Genetics Council worked. They researched each strength and weakness, tested and tortured until the subjects were dead or just too damned numb to care if they lived or not.

Which meant the stakes were raised, as well as the danger.

◆　◆　◆

Dr. Elyiana Morrey was a Breed with dark brown eyes and short, dark brown hair. She was tall, nearly five-ten, with a compassionate expression and a hard-as-nails voice when things didn't go her way. But despite her likability, she made Megan uncomfortable.

"I need you at Sanctuary," the doctor said as she took the final vial of blood and packed it in her case. "The samples aren't going to be enough soon. We need to keep a close watch on the Mating signs, compare them to the others."

Sanctuary wasn't a place Megan figured she wanted to be confined to. She had seen reports on the high security compound the Felines called a home base, and she didn't think much of it. She couldn't handle being watched like that, day in and day out, knowing that the moment she stepped out of those gates any number of people were photographing her, profiling her and attempting to determine her weaknesses as the journalists often did the Breeds and their wives.

"That's okay." Megan rubbed at her arm before rising from the bed and moving stiffly to the robe she had laid across a chair. "I'm doing fine here."

She was living for a change. She restrained her smile, reliving the sheer exhilaration of the chase earlier and the knowledge that no matter how close it had been, they had won.

"The Mating is different with you." Dr. Morrey sat comfortably at the end of the bed, watching her with a hint of confusion. "Biting is normally rarely done, and only during sexual situations. Braden is the first Breed male to bite outside of that situation. The bite is different as well. Deeper than normal and if I'm not mistaken, which I'm usually not, the hormone he's injecting into you is more potent. The scent around the bite is stronger than the others. This will increase instinctive responses and emotions. Be careful of that, especially where anger is concerned. It seems anger and arousal are the two responses it increases first. Judgment can be hindered in some cases, and it's not always easy to control."

No shit. But strangely enough, the bite didn't hurt. Megan reached up, rubbing at the muscle as she flexed her shoulder. It was the only spot on her body that wasn't sore.

"It's already beginning to heal," the doctor pointed out. "That's odd as well, considering the depth of the bite. I can't do the proper tests this way, Megan. And until I can see what's going on, I have no idea what's causing it."

"Ask Braden," she snorted. "He's the one that bit me."

She was no one's lab experiment and she wasn't going to start now. Maybe later, she amended.

"If Jonas had learned anything from him he would have let me know." Morrey shrugged her shoulders gracefully. "I'll get the samples I need from Braden before I leave, but still, this isn't enough. I need you back at the labs."

Yeah, Megan bet she did. She eyed the other woman carefully, uncomfortable with the emotionless core she could sense in the doctor.

"This has to finish here." She finally sighed wearily. "Hiding won't help, no matter the excuse we use. And I'm tired of hiding. When it's finished, maybe I'll visit for a while."

Dr. Morrey stared back at her serenely. "You could die here, and we'll never learn what caused the anomalies you're showing. Just the initial exam is showing several differences between you and the other mates at Sanctuary. Braden's hormones are reacting in a different manner than those of the other Breeds. I need to study this."

"You have blood, skin, vaginal, saliva and a multitude of other samples to go on." Megan crossed her arms over her breasts as she stared back at the doctor. "It will have to be enough."

A reluctant smile tipped the doctor's thin lips. "You don't have much give in you, do you, Miss Fields?" she pointed out.

"Sometimes too much," Megan admitted wryly. "And you're avoiding telling me what this biting stuff is all about. What the hell is going on?"

Dr. Morrey pursed her lips tightly for a moment.

"The hormone we carry during Mating Heat has some peculiar properties," she admitted. "Over time, and the time varies from Mating to Mating, it begins to affect the non-Breed mate on the genetic level. The bite today . . ." She shrugged as she waved her hand in confusion. "That has never happened before. But I've noticed with the other females that their healing rates increase after Mating, as do their immunity levels. I suspect it was an instinctive action that resulted from the extremity of the situation. I'll know more after I test the levels of the hormone in Braden's saliva and semen."

Megan's eyes widened as she swallowed tightly. "It's in the semen too?" A vision of her on her knees, Braden's cock spurting heavily into her mouth, flashed before her eyes.

"The hormone levels are actually much higher there." The doctor nodded as she closed up the case that held the samples and began gathering her tools of torture together. "Especially in the barb. The hormone potency there is amazingly high from the few samples we've managed to acquire." The short, mocking laughter the doctor gave as she leveled a look at her was faintly bitter. "It's almost impossible to get samples from the barb. We got lucky with Merinus, once. The hormone travels so quickly into the womb that it's almost impossible to get a sample. For some reason, the barb only emerges vaginally." She shrugged philosophically. "Such is a doctor's quest, I guess."

Megan kept her mouth shut. No way in hell was she going to reveal the oral injection she received. With her luck, she'd be jerked into Sanctuary so damned fast it would make hers and Braden's heads spin. She wanted nothing to do with Sanctuary right now, despite the edge of guilt that filled her. The Breeds deserved their freedom, and they deserved to know what nature was doing to them. But she knew that the danger surrounding her would only intensify if it wasn't dealt with now.

She cleared her throat carefully. "Well, maybe you'll get lucky one of these days."

"We could only hope." The doctor snorted. "Until then, we do our best with what we have. One day, we'll figure it all out."

Megan nodded with what she considered impressive seriousness. She could feel the betraying blush threatening to rise beneath her skin, and she knew the doctor, being a damned Breed, would have no trouble whatsoever . . .

"It would really help, my dear, if you would at least give me the information I need." The doctor, Elyiana, slanted her look from the corner of her eyes as she leaned over the case and fidgeted with the lock. "I know how to keep my mouth shut in the interests of science, you know."

Shit.

Megan opened her eyes wide.

"I've told you everything I know," she promised as she fought any betraying evidence of a lie.

"Nothing more at all?" Elyiana arched her brow curiously. "Strange, start talking about that barb and the hormone levels and your pulse rate go sky high. Has Braden ever mentioned that subterfuge has a scent?"

"Actually, he says a lie does," she retorted calmly.

Elyiana smiled demurely. "One could say denial comes in many forms," she pointed out. "As do lies. And the scent changes for each. You can keep your secrets for only so long, Megan. Eventually you have to face the consequences of the Mating and its reactions on your body. Hiding it will do you no good, and it will do nothing but make it harder to help you and Braden."

"We're doing fine." Megan frowned at the subtle chastisement. "No problems whatsoever."

"Very well." The doctor tilted her head in a small, mocking nod. "I'll leave you in peace to calm your mate. Jonas is rather good at inciting his anger."

Megan's shoulders dropped. "Yeah, I heard them."

Elyiana shot her a quiet, probing look before flattening her lips and heading to the door.

"I'll leave you to him then," she said again. "If you need me, have Braden contact Jonas and I'll come out. Though I do encourage you to come to Sanctuary." She gripped the doorknob, glancing over her shoulder and spearing Megan with a disagreeable look. "It could mean more than just your life, Megan. It could affect others as well."

"Elyiana . . ." Megan kept her voice soft as the doctor paused in front of the door. "The potency of the hormone in the barb?"

"Yes?" The doctor watched her with a quiet calm.

"Maybe . . ." She cleared her throat. "Maybe it's different if it's delivered in a different way." She felt the flush rising in her face. Damn this was hard. "Rather than vaginally, I mean."

"Orally?" Elyiana's eyes narrowed as Megan nodded jerkily.

"For some reason," the doctor continued, "the reports we have from the mated pairs show that the males do not allow ejaculation during oral sex."

Megan cleared her throat again. "Maybe Braden is just odd."

Talk about uncomfortable. Letting this woman know the pleasures she and Braden shared wasn't easy.

"Thank you, Megan." The doctor allowed a fleeting smile to cross her lips. "I'll add this into my own private notes to investigate further. But I will still need you at Sanctuary as soon as possible. For your own safety if nothing else."

With that oblique comment, she turned the doorknob

and left the room. Now, Megan just had to get rid of her family.

✦   ✦   ✦

The heli-jet lifted from the desert, its engines muted as it hovered for a second before heading back to the Virginia compound.

Elyiana sat in the back, her case of blood, semen and saliva samples carefully locked into a storage compartment beside her. A dim light lit the interior from overhead, casting shadows across the floor as Jonas stepped from the cockpit and sat down lazily across from her.

"The hormonal changes are much more apparent with her. Braden has wasted no time in marking her."

Elyiana met Jonas's intent silver eyes. They were spooky. No, they were damned scary.

"I can't be certain without the proper tests." She sighed in resignation. "But all evidence is leaning that way. The bites he has inflicted could have a lot to do with it. The bites were close enough to the jugular to ensure the hormone was delivered directly to the bloodstream. Her hearing is more acute, as is her ability to heal. I'll know more when I get the samples back to the labs, but I would guess the hormone Braden carries is much more potent than normal."

"Why?" Even his voice was dangerous.

"He's one of the few whose lion DNA is stronger than the scientists anticipated." She shrugged. "It's one of the reasons he escaped the harsher punishments within the Labs and reached the higher assassin status, as you well know. I would guess that would explain why the hormone is more potent. It makes sense."

The growl that rumbled in Jonas's chest was terrifying to hear. It wasn't the normal sound of displeasure that a male lion would utter. But was he upset with her, or Braden? Most likely her; he seemed particularly intent on her lately.

"Don't be deliberately obtuse, Elyiana," he growled, flashing his incisors dangerously. "Why would he need to bite her in such a manner? He's acting on instinct; I can sense this myself. Now why?"

She stared back at him thoughtfully. "I don't know, unless the hormone and his own instincts are attempting to overcome the contraceptive. In the previous human mates the genetic differences in them after conception have led to advanced immunity and healing abilities. It could be a primal compensation of some sort. A way of ensuring either conception or the hormonal balance that would allow that healing and higher immunity. I suspect the latter. She's already showing advanced sensory sensitivity. Hearing, eyesight. I suspect it's one of nature's little tricks to ensure that his mate has every advantage to fight beside him."

And wouldn't others be very interested to know this. Elyiana was very aware of the danger this could place Braden's mate in. The mated pairs so far stayed within Sanctuary for their own protection and to allow the vast array of tests needed to research the Mating phenomenon. Braden and Megan would never stay within Sanctuary. Braden was as wild as the wind, he always had been. And it seemed his mate was no different.

"We need her at Sanctuary. No matter the cost," Jonas informed her coldly, his anger obviously directed at Braden rather than her.

"She won't come." Elyiana was certain of that.

Some Breeds were like that. Confinement only made them more dangerous, more volatile. It was one of the reasons that some of their best fighters had died in the Labs. The Council had been unable to control them.

Elyiana considered herself an able fighter, an intelligent, strong woman. But Jonas terrified the shit out of her.

"I want those test results quickly," he told her softly, his voice cold, demanding as he stared at her out of those eerie, silver eyes. "Very quickly, Elyiana. Is that understood?"

"Yes." She fought to keep her mind blank, her emotions under control. She had been doing it for years, for so long that no one had been able to rattle her until Jonas. "I understand."

"Very good."

She watched as he rose to his feet, a strong flow of movement, graceful and dangerous all at once as he moved back to the cockpit. As the thin panel between the two areas slid shut, she took a deep, steadying breath. He wanted results, but no more than she did. It could mean the difference between her freedom and her own destruction.

The Mating Heat wouldn't be able to stay hidden much longer, which she knew was causing the Breed Ruling Cabinet to become concerned. Once information leaked of the advanced immunity and sensory abilities within the non-Breed mate, and the suspected aging delay, world opinion could turn against them with a violence Sanctuary might not survive.

As long as the Breeds portrayed themselves as weak, unable to fight the evil Council and the Purist societies, then the world would look favorably upon them. They weren't a risk, or a threat. But once the truth emerged, only God knew what would happen.

They were fighting a losing battle though. Already suspicion was gaining among journalists. In nearly ten years neither Callan Lyons nor his mate, Merinus, seemed to have aged a day. The Mating marks on the shoulders of the mates had been glimpsed several times, and various scientists were commenting on it. Several Council scientists, captured during the rescues of the Breeds when word first emerged, had revealed their suspicions of the Mating, though none knew the full extent of it.

At the moment, Sanctuary was their only secure base. The old genteel Southern mansion was surrounded by several hundred acres of forested land and provided the Breeds there a stable, safe haven. They stayed within their own borders and, other than military or law enforcement assignments they were sought for, they rarely ventured among the populace. Though Elyiana knew this wouldn't last for much longer.

Once the Breeds there had adapted to freedom, and their bodies and minds had healed from the cruelties inflicted upon them within the Labs, then they would begin to roam. It was the nature of the beast. The need to further their horizons, to bond, to mate, to begin their own prides.

It would be then that the true battles would begin. And it was those battles Elyiana feared. The fight for survival would seem like child's play compared to what she feared was coming.

· C H A P T E R   1 7 ·

Braden had always considered himself more man than animal. Better able to think before reacting. Clear-headed.
Calm. Concise. Until he met Megan.

Instinct had ruled since the moment he had laid eyes on
her. His body's awareness of her had been instantaneous.
The hard-on that filled his jeans in that second had been
alarming.

The instincts rising inside him now were primitive. And
like the bite he had delivered to her neck after the wreck,
uncontrollable. He had no desire to control them. When it
came to Megan and his hunger for her, he found he had no
will to resist.

He faced her across the living room, seeing the exhaustion, the weariness that dragged at her body. She needed to
curl up in her bed beneath all those fluffy blankets and
sleep for as long as he could allow her to. But he knew that
sleep would have to come later.

"You should be resting." He growled. "You're pushing yourself too hard."

"Isn't that rather like the pot calling the kettle black?" she asked with false sweetness. "You could give a mule lessons in stubbornness, Braden."

Tonight he would be giving her lessons, but not in stubbornness. In submission. In learning the price to be paid in rousing the animal that lurked just beneath the thin veneer of humanity. In obeying him.

His stomach tightened, actually twisted in pain at the memory of her deliberate disobedience when he had ordered her to stay hidden within the boulders. He had meant to do no more than check the situation out, take out the soldiers if possible, if safety's sake allowed, then come back for her.

He had no idea how she would react in such a situation, or how accurate her Academy records were in her training. The possibility of a fatal injury or capture had been highly probable if they had been off by so much as a second before reaching the safety of the Raider.

She had risked not just her life, but his sanity. That could not be allowed to happen again.

"Why are you staring at me like that?" The defiance in her voice had the animal raging inside him.

"You disobeyed me today, Megan." There was a dangerous rumble in his voice. "Before I could gauge your strengths or your weaknesses, you disobeyed me, placing not just my life in jeopardy, but yours also."

"Are you still pissed off over that?" She stared back at him incredulously. "Oh really, Braden. Isn't it time to get over it now? I knew what I was doing."

"But I didn't," he pointed out, his voice soft with the exception of the rough rumble just beneath the words. "I had no idea what you were doing or what you were capable of. I told you to stay put, mate."

Her eyes narrowed in response to his declaration.

"I'm not a puppy to order around, Braden," she informed him coolly. "That is not our most pressing problem anyway. That hormone shit of yours has got to be addressed."

It was too much. Her earlier defiance of him had crossed a boundary he hadn't known existed for him. And now this.

Before she could do more than gasp, he was on her. The fingers of one hand wrapping in her hair as he pulled her head back fiercely, his head lowering, his lips claiming hers.

Braden allowed his tongue a quick lick at her lips before nipping them open. Then he speared it deep into her mouth, wrapping around hers as he felt her lips enclose it, heard her moan of arousal.

The swollen glands along the underside pulsed and throbbed as they spilled their sweet narcotic into her mouth, priming her, preparing her. And she took it eagerly even as she searched for more.

Tonight she had to learn who led, and who must follow. Tonight, she would learn who was alpha, and who was beta. Tonight, she would become more than just his mate.

Holding her to him, his free hand smoothed down the arch of her back to the tempting curves of her ass. The hunger that swept through him as his fingers cupped one cheek shook him to his core.

What he needed he had never needed from a woman before. The ultimate submission, a primal acceptance of his dominance. And by God, he would have it. His fingers tightened on the curve as his other hand slid from her hair to the opposite cheek, gripping it, slowly spreading her as she went on her tiptoes, her nails biting through the fabric of his shirt as she moaned weakly into his mouth.

He thrust his tongue between her lips slowly, pumping into her mouth as he fought to drain the last of the swollen heat from his tongue. He wanted her to take it all, needed her to. He wanted her wild, as mad for the sexual intensity as he was. As desperate for his touch as he was to give it.

"Braden. God, what are you doing to me?" She held on to him as his lips slid from hers, his hands clenching at her ass, spreading the cheeks, allowing her to feel the fiery pleasure of the tiny entrance there being spread minutely.

He didn't answer her. Instead, he picked her up in his arms before leaving the room and moving quickly up the stairs. He had already laid out what he needed on her bedside table, preparing for what would come tonight.

◆   ◆   ◆

Megan stared into his harsh, savage features, amazed at his sexuality. The expression on his face should have been frightening. The way his eyes glittered with fierce hunger, the harsh angles of his face that were only revealed by rage, or this . . . this primitive air of dominance.

It shook her to the core. He was furious. She had known he was furious the moment he bit her, his teeth sinking into her shoulder, attempting to hold her still as his hand moved quickly over her body after the wreck.

And he hadn't gotten over it either. She had felt it building, altering, deepening inside him as he endured his examination. The sensations had reached out to her from his room, even as she fought with her family. Building an arousal inside her that even the hormone that filled his kiss couldn't compete with.

"I thought I could drain this need for you." He growled as he entered her bedroom and tossed her on her bed, staring down at her fiercely. "When I jacked off for those fucking tests, I thought I could spill the fear and anger into that fucking vial and ease this need inside me." He jerked his shirt over his head and tossed it away before removing his boots just as quickly.

Megan could only stare up at him, shocked by the deep baritone of his voice as much as she was shocked by his words and her reaction to them. She imagined him lying in her guest room, his thick cock enclosed by his fingers as he stroked himself, and she felt her juices sliding thickly from her overheated cunt.

His pants came off next. Megan swallowed tightly at the sight of the plum-colored crest, the angry throb of the tight, hard flesh. Oh yes, he was in full rage, a Mating rut she wondered if either of them would survive.

"Come here." He knelt on the bed, his hand gripping her hair, pulling her to him.

She knew what he wanted. They could discuss his means of achieving it later, as well as the repercussions that could result. She hadn't forgotten the doctor's information, but she hadn't forgotten the taste of him either. And she needed the taste of him.

Her lips opened, stretching around the thick head as it slid into her mouth.

"Oh yes," he growled. "Suck my dick, baby. Suck it deep while I play with these pretty tits."

She whimpered around the flesh as he jerked her gown up, his hands cupping her breasts, his fingers tweaking and pulling at the hard nipples. Sensation speared from the hard points to her clit as she sucked ravenously at his cock, her hands stroking the hard shaft as she moaned hungrily. She arched into his hands as his erection thrust in shallow strokes against her lips.

The blood rushed through her body, sizzling in her veins as she felt the hormone adding strength to her arousal. It amazed her, feeling it as she did, rushing across her nerve endings, sensitizing her flesh, making her burn.

Her fingers stroked over the hard length of his cock as she sucked and licked at the throbbing head, moaning at the taste of him. Fresh. Wild. The taste of a storm at sea.

"Beautiful." Her eyes opened, lifting to stare up at him.

A tight grimace revealed the lethal incisors at the sides of his mouth as he watched his cock fuck slow and easy into her mouth. She swiped at the underside with her tongue and watched his eyes flare. On the next thrust she curled her tongue, reaching for the other side of his cock where the barb pulsed just beneath the silken flesh. The hard flesh jerked in her grip as a primitive growl left his lips. The harsh rumble speared through her, convulsing her womb, clenching in her pussy and sending her juices to saturate the swollen lips beyond. His hands clenched in her hair, holding her still for each penetration past her lips.

"Enough." The harsh command had her struggling in his grip, fighting to keep the pulsing head of his erection between her lips.

Within seconds, he had her stripped of her robe and short gown. Naked, her body damp with perspiration and tingling with the need for his touch, she knelt on the bed before him.

"You're mine," he stated then, demanding, dominant. "Do you understand me, Megan? Mine. You will not disobey me in such a way again."

The tone of his voice penetrated the sexual haze fogging her mind.

"In your dreams, bad boy," she cooed.

Braden stiffened. Her gaze flickered to his cock as a hum of appreciation slipped past her lips. It looked harder, flushed and thick and eager for her touch. She reached out for it, only to frown as Braden caught her hands, holding them back from his flesh.

"Lie to me, Megan." He snarled. "Tell me you will obey next time. That you will never do anything so foolish again."

Yeah. Right. That lie would send lightning whipping through both of them.

She pursed her lips instead and sent him a soft, blowy kiss.

"How about I promise to be careful instead?" There wasn't a chance in hell she was going to promise to give up the freedom she had found with him.

His eyes narrowed. The look sent wracking shudders

working through her body as her womb convulsed at the promise of retaliation.

"How about I show you why you will obey me next time?" His voice was deep, brooding. So sexually rough it nearly stole her breath.

"Hmm, why don't you just go right ahead and give it your best shot, sweetie." She moved, stretching out on the bed as she ran her hand along her stomach, stopping a scant breath from the damp curls between her thighs. "I'm sure I'll pay attention."

She knew she should have been worried. Wasn't there some saying about waking a sleeping lion? No, tiger. She smiled slowly at the thought as she watched his eyes darken, heard the dangerous, primal growl that left his chest. Whatever.

Her fingers moved lower, ruffling the soft curls between her thighs as he watched eagerly. Maybe she could just make him forget about punishment. Her fingers dipped in further as her eyelids fluttered at the pleasure.

"Keep going." His fingers curved around his cock, stroking slowly as she dipped into her saturated slit. "Show me what you like, baby. Then I'll show you what you get."

She gasped as her fingers circled her clit, her hips jerking as fire raced through her belly.

"Let me touch you too," she begged, dying to feel his cock spurting in her mouth, the wild taste of his semen sending her careening past arousal, past pleasure.

"How about I do this instead." He came down beside her, lying close on his side as his head bent to one hard, upthrust nipple.

She nearly screamed as his teeth nipped at the tender point at the same instant his hand covered hers, pressing her fingers more snugly against her cunt.

"Pleasure yourself," he ordered roughly. "I want you wild, Megan. Go wild for me, baby."

Her fingers speared the swollen tissue of her pussy as

her back arched from the bed. It was incredible. His mouth at her breast, suckling the dark point to painful awareness as her own fingers sank into her sensitized vagina.

She shook, trembled as powerful jolts of sensation sizzled through her. Her palm pressed against her clit, increasing the pressure, the pleasure, until the sizzling currents turned into a fireball, sweeping over her, leaving her gasping.

"So pretty." He growled, giving her nipple a parting lick before kissing his way down her stomach as he lifted her fingers from the swollen flesh she had caressed.

A whimpering moan left her lips as he brought her fingers to his mouth, licking the slick juice from them before laying her hand at her side and moving lower.

Megan could only watch as he spread her thighs and moved between them. His head dipped low, his tongue swiping through the drenched slit. He raked it tenderly over the painfully sensitive nubbin of her clit. Her hips jerked as a startled gasp left her lips and the fires began to build again. She couldn't get enough of him; even in the heat of danger her body craved his, creamed for him, and never let her forget where pleasure could be found.

"Shhh . . ." The soft, crooning quality of his voice made her realize that the gasping, mewling cries echoing around her were her own.

Despite the release, she was only burning hotter now. Wilder. She could feel the arousal, the heady lust pouring through her, demanding ease.

"I can't wait." Her hands gripped his hair, desperate to end the teasing licks and soft touches he was bestowing on her. She wanted it hard, fast. She wanted him now.

"You will wait anyway." His hands gripped her thighs as he settled himself more securely between her legs. "Just a little bit longer, baby, and you can have what we both need."

His tongue slid through the swollen, needy flesh teasingly.

"Teasing me to death isn't going to get you what you

want." But her hands wrapped in his hair anyway as pleasure washed over her, through her. Each touch was better than the one before it. Each took her higher.

"You taste as sweet as spring, as hot as summer." He growled as she felt his fingers stroking the entrance to her vagina, teasing, tempting.

She arched into the touch, desperate for more. When his finger slid inside at the moment his lips covered her clit, she was certain she would find release. She poised on the edge of it, straining closer.

"Damn you, Braden," she cried furiously as his finger slid free, dipped in again, dragged out, pulling the wet heat of her juices free as he did so.

She could feel the damp warmth easing along her flesh as it flowed lower, encouraged by his diabolical fingers, to heat the sensitive flesh between her rear cheeks.

She shuddered, unwilling to give credence to the pleasure that subtle caress brought her. Blood thundered through her veins as his fingers followed, stroking, pressing.

"Braden." Her hands tightened in his hair as fear lent a new dimension to the pleasure rushing through her.

He stilled, but his finger didn't move.

"Mine." He snarled again. "Before we finish, Megan, you will make that promise to me."

That she would obey? Let him call the shots? She didn't think so.

She shook her head desperately, pulling at his hair, needing him, needing the touch that would send her over the edge. His fingers pressing into her pussy, fucking her hard and strong as his mouth and tongue worked magic at her clit. That was what she needed. What she wanted.

His finger returned to the pulsing depths of her vagina as her hips came off the bed, beseeching, begging for his mouth. He licked, stroked, sucked. His fingers thrust gently, shallowly inside her as her senses began to burn out of control. She couldn't stand it.

"Damn you. Stop teasing me." She pulled at his hair.

"Promise me."

She tried to scream, but what came out sounded more like a plea than a curse.

His finger moved lower once again, caressing the small, hidden entrance with delicate strokes. "Come on, baby, promise to follow my lead. We are partners, remember? I lead, you follow."

That was a partnership? She didn't think so!

"I followed." She gasped breathlessly. "I did, Braden. You know I did. I waited until you went first."

He growled fiercely, nipping at the soft lips he was licking, sending currents of whip-sharp pleasure tearing through her womb as she felt the finger press at her rear, parting the tiny entrance.

"Bad girl," he accused darkly, his head lowered farther, his tongue working closer to her needy pussy.

"Oh, God yes," she screamed as his tongue plunged inside the weeping entrance. At the same instant, his finger pierced the entrance of her ass.

The alternating fire and pleasure tore through her. She didn't know if she should beg him to stop or beg him to continue.

There was no begging for anything with Braden. There was nothing but gasps filled with desperation, the need to breathe, to climax, as he built her pleasure higher, hotter, drawing every nerve ending to fierce, desperate attention.

What he was doing to her was destructive, mind-blowing.

"Turn over." The harsh command sizzled across her senses as images, hungers, desires whipped through her mind.

She whimpered as he turned her, pulling her hips up, pushing her knees beneath her. His hand landed on her ass, stinging, fiery, blending with the overload of pleasure and driving her higher as her hands balled into fists, crushing the fabric of the comforter between them.

"What the hell was that for?" She panted, turning her head to glare at him over her shoulder.

The sight that met her eyes left her stunned. His hand was descending again, the slight smack burning through her flesh as his expression burned through her mind.

Intent. So savagely lustful it stole her breath.

"Promise you will follow, Megan." His hand smoothed down her stinging flesh until it moved between her thighs, cupping her pussy.

Oh God, she was so tempted. But a promise was a promise. She would have to do her best to keep it. It would kill her. He would insist on protecting her.

She turned, burying her face in the covers as she felt him part the cheeks of her ass, his fingers moving dangerously close to the already tormented little entrance there.

"Say it, Megan." He growled as she felt him probing at the anal entrance. "Tell me, and I'll give you what you need. Otherwise, I'm going to have what I want instead."

The tip of his finger pressed in as a long, keening cry left her lips. She couldn't give him that much control. It would never work.

She shook her head desperately. Surely she could hold out. He wouldn't hurt her. She knew that much about him. Whatever he did to her would make her mindless with pleasure instead.

Her thoughts scattered at that moment as she felt his finger slide deep, hot and thick inside her rear. The fiery pleasure was unlike anything she could have imagined.

His finger was slick, the lubricant covering it cool to her overheated inner flesh. But nothing could dim the fires igniting inside her.

The sensations filling her were more than physical. It was more than pleasure. As she knelt before him, her shoulders tight against the mattress, her rear raised in preparation of his invasion, she began to understand what he wanted her to feel. To know.

Submission.

Not weakness. Not protection or a sense of smothering restraint. What she felt sent her flying headlong into a knowledge that she knew would change her forever.

The spanking had only primed her. The short, fiery slaps of Braden's palm only drove her higher, made her hungrier. The blending of pleasure . . . Braden's fingers stroking her pussy, dipping in, filling the slick recess of her vagina, had her screaming for orgasm. The pain, a light spanking, the fingers working inside her anus, opening her, preparing her, was driving her mad.

"There, baby." The rough croon stroked her senses as finally, blessedly she felt the blunt tip of his cock stroking against the back entrance rather than his fingers.

She couldn't believe she was backing into him, desperate mewls of need escaping her lips as his thick width began to press in, stretching her, burning her.

"Oh my God. Braden. I don't think . . ."

"Don't think." His hand landed on her ass once again as she felt the fiery head of his cock breach the virgin portal.

Her eyes widened, dazed, shock and pain-filled pleasure rioting through her system as his erection continued to sink inside her. Nerve endings she had never known she possessed flared to life as Braden growled harshly behind her.

His hands gripped her hips, holding her firmly in place as he began to work inside her. Slowly, too slowly. Inch by inch she felt the invasion, spreading her, sinking into her as rapid bursts of pleasure-pain began to sizzle along her nerve endings.

It seemed to go on forever, slow, easy thrusts that stretched the tight opening, sent her spiraling further into rapture. Until he paused, his breathing harsh behind her, his erection inches from filling her fully.

"I am your mate." He snarled as a final thrust sent him in to the hilt, causing her to scream breathlessly against the invading force. There was no protest as the muscles of her ass began to milk the hard length. Only pleasure. Only ecstasy. "You will follow. I will lead."

She shook her head desperately, the muscles of her ass clenching around Braden's throbbing erection as it pierced her body.

"You will follow. I will lead." He snarled again, his hand landing on her ass once more.

She should be furious. She should be raging and attempting whatever it took to escape his hold. Instead, she was whimpering like a pathetic love slave eager for more.

"Feel me, Megan." He came over her then, moving his hips, pulling back marginally before plowing inside her once again.

"Yes . . ." She could only pant, beg for more. Oh God, this was incredible. It was past incredible.

She felt her hair being brushed from her shoulder, felt his teeth raking it warningly.

Oh man, he was going to bite her again. She could feel it coming.

He chuckled instead, raking his teeth over her flesh, licking at the wounds already there as he slowly began to withdraw his swollen flesh from her rear.

Megan gasped for breath, amazed at the sensations rushing through her. The ultrasensitive flesh burned in near ecstasy, gripping, clenching on the retreating erection as she moaned in disappointment. He couldn't leave her now. He couldn't withdraw . . .

Her back arched as a scream tore from her throat. The fierce thrust inside her ass had fiery pleasure ripping through her womb, her clitoris. She shook beneath him, pushing back, driving him deeper.

"I lead, you will follow." He growled in her ear, his voice harsh. "Give me your promise, Megan, and I will give you ease. I can do this for hours. As long as you wish. As long as I wish. Your ass is so hot, so tight," he crooned.

She knew she was going to give in. Perspiration dripped

from her forehead, coated her body. She could feel the juices flowing from her pussy, her nerves rioting with the need for orgasm.

"Let me guide you, Megan." His voice tempted her, teased her. "As I guide you here, let me guide you in battle as well, baby. Let me show you how . . ." His thrusts increased in intensity, sending her senses careening as pleasure exploded through her system.

"God yes," she screamed. "You bastard. But swear to God, you try to coddle me and I'll kill you. I'll kill you, Braden."

"Coddle you?" He groaned, his voice a fierce, triumphant growl. "How's this for coddling?"

This was not coddling. It was dominance in its most primal form. It was a claiming. A demand for submission that she had no choice but to answer.

"Now promise me." He held her on the edge, refusing to let her fly, keeping his thrusts deep and measured.

"I promise, dammit," she screamed, desperation pounding through her. "Now do it, damn you."

He reached one hand beneath her, curving between her thighs and plunging two fingers deep inside her aching pussy as he thrust hard and deep inside the tight, gripping tissue of her ass.

Stars exploded behind her closed eyes. No, this wasn't coddling. It was lust in its rawest form. It was a taking, a giving. His cock speared into her ass as his fingers fucked her pussy below, driving her higher as pleasure exploded across her senses.

Her orgasm ripped through her. She tightened on the pistoning erection, gripping it, milking it as she was flung past reality, worries and cares into a world of light, of rapture. A world that consisted only of Braden and of pleasure.

"Good girl . . . So hot and sweet."

She came back to earth slowly, shivering beneath his

hard body as he stroked her stomach and whispered wickedly in her ear.

"I'm going to kill you." She was gasping for breath. "Honest, Braden. You're dead. As soon as I can move again."

She moaned harshly as she felt him withdraw. He was still hard despite the orgasm she knew had swept through him as well. She had felt that damned barb stroking inside her ass, making her crazy as her orgasm powered through her.

"Then I'll just have to make certain you can't move until you change your mind." His voice was lazy, by no means sated, but satisfied.

She snorted at the thought, rolling over to watch as he disappeared into the bathroom.

"You think you're tough shit, don't you?" she called into the other room. "Big tough Breed got what he wanted." It rankled that she was so weak against the sexual impulses he could make power through her.

She stared up at the ceiling as she listened to the water run, a small frown creasing her face at the thought of how easily she had given in to him. She never gave in, not unless she wanted to. Realizing that in the end she had wanted what he could give her more than she wanted the freedom she had barely tasted, was confusing.

"You didn't give anything up, Megan." Her head jerked to the side, her gaze locking on his naked, powerful form as he leaned against the bathroom doorway.

Naked, he was damned intimidating. Even more so than when he was dressed. Hard muscle rippled beneath golden flesh as he stood before her like a fucking sun god. How had nature ever messed up so bad as to pair her with the golden creature standing across the room?

He was wild and free. It was in his eyes, the way he held his body, his expression. There was nothing restrained about him, nothing tamed. Not like her. Fighting to hide, to bury her dreams.

"How do you figure that?" She rose from the bed, jerking her robe over her naked body despite the frown that furrowed his brow at her movement.

"Because I like you wild." He straightened, moving slowly toward her, the still-hard length of his cock gleaming wetly. "Because I'll take nothing from you. Not your freedom, or your choices. But I will know your strengths and your weaknesses. I have to, otherwise there can be no trust between us as partners."

Partners. A chill raced through her at that word. She had never really had a partner, just some very close friends that she had nearly gotten killed.

Megan clenched her teeth, remembering the training mission during her final year in the Academy. It had been a disaster; her only salvation had been the fact that no one had realized just how horribly she had messed up.

The overwhelming rage and hatred of the perpetrator had frozen her, locking her mind down, filling it with pain as he slipped past the net they had set for him. The disaster had almost been fatal, and she had sworn then that it would never happen again.

"Megan." He stepped closer, ignoring her as she backed away from him, his expression quiet, calm. She hated that expression. It meant he had made up his mind about something and she was going to agree with him or else.

"I need to think . . ." She drew in a deep, hard breath as he pinned her against the wall, the heat from his body seeming to wrap around her as she pressed her hands against his chest in protest.

At least, she tried to tell herself it was in protest. She was going to push him away . . . in just a minute.

"Thinking will only get you in trouble." He grunted again. "I've seen you when you start thinking. You get strange ideas."

"Like what?" That took her by surprise. Her ideas always seemed perfectly sensible to her.

"Like aiming a Wounder at my dick in that canyon." He growled as his gaze lit with amusement. "Bad girl, Megan. You could have fired by accident."

He pressed against her, dipping his knees as his hands cupped her ass to lift her closer to that hard, hot flesh. Her robe parted, giving him perfect access to her as his cock slid against the slick, aching flesh of her cunt.

"I knew what I was doing." She gasped, feeling her knees weaken as the head of his cock parted her inner lips.

"Sure you did," he crooned as his head lowered to allow his lips to smooth over her jaw.

"Maybe I didn't." Her head fell back against the wall as a teasing smile curved her lips. "On second thought, maybe I should have fired . . . Oh God . . . Braden!"

The fierce, hard thrust inside the slick depths of her pussy sent shudders of reaction racing through her body. He was lodged into the very depths of her, the head of his cock rubbing sensually over the entrance to her womb as he flexed within her.

Racing zephyrs of electric awareness seared through her nerve endings as pleasure began to tempt pain, creating a mix of sensations that stole her breath and left her gasping. Her hands held tight to his muscular neck as the flaming lust and emotion in his gaze seared into her brain. His eyes were locked on hers, refusing to allow her to close them. She didn't want to close them. She wanted to watch the flare of pleasure in the rich gold depths of his eyes as he began to move slowly, dragging his erection from her until only the swollen head remained. Then with a hard jerk of his hips he was buried inside her again.

Fiery pleasure. A whiplash of heat and mind-numbing intensity. The heavy strokes of his engorged erection filling her, overfilling her, stretching her with such erotic force that she could only cry out, beseeching, pleading for more as he fucked her with lazy, deep thrusts. His lips played with her, his tongue stroking in and out of her mouth, the sweet taste of the Mating hormone driving her pleasure higher.

It wasn't the hormone that made her want, made her need, she decided. The hormone turned ecstasy into something more, made the pleasure more vibrant, her body better able to relax, to accept the intensity of a lust that would have terrified most women.

But this was Braden. Her Braden.

Her lips captured his tongue, drawing on it. She wrapped her own around it as his hips began to move faster, his cock powering into her with jackhammer strokes that destroyed her senses.

Wild. Free. She was flying.

The resulting explosion tore through her womb, spasmed her pussy and sent her screaming into orgasm. She felt her muscles clamp down on his erection, heard his harsh, animalistic snarl and felt the sudden, heated impression of the barb extending from his cock.

It locked inside her, holding him in place and sending her into another cataclysmic series of explosions that seemed never ending. It stroked and caressed the ultrasensitive area it was snuggled into.

Hard, pulsing shudders tore through her as Braden's head lowered to her neck, his teeth nipping, his tongue stroking at the small wound he had left there. His hands flexed on her ass as his cock flexed inside her until finally, mercifully, the almost painful pleasure began to ease and she collapsed in his arms.

Megan was only barely aware of Braden moving then until she felt the slow exit of his erection from her tender vagina and, a second later, the comforting cushion of the mattress at her back.

"Stay out of trouble," she murmured as she turned her head into the pillow, allowing the exhaustion to finally claim her. "I'm too tired to save your ass."

Braden watched silently as sleep stole her from him, stilling the chaotic emotions that had swirled between them. Her mind had shut down all thought processes, finally. The chase, the wreck, the sex. The combination of adrenaline-laced activities had finally crashed inside her. As they were crashing inside him.

He lay down beside her, pulling the sheet over them to protect her from the chill of the bedroom before closing his eyes as well. The Breeds guarding the house would keep them safe for tonight. They would leave when he arose, heading overseas to fight a much more important battle than the one he was waging here, in this desert. He was one Breed whose stubborn mate refused the safety of Sanctuary. There were many others out there in desperate need of a ride out of hell. The Feline community had no choice but to concentrate their efforts there. There were so few of them left.

He allowed his hand to smooth down the long strands of her silken hair, glorying in the feel of it, the memory of it wrapping around his body, caressing him with sensuous little ripples of pleasure.

She was a treasure, one he had never expected to find in his life. Now, protecting her could become his greatest battle. Because he knew that whoever or whatever was closing in on them had no intention of leaving either of them alive. He could only pray his experience and training could pull them out of it.

CHAPTER 18

It was a dream; she knew it was a dream. Megan stood in the center of the training room at the Academy, her breasts heaving as she fought for breath after putting herself through the grueling series of exercises designed to strengthen and tone her muscles.

She was tired. The exhausting Academy courses during the day, combined with her nightly routine was getting the best of her.

The agonizing drain on her strength from the emotions, hopes, dreams and hatred that filled her fellow classmates had driven her to the training center at night. There, she tried to exhaust herself to the point that her mind just didn't give a shit what it sensed.

She couldn't seem to shut things down though. Exhaustion was eating her alive, fuzzing her brain, making it impossible for her to separate or distinguish among the individual thought patterns.

A whimper of agony sizzled through her. Not her own

pain but another's, blinding and soul deep. A blistering wave of inconsolable grief and rage that brought her to her knees and left her gasping for air.

It wasn't the first time the emotions filling the Law Enforcement Academy had incapacitated her. The recruits were young, some more violent than others. And this late at night their twisted dreams and nightmares reached out to her and tortured her sensitive brain.

This was worse though. Perhaps the mix of exhaustion and her own fears had caused it. Or the stress of attempting to hide the curse that haunted her every step from her superiors while assuring her parents that her shields were developing against the talents she had inherited. Whichever it was, she was left trapped within the pain now, fighting for control.

She dragged herself wearily to her feet, swaying beneath the rush of rage that slammed into her head. The pent-up horror was agonizing to feel. The wail of silent screams, the determination to hold back the nightmare.

Escape . . . The word whispered through her mind.

Freedom . . . It wasn't a word, it was a plea, a soul-deep hunger that shook her to her core.

With one hand clutched to her head, she stumbled toward the closed double doors that led from the training room. Her vision was dim and unfocused as brilliant shards of light exploded behind her eyelids. Shaking her head, she gripped the metal handle, pushing at the heavy panel as she fought the whimper that built in her throat.

Freedom . . . The scream echoed in her head as her stomach clenched with pain. God, had she ever known such pain? It rose unbidden, whipping through her mind, building in strength as she forced herself into the hallway.

"Whoa! Megan. Sweetheart. Is that you?"

Megan jerked back, nearly falling in her desperation to escape as she fought to focus her gaze on what she knew was the enemy. No, another's enemy. She shook her head, fighting to separate herself from the confusing impressions beating at her.

But no enemy faced her. Frowning down at her was her father's best friend, former Congressman Mac Cooley. His pale blue eyes were filled with compassion, concern. She shook her head, fighting to clear it, confused by the evil she had felt in his touch.

"Mr. Cooley." She cleared her throat, fighting for a semblance of normalcy. "I'm sorry. I'm not feeling well."

She could sense the pain growing stronger. The agony it caused was tearing through her head, ripping her apart.

"You're very pale, Megan. Let me help you to the medic's station." He moved to touch her once again.

"No." She shook her head fiercely. "I'm fine, really." She breathed in deep, pasting a smile on her face as she stared into his pale blue eyes.

Ice. They were cold, bitter chips of frozen malice.

She blinked and it was gone. She saw only concern, only compassion.

"Congressman Cooley, your helicopter is waiting." Her head swung around.

There were four others with him. Young people. Or were they old? Definitely bodyguards; she knew the type. She glanced into the eyes of the one who spoke, a pleasant young man with quiet features and dead eyes.

Rage ate into her stomach, boiling inside it, threatening to spew from her it was so sickening, so painful. Was it his rage? Or another's? Where was it coming from? Her gaze touched on each of the five as she fought to pinpoint the origin of the emotion.

But there was no origin. As always, she couldn't follow the path reaching out to her; she knew only the pain.

"One moment." Did Mac's voice harden? Did she hear the promise of retaliation in it? She couldn't have. Mac was one of the kindest people she knew.

"I'm fine, Mr. Cooley." She straightened despite the cold sweat that covered her, the icy fire that seared her. *"I've been trying to finish early. I guess I pushed too hard tonight."*

"I would say you have." His voice was filled with disapproval. *"I'll call your father tomorrow and have him check on you . . ."*

"No." She winced at the fear in her voice. Her parents would only worry, and would realize she had been lying about her ability to handle the strength of the emerging talents. *"I promise I'm fine. Dad will just worry. You know how he and Mom are. I'll see the medic in the morning, I promise."* She would have promised anything at that point.

"Very well." He finally sighed in resignation. *"But I will be calling the medic for sure. Make sure you check in with him."*

She nodded gratefully. *"I promise."* She drew in a long deep breath as she gave Mac a wry smile. *"I'm just exhausted. I'm going to go on to my room now."*

"Of course." He nodded, his eyes watching her warmly. *"I'll watch you down the hall to make certain you have no further problems. Be careful, Megan."*

She nodded before turning to walk away.

Remember me . . . She almost stopped at the demand that ripped through her head. Another's thought, a split-second demand that she wasn't even certain she had felt. She bit her lip, confident that it would be gone soon. It was already dissipating, the last lingering sensation of sadness, of grief, before it was gone.

As she rounded the hallway, she stopped in shock.

She had been certain that one small event in her life meant nothing. A moment in time. A coincidence. Until the dream shifted and she looked up and saw the bullet-ridden SUV in the gully and the young man at the wheel. The pictures from the computer flashed before her mind then.

Mark and Aimee. The same couple she had seen with Senator Cooley.

❖   ❖   ❖

"Megan, God dammit, I said wake up."

Megan came awake with a gasp, shaking in Braden's grip as she realized she was standing in the middle of her bedroom floor, naked, shuddering with cold as she stared up at him in shock.

She breathed in harshly, great, gulping breaths, as though she were starved for oxygen. Her head bounced on her shoulders.

"Stop." She tried to raise her hands, pressing against his abdomen rather than his chest as the shaking stopped and she stared back at him in shock. "What are you doing?"

"What the hell were *you* doing?" He snarled down at her fiercely. "You get out of the bed muttering about training and exhaustion only to start jerking as though someone were stealing your breath. I barely caught you before you fell to the floor."

She shook her head, trying to remember. She had to remember the dream. She bit her lip as he dragged her back to the bed and wrapped the quilt around her shuddering body.

"What the hell were you dreaming about, Megan?"

Dreams. No, not a dream, a memory. She frowned as disjointed images flipped through her mind.

"I don't know." She shook her head, putting her hand to her forehead as the images tried to solidify. Faces. Closed. Eyes. Dead eyes. Without hope. Without freedom.

Remember me.

She flinched as the voice resonated through her head. The sensation, an animal's pain, a young woman's scream. She raised her eyes to Braden, seeing the concern in his gaze as he hunched before her, his hands rubbing at her arms as she blinked in shock.

"I've seen them." She stared back at him in horror. "Oh

my God, Braden. I have seen them." She stumbled to her feet, batting away his hands as she tripped on the blanket and fell against him.

"Megan, calm down." His harsh order, the whiplash of his voice had her stilling, but her mind was still in chaos.

"Let me go." She shook her head fiercely. "I have to dress. I have to see those pictures again. The ones you showed me before."

"Mark and Aimee?" His tone was sharper now.

She nodded jerkily, her mind racing as she fought to pull together the dream. Most of it was still fuzzy, but she remembered faces.

"There were four. Where are the other two?" She jerked away from him as she moved to the chair and pulled on the soft, long flannel gown.

"There were four?" He was dressing as well. "Four what?"

"Breeds." She pushed her fingers through her tangled hair. "I was dreaming, but it wasn't a dream. It's so fuzzy . . ." Her voice was thick with the desperation raging through her, causing her to wince at the sound.

"Come here." He turned her around, pushing her gently to the chair as she realized he was fully dressed. "Put your socks on, the floor is cold. You keep this place like a freezer."

She frowned as he pulled a pair of socks over her feet. She felt frozen, but not from the air conditioner.

"Stop, Braden." This sudden intensity in him was making her head hurt. Or was it the dream? "I forgot to turn the air down, but I like it cold at night. That's all. I have to see those pictures of the Breeds who died again."

She remembered their faces now. High cheekbones, exotic eyes. Dead gazes. She swallowed tightly at the memory. Their eyes were dead, but something raged inside them, something so deep that it had nearly broken her when she had experienced it.

"They knew . . ." she stated then. "Mark and Aimee, they were there at the Academy when I stumbled into the hallway. They were with someone . . ." She fought to remember who. "They knew I could sense them. As I turned to leave, it was in my head. I never hear thoughts. But I heard it in my head, someone telling me to remember them."

He straightened quickly, grabbing her hand as he helped her from the chair and led her from the bedroom.

"Tell me about the dream," he demanded as they started down the hall. His arm went around her back, steadying her despite the fact that she was now moving fine.

"I told you, it's fuzzy." She had to fight to hold back the snap in her voice, the instinctive anger that was more a remnant of the dream than any real anger she was feeling. "But I remembered Mark. He spoke; he was reminding someone of a flight. Someone who was angry with him. There were three others with him. The girl that was killed with him, and another couple."

"Four Breeds?" He glanced down at her as they moved down the stairs.

"Two men, two women." She nodded. "I remember their faces. I remember someone's pain. It was horrible. A mix of rage and grief that made no sense. None of it made sense. I thought it was something else, because when they approached, it began to lessen. I thought I was just tired, weak, and that the thoughts and dreams of the Academy's recruits were stronger because of it. That happens when I'm tired."

"They would have been aware you were picking it up," he said grimly as they stepped into the kitchen. "Can you handle making the coffee? I'll power up the laptop and call Jonas. We need to get you to Sanctuary immediately, until you can remember who they were with. We can't take any more chances."

She clenched her teeth at the thought of the Feline compound but said nothing as she made her way to the coffeepot. Maybe he was right. She couldn't remember who had been with those Breeds, but she knew that the memory would return soon. She could feel it, just beyond her reach, but moving closer.

Who had she seen with them? She clenched her teeth as she fought to remember who had been there that night. She remembered the evil that touched her, the impression of depravity, of perverse lusts.

As she made the coffee, she heard Braden on the phone, his voice low, controlled.

Despite the shock the dream had delivered to her system, she felt a curl of warmth traveling through her body as she listened to him talk. It was disconcerting, this reaction she had to him. She wanted him, no matter where they were or what they were doing. In the middle of a desperate race to safety or fighting him over his arrogance, it made no difference. And though she knew the hormone had added to the arousal that pulsed within her, she also knew she would have wanted him anyway.

She would have loved him anyway.

She stilled at the thought. She hadn't wanted to admit to loving him. He was arrogant, proud; he was larger than life at times and made her crazy with his deceptive laziness and dry humor. But he was growing on her. Hell, he had already grown on her, around her and inside her. She couldn't imagine life without him.

"It will be later before Jonas can get here. The fucking jet is in Israel collecting information on several former Middle Eastern Labs. He has to call it back then head out."

"It's the only one?" She hated the sick feeling in the pit of her gut at the news.

"The only one on standby," he said roughly. "The others are on missions and farther away. They can't be called back. Besides, even waiting for it to return to Sanctuary before heading out, Jonas would be faster."

"What's their ETA?" She watched the coffee begin to drip into the pot.

"Almost midnight." He growled. "But, on the other hand, you slept most of the day away. We have three teams outside the house and plenty of protection until he arrives. We'll go through the pictures, get the information we need and be ready by the time the jet gets here. No problem."

No problem.

She pressed her hand to her stomach, hoping to still the instinctive fear rising inside her. Sometimes it meant nothing. Absolutely nothing. Other times . . . She couldn't think about the other times. She wouldn't think about them. She couldn't afford to lose her cool now. Not when they were so close. Not when she could feel the answers moving inside her head.

Her hand rose to her hair, her fingers clenching in it as she fought to force the memory forward, to understand what was going on and why.

She clenched her fists to keep from calling her father. He would come for her. He would call out her uncle from the reservation and throw a net over her that would make her feel safe, at ease.

She almost shook her head at the thought. She couldn't involve her father in this. No matter how sickening the feeling in the pit of her stomach was growing, she couldn't involve her family.

God help her if she caused even one of them to die. She couldn't live with herself. It would be more than her conscience could bear. Besides, she wasn't defenseless, she reminded herself. Braden and his teams were here. They were well trained, too well trained. They would surely be a formidable force against anyone who might try to attack. Again.

She watched the coffee pour slowly into the pot, her frown deepening as she fought the mists that swirled around the memory, fought to understand why she had forgotten the event.

Because it hadn't been the first, she answered herself. It wasn't the first time emotions and sensations had attacked her with no clear reason. During those days at the Academy, confined to an area filled with so many different people and personalities, she had often suffered such episodes.

Pushing her fingers restlessly through her hair, she turned from the coffeepot and walked to the shade-covered window. She lifted a slat and stared out bleakly as she remembered the emotions that had poured from one or perhaps even all of the Breeds she had seen that night.

The grief had been horrible, and it had been feminine in nature. She remembered that from the dream. She stared into the distance, focusing on the ridge of low mountains rising beyond her home.

It was early evening. She was amazed she had slept that long. The sun was already beginning its slow trek along the horizon before allowing the dark sky to converge over the land.

She closed her eyes, and as she did, a face wavered before her inner sight. A familiar, affectionate smile. Pale blue eyes filled with laughter . . . with ice. Her heart rate increased as dread began to quake through her veins.

It couldn't be him, she told herself fiercely. She had to be mistaken.

"Megan, come sit down and have some coffee." Braden's voice was low, soothing. "Calm down and then we'll go over the pictures again."

She turned back to him, surprised. "I am calm."

"Are you?" His gaze met hers solemnly. "I can feel your mind raging, baby. You're not going to find answers like that. You have to learn to sift through the information. How to set aside what isn't important to get to what is."

She dropped the slat as she crossed her arms beneath her breasts and turned fully to him.

"They've been watching us." She knew it; she could feel it in the sick rolling of her stomach.

He knew. She saw it in his eyes. Lucky for him he didn't try to lie about it.

"At odd times." He nodded. "Two of the teams I brought with me were searching for them. I've called them back in closer to the house for full surveillance until Jonas arrives. We're not taking any chances."

"I'm not scared," she assured him. "But I can feel them. They're watching now."

She couldn't feel their emotions, just a sense of being watched, of being targeted.

"My men are waiting for them too." He moved from where he stood by the doorway, pacing over to the coffeepot and pulling two cups from the cabinet. "We need to eat. I want you at your best tonight and before you go over those pictures. Your system moves more slowly when it's hungry."

The words were very domesticated. The man moving around her kitchen wasn't. She could see the tense lines of his shoulders, the prepared readiness of his body. He was on full alert.

He poured her coffee and sat it on the table, waving at her to sit down before he turned back to the counter. As she watched him and sipped the dark liquid, he put together a quick meal of eggs, sausage and toast. Eating was a silent affair as Megan fought to find balance. Again.

She could handle the danger. The chase the day before had been exhilarating, despite the chances of death. Pitting her wits against those bigger and tougher than she was and coming out on the winning team was a high she found she craved. But that dream had thrown her as nothing else had so far. The knowledge that someone she knew could kill so cruelly was tearing her apart.

"I need to dress." She pushed her plate back, satisfied that she had nearly finished the huge portion he had put out for her.

"Go on. Shower while you're at it." He nodded to the doorway. "I'll make a few more calls and we'll go through the pictures when you come back down."

"You're trying to protect me." She sighed wearily as she came to her feet, staring back at him as he came toward her. She watched his expression closely as he reached out, his fingers caressing her cheek.

"A different sort of protection," he assured her gently, his voice rumbling with emotion. "I can feel your confusion; hell, I can see it. And your pain. It . . ." His gaze flickered with a small amount of his own confusion. "It affects me, Megan. I would kill to hold back what I see haunting your eyes. It breaks my heart."

He was breaking her heart. Her throat tightened at the emotion in his voice, the sincerity. The bonds holding them to each other were only deepening. Tightening. And rather than running as she had always done in the past, she wanted nothing more than to rest in his arms. Just one more time, before fate had a chance to tear him away from her.

The thought of that terrified her.

She nodded without speaking and escaped. She needed silence. She needed to feel alone, unwatched. She needed a shower, because as sure as she was standing there, she had finally realized why the grief from that female Breed, Aimee, had been so strong. And it made her sick to the very core of her soul, because she was terribly afraid she wasn't wrong about the face materializing in her memory.

Mac Cooley. Her father's best friend. And Aimee's rapist as well as, most likely, the reason for her death.

He could feel her crying.

Braden stood at the kitchen counter, his arms braced on the edge, his head hanging low as he fought the tightness in his chest.

She was breaking his heart and she didn't even know it. Hell, he hadn't imagined this could happen, but he could feel her pain. There were no blocks, no shields strong enough to allow him to escape it. Just as he had felt her elation, her triumph during the chase the day before, now he felt her grief.

He had never allowed himself to let others' emotions in. Staying separate, keeping that part of him unhindered had been imperative if he was going to survive in a world where littermates were killed in front of your eyes, and depravity was the norm rather than the unusual.

But he couldn't escape his mate.

Whatever the dream had been, it was such a shock to her

mind that recovering from it was now taking all her strength. He had felt her need to escape him, the need for silence, and he had allowed it. This had been hard enough on her, but now that the truth was so near, she was off balance, unwilling to accept whatever truths she had been shown.

An Empath's dreams were rarely pretty. No matter how hard one tried to block the darkest parts of a human's thoughts and fears, it never fully worked. At least, not for a human Empath. The natural shields the Breeds had been born with, courtesy of their animal DNA, changed the rules just a bit for them. Megan had none of those natural blocks. Her senses were getting stronger though.

She had become aware of the eyes watching the house as she stared beyond the window, whereas before she had been blessedly ignorant of them. And Braden had allowed that ignorance, certain it would serve her better to be comfortable rather than always on guard.

He grimaced tightly as he fought to keep from going to her. It was a wasted battle and he knew it. He could no more keep from attempting to comfort her than he could keep from breathing.

He pulled his cell phone from the holder at his side and quickly punched in the secured line to the team leader outside.

"Tarek." The voice that came over the line was a surprise.

"Your ass should be back in Fayetteville." Braden growled. "Keeping your mate warm. Does she know you're out playing?"

Tarek laughed. Laughter was something he had rarely heard from the other man until he found his mate.

"She's safe and sound with her family at Sanctuary visiting with Callan's and Taber's wives while the brothers coordinate with the security forces there."

"In other words, no," Braden retorted. "She'll skin you when she finds out."

"We're heading back with you when Jonas arrives to-night. She'll forgive me." His voice held the confidence of a man well loved by his woman.

"You hope." Braden grunted. "Cover the house tight un-til further notice. If the watchers make a move, we'll need a good five-minute head start if possible."

"We'll spread back and take post above then." Tarek's voice firmed as the Breed commander slid easily into place. "Be on call by nightfall though. I have a bad feeling the closer it gets."

Yeah, so did he. Enough so that he was close to dis-obeying Jonas's direct command to stay put until the heli-jet arrived.

"We'll be fully prepared to move if needed by nightfall." He finally sighed. Town was a bad idea. Drawing innocents into the crossfire was not a reasonable solution.

He disconnected, slid the phone back into its holder and made his way up the stairs. Each step brought him closer to the threads of mental pain he could feel emanating from his mate.

His mate.

God had gifted him with something so precious, so pure, he was terrified of seeing it broken. He now under-stood why Megan's family gathered around her, fighting to protect her, to keep the evil of the world from touching her. She was like a breath of spring, of hope. She had blown into his life, his heart, and stolen any chance he had of de-fending himself against her.

He had never thought he had a weakness before; now he knew he did.

He had never believed he could find the strength he needed outside himself. Now he knew he had been wrong.

Megan was his weakness, but she was also his strength.

He pushed open the bedroom door and undressed silently before padding to the bathroom. The door wasn't locked and opened easily beneath his hand. The sound of the shower running should have drowned out her sobs. The smell of chlorinated water should have covered the salty scent of her tears. But it didn't.

He stepped to the tub, pulling back the shower curtain slowly and staring in at her. She had known he was there. She was fighting for composure, to rein in the tears, the pain.

"I'm sorry." Her voice was husky, endearing in the strength he saw.

"For what?" he whispered as he shut off the water, pulling her to him. He took a towel from the rack on the wall and helped her step from the tub. "For feeling? Or for being strong enough to cry when others can't?"

He had never cried.

She gazed back at him. The blue of her eyes, as deep as the oceans they reminded him of, stared back at him from within her dusky skin. The sodden silk of her hair hung down her back, nearly brushing her hips. He began to dry her slowly. He wrapped the midnight tresses in another towel, then worked to dry the moisture from her body.

She was exquisite. Her body was shaped by nature, with smooth female muscle beneath her silken flesh. Enduring. She curved where she should in her full breasts, the perfect size to fill a man's hands. Her flared hips, which his hands cupped easily to hold her in place beneath his thrusting body. Her tummy, slightly rounded, smooth and shimmering with a life all its own.

His palm flattened over it as he marveled at the differences between his rougher, tough flesh and the soft burnished silk of hers.

One day, his child could rest there, he thought. Despite the scientists repeated attempts to force conception, they had never managed to achieve it through the more accepted means. A Breed female could not conceive without Mating. A Breed male did not develop semen compatible to breeding without Mating. And Mating required something those bastard scientists hadn't believed in: a bonding. The coming together of two halves of a whole. The Breeds had been blessed by nature in a way a normal human being was never certain of—the assurance that that one man or woman was meant for them and them alone. Then nature had played a trump card no one could have expected. Only through the Mating could conception occur.

Braden closed his eyes as he felt her fingers in his hair, combing through the strands, stroking his scalp. The sensation sent pleasure racing through his body. Her lips were damp, parted, waiting for his kiss.

He licked at the silken curves, catching her gasp as his hands smoothed up her back. His fingers relished the feel of satiny skin as they moved along her side, smoothed over the golden globes of her breasts and whispered across her nipples.

Her response was immediate, hot. A small moan drifted past his lips, spearing straight to his cock as it jerked in demanding hunger.

Braden allowed a small smile to tip his lips as he turned her, backing her against the sink counter before gripping her hips and lifting her until her rear settled against the cool top.

Her eyes widened.

"Spread your legs for me." He knelt before her, propping her small feet against his shoulders as his palm pressed against her stomach. "Lean back, baby. Let me have my dessert. Sweet, soft cream, just the way I like it."

His tongue licked up the small parted slit, his taste buds exploding with the taste of spicy sweetness as her hands clenched in his hair.

"This is so depraved." A small, arousal-filled sigh whispered around him as his tongue circled her clit.

The swollen little bud was so responsive that each lick around it sent her inner juices flowing against his fingers as he massaged the sensitive entrance.

"Uh-uh." He growled. "We haven't gotten to depraved yet."

"We haven't?" She gasped as he worked one finger inside the small entrance of her pussy, stroking the tight little muscles that gripped the digit so erotically.

"Hmm, not yet." He pursed his lips and kissed her little clit slowly.

Her hips jerked as her thighs tightened, a needy little cry leaving her lips. God, she tasted sweet. And so fucking hot. He let his tongue circle the swollen bud, feeling the small, shivery little pulses of response as he lingered against it before suckling at it lightly.

She was breathing harder now, but hell, so was he.

As he caressed her clit, his finger delved into her pussy, rubbing, stroking, finding all the soft little spots that made her gasp, made those hot little moans leave her throat as she begged for more.

As he began to work another finger inside her, he suckled harder, feeling her orgasm building as her pussy clenched and spasmed around his finger. Damn, pleasuring her was mind-blowing. Hearing those hot little moans, feeling her tighten, hearing her beg. It went to his head like a narcotic, knowing he could make her lose herself in his touch.

But he lost himself in her touch as well. Her fingers gripping his hair, stroking his neck. Her thighs pressing against his cheek, holding him in place as he pushed her closer to the release she was reaching so desperately for.

Her cream flowed from her. It made his fingers slick as he worked them deeper, stroking her, building the heat raging inside her body. Her hips began to writhe, raking her clit harder against his tongue as he sucked at the little bud.

She was so close. So swollen and begging for release. Her cunt tightened on each retreat of his fingers, milked him back in with each entrance.

"Braden. Oh God. Braden, let me come." Her voice was husky and rich with hunger.

He murmured softly against her cream-coated flesh, his tongue flickering her clit, his mouth suckling her harder as he pushed her headlong into the explosion she was seeking so desperately.

He felt it hit her. She tightened, clamping down on his fingers with a strength that had his cock jerking in hunger to feel it as well. But first, he had a need to taste her. To feel and to consume the pleasure that would pour from her.

He moved his fingers faster, deeper, driving into her as her clit swelled, pulsed. Her scream of release echoed around him. A final sucking pressure at her clit to ensure he had given her maximum satisfaction before he pulled back quickly, removing his fingers and driving his tongue inside her weeping pussy.

She screamed again as he licked. Her hips jerked violently as the next orgasm tore through her. He licked and probed, filling his senses with her taste, her pleasure, before jerking to his feet, aligning his cock to the sweet warmth, and driving home.

Her head had fallen back against the mirror, her expression filled with ecstasy as her parted lips gasped for breath, for strength as a keening cry left them.

Sharp little nails dug into his scalp as he leaned close, his lips covering the small mark on her shoulder, his tongue licking, stroking as he fucked her relentlessly. Driving into her as he rushed headlong into his own release and triggering hers as his teeth sank into her flesh.

It was heaven. It was rapture. It was the most incredible pleasure he could have ever known. He felt the barb extend, locking into the muscles of her pussy as his cock spewed its release and the small extension vibrated with the cataclysm.

In that second he was reborn in her. He felt his soul touch hers as his gaze met the deep, dazed blue eyes staring back at him. He felt a rush of elation, of possession a second before his head fell back and a roar tore from his chest.

His mate.

God only knew how much time had passed before Braden was able to loosen his grip on her. His head was buried in her long fall of hair as he crushed her to him, holding her, soothing her.

He cleaned her gently, drying the soft, swollen flesh he had invaded.

Such pleasure should have never been possible. It wrapped around the soul and filled it with a light that heated from the inside out. Warming where once it had been cold. Soothing it where there had been only pain. Just as Megan did. She was the miracle.

"I wanted to be strong," she told him moments later as he stepped back, steadying her as she stood before him. "I wanted to accept what I was remembering and then go on." Her voice was husky with spent passion, with a renewed sadness. "I can't accept it, Braden."

The heaviness in her voice tore at him. God, he had never believed that another's pain could affect him so deeply.

"Accept what, Megan?" He kept his voice soft, gentle. It wasn't the time to push her. He couldn't push her. Whatever tormented her memories, she would have to release on her own.

"Aimee." Her answered surprised him.

She moved away from him, reaching for the clothes she had laid out earlier. "I remember feeling the grief in that dream. God, it was so strong. I thought my soul would rip from my body, it hurt so bad. And I didn't know why."

He knew. He had felt that grief himself as it poured from the young women in the Labs. The horror, the bleak knowledge that no part of their bodies or their souls was sacred.

"She was raped." Her voice was a mere breath of sound. "It couldn't have been long before I saw them at the Academy. And she looked so calm. Her eyes were as dead as the others, but it poured from her." Anger thickened her voice.

"And the rage." Her voice was thick with the memory of it. "The rage was male. Mark knew, and there was nothing he could do about it."

Braden grimaced. God above have mercy. He couldn't imagine living with the knowledge that some bastard had forced Megan in such a way. He had been unaware that Mark and Aimee had mated, but he remembered clearly the days when their futures had been uncertain. Had Mark and Aimee been that unfortunate, then Mark would have had no choice but to endure. The life of his mate would have transcended pride, and the rage would have eaten him alive.

Braden stalked from the bathroom to where he had dropped his clothing in the next room. He dressed quickly, but it was several long moments before he could glance up from where he was tying his boots, watching as she stepped into the room.

"Who was it?" He had to know who she saw. The need to kill filled him with the fury of hatred. He wanted the bastard's blood.

He felt her hesitation and wondered if she sensed the fury he was fighting to hold back. He didn't want her to feel it, didn't want her to know the black hatred welling inside him.

"I thought he was a friend." She kept her voice low, fighting the pain rising inside her. Confusion filled the room, the fight to accept, to get past the denial of the answers she had found within herself.

"Megan." He stood slowly and moved to her, catching her shoulders as he stared down at her. "I need to know who it was. I have to know what we're facing."

"It makes sense now." A brittle, bitter laugh left her lips as she stared back. "How he managed to pull in the military. How he could find my schedule. All of it."

An eerie foreboding began to fill him.

"I thought he was a friend," she said again, her voice

hoarse as betrayal filled her. "But he wasn't. He killed those Breeds and now he wants to kill me, because he suspected their deaths could trigger the memory of seeing him with them. And he's my father's best friend, Braden. It's Senator Cooley. Senator Mac Cooley."

Bingo.

◆ C H A P T E R   2 0 ◆

Senator Mac Cooley. It all made sense now. He had been one of the strongest opponents of Breed Law, the new legal mandates that gave Breeds autonomy and had declared them human despite their DNA. He was also the reason why two military advisors were now required to be at the Bureau of Breed Affairs in Washington as well as two to oversee all security and interrogation at Sanctuary. Not that it wasn't easy to fool the bureaucratic twits, but the thought of a spy in the house made Braden's ass itch.

The spy was most likely the reason why the attacks at Sanctuary were always so precise and why their weaknesses were exploited so easily.

"Show me your weapons." They were moving down the stairs as Braden glanced toward the shade-covered windows. Night was falling quickly.

"Hall closet." They made the turn and moved to the door. Megan threw it open, pushed boxes to the side and ripped coats from their hangers, tossing them to the corners of the closet to reveal a heavy metal safe door.

"I rarely keep it locked." It clanged open to reveal an impressive display of weapons and ammunition. Nothing on par with what he could have found at Sanctuary, but impressive all the same.

Until she threw open the back. Braden lifted his brows at what lay in there.

"Do you have night vision?" She jerked a pair of the most advanced military field goggles from their protective pouch and strapped them to her head before pushing them to her forehead.

Held by secure elastic straps, the small eye socket–sized goggles were the most technologically advanced in the field. They eliminated the need for unwieldy larger models, and had several little fringe benefits thrown in as extras in the lenses.

They literally saw through the dark. Instead of the confusing green illumination, the wearer saw in shades of gray, with pretty little neon colors to pick up anything with a heartbeat.

"Not as good as yours." He snorted. "How the hell did you get those? Even the SEAL teams haven't been blessed yet."

"I have friends." Her comment wasn't satisfactory, but he let it go for the moment. He was more concerned with the other toys she was pulling out. Knives that belonged in sci-fi flicks and a laser-guided pistol that hadn't even hit the military yet.

"Shit, Megan, I think your friends are a bad influence on you." He watched as she strapped the knives along various points of her body—her forearm, her lower legs—and tucked the gun behind her back.

"Us psychic freaks tend to stick together," she informed him breathlessly as she finished, then slammed the inner door closed again before giving him a glare. "And Lance really doesn't need to know about that other door."

"Hell, I don't think I needed to know."

He jerked the cell phone from its holster and hit the command button.

"Tarek." The other man was on the line as Megan passed the ear-held comm links they had stored there the day before.

"Activate field link." He gave the order quickly. "Prepare for early extraction and removal."

"Link active," Tarek reported through the link, which would now be received by the six Breeds outside.

"Secure. Set Field Beta Three." Beta Three was the only code the advisors at Sanctuary did not have.

"What the fuck is up, Braden?" Tarek's tone was hard, concerned. Secure Field Beta Three was also the channel set for use only if top command was considered compromised. And Tarek's wife was in the same compound as top command.

"We have a rat at headquarters," Braden confirmed. "Preparing for removal now. Pull in. I repeat, all teams pull in."

The closest point to contact Pride Command securely was the sheriff's office. Braden knew the risk; Cooley had connections within the military who could make the drive to town a fatal one. There was no doubt the roads were being watched, just as the canyon had been watched the day before.

Next, he keyed in Lance's number, waited for the first ring.

"Lance." The other man was alert.

"Extraction in progress," Braden informed him quietly. "We have possible military alerts and a high level breach of security. We're coming in."

He heard the other man cursing as he disconnected.

There would be only way out of this mess. The senator wouldn't dare send the regular military into Broken Butte, the political repercussions would be too severe. Braden bet the men in the canyon the day before had been malcontents, or part of the senator's private force drawn from those who were dishonorably discharged, or considered too violent for the government forces. He bet they were military-trained mercenaries and nothing more.

Braden gathered up several powerful submachine rifles and ammo cartridges, then watched as Megan continued to weapon up. The single submachine handgun was strapped to her hip and secured at her thigh. A heavy knapsack filled with ammo was tossed to him.

"We won't be able to take the main road," she verified as she closed the closet door, turning to him. "I suggest heading to Carlsbad rather than Broken Butte. They won't expect that."

"Broken Butte is our only option. We'll never make it to Carlsbad," Braden disagreed as he disengaged the tracker on the cell phone, knowing the emergency signal it would send through to Sanctuary. If there was a way to get to them, Callan would do it. He would also immediately isolate the military advisors on site. It was a clear signal to the compound that security had been breached. Until then, Braden was taking active measures to protect their asses now.

"Carlsbad has a military post, manned and operational," Megan pointed out.

He shook his head, then tilted it to watch curiously as she lifted and unbuttoned her shirt and stuck two sheathed three-inch blades beneath the lace of each bra cup.

"Sweet." His cock jerked at thought of the weapons lying so close to intimate flesh. "Remind me not to piss you off when you're armed and ready to go."

She flashed him a wicked smile, her gaze almost electric as she rebuttoned the shirt.

"It occurs to me you might like the danger a bit more than could be healthy," he pointed out with no small amount of amusement. And damn if the thought of it didn't make him just want to throw her to the floor and fuck her for the sheer pleasure of being inside a creature filled with such incredible daring.

"And you don't?" She arched her brows mockingly. "Takes a junkie to know one, Braden."

This was too true. They were doomed. He'd be damned if he hadn't found a woman who loved adventure and life as much as he did. It wasn't just the rush of adrenaline. It was fighting for what was right, it was pitting his strength and his intelligence against the enemy and coming out the victor. Not that he had won every battle, and he knew death could lurk just outside the door. But by God, he would die free. And freedom was worth dying for.

"Well, if we live through this one, remind me to spank you again." He tied his hair back quickly with the leather strip he carried in his jeans before flashing her a wicked smile.

"For what?" Incredulity filled her voice as he turned on his heel and headed for the back door.

"Just 'cause I like to make your bare ass blush." Turning quickly, he grabbed her around the neck, pulled her close for a quick, brief kiss then released her just as suddenly. "Ready to party, baby?"

"Let's party."

Braden opened the door slowly, his eyes narrowing then adjusting to the darkness to allow for near perfect vision. The DNA he carried had given him eyesight superior to any normal human as it pierced the dark, shadowy night.

"Ready?" Tarek stood at the side of the door, the five Breeds assigned with him placed at various points close to the Raiders.

"Stop baby-sitting me." Megan punched his arm. "Let's

get the hell out of here before they have time to move. And trust me, they are getting ready to move."

◆   ◆   ◆

Megan could feel them. She didn't know how many there were, or where they were, but the vibrations were pouring through the air.

"Interstate or back roads?" Braden snapped as they began to move, rushing to the Raiders and jumping into the opened doors quickly.

"Back roads." Interstate was out of the question. It was the quickest, most likely route. It was sure to be heavily guarded. "If Cooley has pulled a military unit in on this, our best bet is back roads, no lights. Even a mercenary force could have better gadgets than I do. A deputy's pay sucks, you know."

"Not a problem." The Raider shot from the driveway and headed into the desert, away from the ridges that surrounded Megan's home on three sides.

"Security engaged, GPS location and override deactivated."

"Here." Megan punched a map up on the screen, laying out the coordinates to one of the back roads that led into town. "It's not the best route but it's the most defensible."

The road was little more than a dirt track that bypassed the gullies and caverns that could provide easy ambush. "They've seen us leave though, tracking us by sight won't be that damned hard," she added.

She could feel them. Her neck itched, and just behind her left ear she could hear the strange little sizzle in her brain that heralded a rush of information. Not military, but heavily armed, and heavily payrolled. They would have the gadgets.

She shook her head, tightening the shields around her mind that she pulled from Braden as her pulse began to throb in her veins. Someone was betraying the senator, but who? And why?

"Someone isn't good at blocking. I have an unknown pouring information at me, Braden," she yelled over the whine of the Raider's motor as Braden pushed it to its highest speed.

"Keep the path to him open, Megan," he barked out. "Doesn't matter if he's friendly or enemy. I'll block him from taking info but draw in as much as you can."

This multitasking was going to get ugly, she thought with a grimace as she fought to do just as Braden had asked, to keep the channel open as she began to plot the best course into town.

"They're on the move, and tracking. Son of a bitch, I knew I should have gotten that loan for those nifty little radar and laser blockers I saw last month," she yelled as she felt the information stream into her head.

"Loan?" She ignored the incredulous look he shot her, as well as the snickers of the two men behind her.

"Sure, you think the outside of my house looks like shit because I'm lazy." She laughed in sheer delight. "I'll owe my local bank until I'm eighty, Braden. They finance my little playthings."

She flipped the Raider's radar and laser tracker, cursing as it came up empty.

"Son of a bitch. I hate it when they don't play fair." She tapped the screen roughly, knowing the pinpoints of movement should be there, snarling at the thought that they were jamming their signals.

She lifted her hand to her head as she shook it fiercely. She needed more information.

"Bastards should know to be blocking," she bitched as she felt, literally felt, one of the soldiers as they headed from the nearest ridge into the desert. "We have them on our asses, tracking our location and coming up on us."

She hit the lock to the dash keyboard, punching in commands before it fully leveled out over her lap.

Instantly, the windshield displayed a subtle glowing map.

"There, seven dash four," she snapped as the turn came up. "To your right. It will be harder to follow."

There was nothing ahead. No ambushes, no one lying in wait. The clarity of the information was disturbing, almost familiar.

"Can you trust this, Megan?" Braden jerked the wheel to the left and headed into a more hilly part of the desert, toward the canyons that crisscrossed the desert.

"Someone's opened up to me." She continued to input the information into the map. "The information isn't a trap, but I'll be damned if I know why. They can't be as damned stupid as they're acting."

Perhaps she was stronger. She bit her lip fiercely, disturbed by how quickly the information flooded her mind, without the pain.

"Tarek's behind us, riding us close. Is he being fed the map?" one of the Breeds behind them snapped out with a tone of imperative demand.

"As I put it in, they get it."

"What about those bad boys coming up behind us?" Another snarled. "I can see the dust trail behind us."

"Vehicle to vehicle only." Megan kept tapping, keeping the link to the other vehicle secure against any attempt to hack. "I know what I'm doing."

At least, she hoped she did. It had been a long time since her uncle Steven and his military buddies had been out to play. As she kept the communication link between the two vehicles clear, a sudden burning at the back of her neck had her eyes widening.

"Break off!" she was only barely aware that she was nearly screaming as she felt the sudden order shoot through her brain. "They have missiles . . . You fuckers!" The blast rocked the Raider as Braden twisted the wheel, snarling as the vehicle behind them swerved and nearly rammed into them before righting itself.

"Attempted radar lock." The computer voice came

through as three furious Breed snarls echoed around her. And she swore the link at her ear was filled with the same sound.

"Yeah, snarling is going to help," she yelled back at them, fighting to stay in place as Braden began twisting the wheel while the computer continued to warn of the attempted lock.

"Canyon ahead." She pointed to the turn on the map. "Two hundred feet. We have a series of roads through several canyons we can use. It will block the missiles."

"Missile lock."

"Bastards! Where the hell is the speed, Megan?" he yelled out.

"Empty. We'll make it." She braced for the turn, gritting her teeth as the Raiders took it on two wheels only seconds ahead of the strike.

The missile exploded into the wall of the canyon entrance as the vehicles shot through it.

"Road's narrow," she warned him as the night-vision goggles she wore picked up the canyon walls. "Radar is showing no obstructions ahead. That's all we have to watch for."

"How far does this canyon last?" A voice snarled in her ear. That voice was just as dangerous as any Braden had ever used. Pure male fury-laced testosterone.

"Five miles, less than three minutes, but it's a shortcut. There's no way they can keep up unless they take the canyon, and with any luck they'll have to go a hell of a lot slower." She glanced at Braden's set face. "I could drive it faster."

He threw her a look of utter incredulity. "I remember your last chase, Megan. Not a chance in hell."

They shot out of the canyon minutes later, Megan hunched over the keyboard as she fought to stay one step ahead of the bastards chasing them, as well as the psychic impulses rushing into her brain.

"Left." She pointed to the next canyon ahead. "Fuck, I think they're using satellite tracking with GPS. They have some handy-dandy gadgets, Braden."

"How far are we from town?" He kept his eyes on the narrow path they turned onto, and was forced to slow their speed to navigate the turns.

"This takes longer than the interstate. We could be a while."

"Jonas will find us before we ever hit town," one of the Breeds behind her snapped out. "Just keep us one step ahead of those damned missiles and we'll survive."

"Tarek, your Navigator have anything?" Braden suddenly yelled into the link.

Megan threw him a surprised look. "Navigator?"

If the bastard behind them was driving a Navigator Raider then she was going to hurt someone. The Navigator was the elite, the best of the best with full satellite links and blocking capabilities.

"Blocking is out," Tarek answered. "And we have bogeys coming up our ass."

"Left." The next turn was sharp, almost hidden, while the main canyon road continued on. It was also quicker.

"We need to find some speed," she muttered, her fingers flying over the keyboard as she pulled up the maps she had inputted into the Raider over the past year.

"We can come out here." She pointed to the next turn. "We have to get some speed and get to this next set." It was close to fifteen miles away. "If we can get through there we'll be close enough to Broken Butte to call Lance."

"Lance has been notified. The bastard better be on his toes."

Megan turned, staring into the rearview as they sped through the twisting canyon road. Something wasn't right. The Raider behind them was in view, but something else was beyond, too close.

"Faster." She snarled. "Put that damned pedal to the floor

or we're all going to burn." She knew she should have made him let her drive, dammit.

He added speed, cursing every breath as the walls of the canyon brushed the Raiders as they raced through it.

"Radar lock in progress," the computer warned in that damned monotone.

"I'll kill those bastards," Braden yelled.

"Stand in line. Tarek do you have flares?" Megan snapped.

"Flares loaded and on track." The voice was a snarling, growling exclamation that indicated the fury she could feel pulsing around her.

They shot out of the canyon. Megan was aware of Braden flooring the gas as the computer warned of radar lock. The flare from the back Raider illuminated the night and seconds later the resulting missile explosion shook the canyon walls.

That was when they got dirty. The next missile was shot before lock, giving Tarek's people little time to set the flare. It was close. The next was closer.

"Hold on. Hold on." Megan felt it coming a second before the Raider pitched to the side.

She gripped the roll bar overhead, cursing as the vehicle flipped, righted itself, then came to rest against a boulder.

"Haul ass. Motor's shot," Braden ordered as he pushed Megan through the door she had only seconds to open. "We're on foot. Let's roll."

He grabbed Megan's arm, pulling her into one of the smaller turns that led back into the canyon. "Spread out. Jonas is less than half an hour away. He'll find us. Full sanctions, shoot to kill."

Megan jerked her pistol from its holster as they entered the rocky, brush-crowded path that led back into the canyon. Gunfire erupted behind them as she listened to the transmissions of the Breeds in her ear.

She could feel the enemy soldiers in the canyon, a full

dozen or more, and one who seemed to see everything. He was doing nothing to hold back his thoughts as the soldiers had the other day. He watched, and he thought. They were after her. Nothing else mattered. Not the Breeds with her; whether they lived or died held no importance. Her death was uppermost.

"Soldiers are moving in ahead of us," she gasped out as they moved through a thick, bramble-coated path.

"I hear them." Braden's voice was soft, predatory. "I can also feel your link. He's doing it deliberately."

"Yeah, I figured that out." She was breathing roughly as he pulled her along behind him. "It's familiar. I just can't place it."

Gunfire behind them had them ducking quickly, listening to the comm link as Tarek gave his men brief, coded orders. So far, none had been hit. Thank God.

"Cooley is with them." Her finger lay firmly on the trigger of her own weapon as she scanned the area where they were hidden. "As well as a Coyote. He's determined."

"So am I." Braden's voice was quiet, but the threat of black rage beneath it sent a chill up her spine.

"We have to take out his Coyote," she murmured as she searched for the best vantage point. She had trained in these canyons with her family from the time she was a teenager.

"We stay upwind of him and we can do that." He began moving again, easing his way through the young pines, piñon and cottonwood trees that grew along the path.

"Cooley is hunting. He's good." She knew he was good. She had heard the tales her father told of training with him when they were both in service together years before.

"I'm better," Braden said. There was nothing like male confidence, Megan thought as she barely refrained from rolling her eyes.

The comm link was filled with the Breeds' low-voiced reports; the night echoed with the sound of gunfire and men's raised voices, and the feel of evil, of death.

Megan felt the pressure tightening in her head as she breathed in deeply, staying low as she followed Braden through the overgrown brush that led along the slanted walls of the canyon. They should be above the soldiers. They should be safe.

She gasped as the pain sliced at her head. She gripped a nearby branch as she fought to keep her footing. Cooley knew what he was doing. She could feel the pleasure he felt at the loss of life, at the pain he had caused. He was deliberately thinking about the deaths of the Breeds, the women he had raped.

Bile rose in her throat as she clenched her teeth and forced herself to move to keep up with Braden.

"Block him. Search out the information and bypass the pain," Braden ordered in her ear. "Don't let him weaken you."

She breathed in deeply, nodding fiercely as she fought to drive the images out of her head.

"He's close." Her eyes searched the night, catching brief glimpses of the soldiers rushing through the canyon below. "He's using the Coyote to track me psychically."

"They aren't dependable." She felt him surrounding her, his thoughts, his warmth, flowing around her like a comforting fog.

He was good. She let a smile cross her lips as she felt the slightest touch of his lust kiss her mind. He was bad too. But the deliberate distraction eased her mind and helped her to follow the mental threads she needed to connect to, rather than the ones Cooley was throwing out to her.

The sudden spray of dirt above them and the *rat-a-tat-tat* of ammunition firing from the opposite side of the canyon had her ducking and rushing to follow Braden behind an outcropping of boulders.

He motioned her to lay cover fire in the direction of the gunfire. As she lifted her weapon and began firing, he ducked and threw himself to the next covering—a thick fallen tree lying precariously on the canyon edge—and began firing back.

Rocks and clumps of dirt exploded on each side of her as she sought the direction the bullets were coming from. Heat. Cold remorselessness. She didn't need to aim. The next volley of shots rewarded her with a broken cry from the enemy as he fell to the canyon below.

"Move." Their position was compromised and she knew it.

They rushed along the canyon face, heading lower for the safety of the caves that pitted the walls below.

As they jumped the final feet, Megan bent to one knee and reached out for the information she needed. She felt Braden close by, the strength of his own focus fueling hers as she reached out.

Her breath caught in her throat the same second she felt Braden tense.

"Very impressive, Megan. You're better than I imagined you could be, hiding like this."

She came to her feet, turning slowly to meet the deadly cold gaze of Mac Cooley. The man her father called friend.

She felt Braden behind her, the silken threads of warning emanating from him, flowing into her.

"I didn't want to believe it was really you." She lifted the goggles from her eyes as she became aware of one of the soldiers moving up on them, covering them from the side.

Mac looked older than she remembered, but he was still in good shape. At five foot eight, with silver-gray hair and cold, merciless blue eyes. Eyes she had always thought held compassion and warmth. He stared back at her, the pistol he carried pointed at her chest.

Her gaze flickered to his side. Deputy Jose Jansen. The betrayal from the other deputy shouldn't have been a surprise.

"Yes, it's really me." Mac's smile was evil, a flash of teeth as his lips curled into a sneer. He glanced at Braden.

"I should have known you'd dirty yourself with him. My Coyote here tells me he could smell the scent of sex from miles away. Such a pity."

Megan played with the trigger of the gun she had lowered to the side of her thigh, wondering if she could be fast enough to blow his heart from his chest as he stood there with that nasty smirk on his face. She looked to Jose again.

"Lance will kill you." Lance would blame himself.

Jose smirked as she watched him warily. She should have known. She had felt the emanations of violence coming from him since she had first joined the force. But she hadn't believed he could actually sell out.

"Drop the weapons, children." Mac shook his head as though disappointed in her. "You surely don't think I'll let you keep them."

Megan breathed in deeply before tossing her gun to the ground next to Braden's.

He was too quiet. She could feel his mind working with fierce intent, but he was playing the lazy, easygoing lion. He wasn't predictable in the least when he did that.

She could feel his demand that she keep Cooley talking though, keep him distracted.

"Check them." He motioned to the soldier at his other side. "Knowing the lovely Megan, she has several other weapons hidden on her."

The gun at the small of her back was her only hope.

The soldier came forward. Tall, muscular, his facial features hidden by the black stripes of camouflage paint he wore. He stripped Braden of his weapons, but she noticed that he never checked beneath the jacket Braden wore. That was too odd. He should have known better than that.

The soldier came to her then. The knives were stripped off her, pulled from her legs and from beneath her jacket. Behind her back, the hand barely glanced over the knife tucked in her belt at her hip, covered by her own jacket, or the weapon strapped at the small of her back.

Caution. The warning whispered over her and it hadn't come from Braden.

She inhaled slowly. She couldn't tell who he was, but evidently he wasn't exactly on the senator's side. He was familiar though, the touch of his mind against hers. She had felt it before, a long time ago. But where?

She shook the thought away before concentrating on the senator again.

"You're not going to get away with this, Mac," she warned him, hoping to keep his attention on her as Braden came up with a miracle. That was his job and he damned well better do it right.

"Of course I am." Mac laughed gleefully, like a child enjoying a joke. The bastard had lost his ever-lovin' mind. "I've been doing it for years, Megan. In the bosom of the family, knowing every move you made with Jose's help. I knew you wouldn't remember seeing me at that Academy without help. It was just a matter of watching the two Breeds and knowing when they would decide to contact you. It wasn't hard to do, my dear. Though it is unfortunate that Mark and Aimee necessitated it. They weren't nearly as careful as they should have been while we were at the Academy."

It was deliberate. She could feel it now. Mark and Aimee had known she would sense them, had allowed their shields to let just enough through to get her attention. It had been the pain that had been a double-edged sword. They couldn't have known how she would react to it, how quickly her mind would reject it and that the memory would pass amid the knowledge that such events had been nearly commonplace at the time.

"You raped them." The gun burned at her back while Braden demanded caution. She had to keep him talking. Had to give Braden time to save them both.

"Of course I did. And I'll rape you as soon as my men have taken care of your pesky little Breeds. I might even rape your little boyfriend before he dies. That's particularly pleasant, making them bend over and take it up the ass. Showing them who's alpha and who's not. It just seems to break something inside them." Satisfaction filled the air as vicious glee attempted to rip into her mind.

She wanted to scream in pain, in rage. She could feel something shattering inside her at the thought of what the Breeds had suffered under him.

"They learn how to take it easy, Megan. I bet your big tough Breed will tell you that. If he can." His gaze shifted to Braden. "You're awful quiet, Breed. Don't you want to share that particular little pleasure you experienced at the Labs?"

Braden shifted slowly, the moonlight that filtered into the canyon, illuminating his predatory smile. "I'm Class A, Senator, Elite status. We did the fucking, remember?"

Cooley's smile froze for a fraction of a second as a thread of fear slipped free of him.

"Ah yes, I nearly forgot." He sneered. "Elite status. I'm disappointed in you. You should have been harder to catch."

"You would have thought." Braden's voice was too soft for Megan's comfort. "I learned how to break men like you, Senator. I believe you were even on the shortlist of potential targets when we were rescued."

Megan barely contained her surprise.

"And now I'm one of their best assets. How far the Genetics Council has fallen. But I'll build them back." Cooley's smile was evil, chilling in its insanity.

"Why kill the Breeds?" she asked him then. "Why wait until they sought me out? You could have killed me at any time."

The destruction made no sense. Neither did the potential for discovery.

"Because it was fun." He shrugged his powerful shoulders as he tilted his head and watched her with maniacal pleasure. "All I had to do was watch Mark and Aimee. I knew they would come for you; it was just a matter of time. And honorable cretins that they were, I knew they would attempt to do so secretly, to give you a choice in betraying me. And I wanted to watch you run, Megan. It makes me hard. It will make taking you so much more pleasurable."

The thought of it sickened her.

"I understand." She nodded solemnly. "Can't get it up the normal way, can you? You have to shed blood to do it."

His smile dropped for a second before returning with sickening force.

"Blood is nice." Excitement laced his voice. "Or maybe I'll do you as I did little Mark and Aimee. Put a gun to your head and make Braden hold you down while I take your ass."

"What is with the ass thing?" She propped her hands on her hips as she feigned incredulous confusion. And no fear. "Have you heard about germs, Mac? Disease? How do you know they haven't infected you somehow? Is insanity contagious?"

His surprise was almost laughable. For a moment, he looked lost, uncertain. And her hand was so close to her gun. *Caution*.

She flashed Braden a glare as she felt the command. Caution be damned. Cooley was making her sick and it had nothing to do with the pain he was trying to cause her.

Gunfire continued to echo through the entrance to the canyon as the comm link at her ear went silent. She knew the Breeds were well aware of what was going on. She only prayed a few of them were at least getting into firing position.

"We don't have long, Senator," the Coyote at his side growled out. "They'll have reinforcements coming in soon."

Stupid mutt, why couldn't he keep his dumb mouth shut?

"Yes, unfortunately." The senator breathed in deeply.

"There will be no time to teach her Breed how lowly he truly is. But take her alive and bring her with us."

Megan laughed. She forced amusement to fill her voice, mockery to shape her expression.

"Nuh-uh." She shook her head slowly. "I don't think so. You may as well go ahead and kill me, Cooley. I won't let you take me."

He smiled serenely as he turned the gun in Braden's direction. "I'll make him hurt as he dies, Megan."

Satisfaction. For some reason, Braden was immensely satisfied to have that gun pointing away from her. Men.

She felt the soldier at her side shift position as the gun-fire seemed to come closer.

Megan shifted her own stance, allowing her hands to press close behind her hips.

"He's going to hurt anyway." She shrugged, feeling Braden's amusement now, as well as the careful preparation of his body. His hands were still held loosely at his sides, but she knew how quick he could be.

Cooley turned his head back to her, his gaze piercing.

"Is he your mate?" His lips twisted in disgust. "Aimee would scream in pain as I held her down. I warned the scientists then that there was a Mating, but they wouldn't listen."

"They knew you were a nutcase too?" she questioned sarcastically.

Anger flowed from him. He wasn't calm any longer, nor was he in complete possession of all his marbles. A few had rolled away somewhere.

"They lost sight of what they were created for," he spat out. "To kill. To be killed. They are nothing." His gun wavered on Braden. "They are animals."

"At least they can get it up without blood." She snorted. "Or is that your problem—penis envy, Mac? I bet their dicks are way bigger than yours anyway. You should feel slighted."

Fury surged through him as his hand trembled.

"Cooley, we're pulling back. The Breeds are moving in." Half a dozen soldiers poured into the area, their faces streaked with shielding paint, sweat, and blood. "Get it over with. We're out of here."

Rifles pointed toward her and Braden. She saw the flash of fear in Mac's gaze, the blood lust in Jose's.

There were boulders to her side, a deep depression to Braden's. She felt him reaching out to her, guiding her, slamming the information into her as they faced the newest threats.

"Kill the bastard . . ." Mac ordered.

Move.

The mental order screamed into her brain as she threw herself to the side, grabbing her gun from the small of her back and aiming for Jose as the senator swung his gun her way a second before she fired. She managed to get a shot off, straight into Jose's heart, but she was a second too slow in firing at Mac.

Suddenly the night exploded with light. War whoops and Breed roars filled the canyon as Megan felt a blaze of fire erupt along her side. Shit, she was shot.

She kept rolling, throwing herself beside the boulder as she fired at the senator again, watching him take more than one hit and fall. His expression filled with amazement as he went to his knees then slowly toppled to his side.

Lance and three other tall, hard-eyed warriors materialized from the dark as the soldier who had so carefully sent her the information rose from his position and stepped forward as well. As moonlight sliced through the cavern and reflected off his gem-bright blue eyes, recognition slammed through her. He had hid his eyes earlier, which was why she hadn't known who he was.

Uncle Steven. She stared at the soldier, well, Special Forces member really. She sat still and silent as the commotion washed over her. The soldiers still alive were being cuffed quickly as the soft hum of a heli-jet could be heard moving in. Lights, voices, too much movement.

Family could be a bitch, she thought. How the hell had her uncle managed to infiltrate the senator's forces? Who cared how, she decided just as quickly, she was only thankful that he had.

Megan closed her eyes as everyone seemed to be screaming at once, throwing out orders, cursing Breeds, radical military dumbasses and senators in general.

All she wanted to do was sleep. She could feel the blood weeping from her side, the pain lancing through her body as shock began to set in.

"God dammit Megan, open your fucking eyes." The sound of Braden's enraged voice had her doing just that.

She grimaced as he tore the night-vision goggles from her head, tossing them aside and tearing her jacket from her body.

"You're fucking crazy," he finally said, as though just realizing that. Hell, he had been with her . . . how long now? Surely forever. And he was just now seeing that? Poor guy, he was just slow.

"I wouldn't mention this to Lance if I were you," she suggested as someone hunched beside them, handing Braden a thick square of gauze that he pressed quickly to the wound at her side.

"Get a stretcher," her uncle Steven yelled out commandingly to someone. She wasn't certain who. "Contact the clinic; we're bringing her in."

Uh-oh.

"The clinic." She leaned against Braden's shoulder. "This is all going to get interesting. Especially considering the fact that Lance has probably already called the whole damned family. Stupid warpaint shit. No wonder I didn't recognize Steven. What the hell was he doing holding a gun on me?"

She felt fuzzy, but she remembered him standing there, watching. Waiting.

"What the hell was he doing here?" she asked again.

"Would you shut up?" Braden snarled, though his hand pawed at her head roughly. She guessed it was some form of comforting gesture. Damn, he seemed kind of upset.

"It didn't go in deep." She tried to look at the wound, but gave up when the growl became an animalistic snarl.

"Damn, you're grouchy," she muttered as he rocked her. Sitting in the damned dirt and he was rocking her. It felt kind of nice; a little odd, but nice.

"And you're shot, Superwoman," he snapped. "Act like it."

She frowned at that. "There's a way to act?"

He groaned. And he didn't sound pleased.

Thankfully, that thought didn't seem to bother her much. She closed her eyes, resting against his warmth, and let the darkness edging along her vision finally surround her. She was just going to nap for a minute. Just for a minute . . .

"Pass out on me and Lance will see it," Braden's voice suddenly cut through the fog in her veins. "He showed up with the rest of the damned males in your family, Megan. What did you say? The wound wasn't deep? Are you wimping out on me here?"

Oh, now that wasn't fair. Her eyes snapped open as she tilted her head back defiantly.

"I'm going to kick your ass." The threat lacked heat. It actually sounded rather weak.

But Braden's smile, it lit up the night. Those sexy lips curved slowly, wickedly.

"Talk like that is just going to make my dick hard."

She lifted her hand, cupped his cheek, and smiled. God she loved him.

"Your dick stays hard."

"Just for you, Mate." He turned until those perfect lips were pressing to her palm. "Always, just for you."

Always. That sounded good enough for her.

She sighed as Lance and her uncles were suddenly converging on her. Thankfully, there was no coddling.

Steven checked the wound, his fingers probing but gentle, his gaze . . . proud. He watched her with pride. With understanding. Seeing those emotions in his eyes helped her to hold back her instinctive rejection of his touch. The discomfort wasn't as severe as it had been, but still, it wasn't comfortable.

"Come on, bad ass." Braden moved in front of Steven when he finished, lifting her into his arms. "You're a crazy woman. Not too deep, my ass. That bullet has to come out, Megan. Looks like you get to wimp out on me after all."

Still in? She stared up at him in horror as she felt her head whirl. Oh hell . . .

She never saw the shock on her mate's face as she passed out, or the surprise in her cousin's and uncle's. But it was her first bullet, she would be careful to assure them later. She deserved a little faint.

· CHAPTER 2I ·

SANCTUARY, FOUR WEEKS LATER

Megan stared at the shafts of sunlight spearing through the windows of the cabin she and Braden had occupied during the weeks of testing they had agreed to. They had left the hospital after the surgery that removed the bullet from her side and flew straight to Sanctuary, where she had been watched over with such careful observation that it gave her the damned willies. The doctors here were way too intense.

But it had saved her from an influx of family members. They had visited a few times, but her father and grandfather seemed to understand that her dreams were finally materializing. Lance was less than happy. For some reason, the thought of working with the unknown female deputy Washington promised to send him wasn't sitting well with him.

Her uncles, Steven, Nash and Blake, had returned to their tribal lands after the completion of a mission they had begun with their resignation several years before. Cooley's name had been associated with the Genetics Council due to

the sensitive files recovered from one of the larger genetics
Labs. How they had managed to fool the senator, she
wasn't certain. She had been a little groggy when that one
had been explained. Something about alternate identities
and facial reconstruction. No wonder it had taken so long
for her to recognize Steven.

None of them were overly pleased with her. She snick-
ered at the thought. They hadn't wanted her in the thick of
the fight, and they sure weren't pleased with the little they
had learned of the Mating between her and Braden.

Mating Heat. She snorted at the phenomenon as well as
the surprising information she had learned. It wasn't a comfortable feeling, knowing that something as basic as her
DNA had been altered in any way, even as minutely as the
Mating hormone had altered hers.

She wasn't a Breed, but she might as well be.

Longer life. She had groaned at that piece of knowledge.

Higher immunity and advanced healing she could deal
with. She liked that part, actually. The rest was going to
take some getting used to.

And then, there was Braden. A small smile tipped her
lips as she stood by the bed, watching him sleep. His long
golden hair framed the savage features of his face, giving
them a stronger, more primal air. The streaks of dark
brown, russet and black that threaded through the thick
golden-brown strands tempted her fingers to sift through
the mass to watch the parade of color as it drifted through
them.

"Wake up, sleepy head." She leaned close to nip at his
lips, only to squeal in surprise as his hands caught her
waist. Before she could counter his move, he had her flat
on her back beneath him.

"You are dressed." He growled as he stared at her from
narrowed, dark gold eyes, his firm lips curving into a smile
as his hands pushed beneath the snug black top she wore.

He was so sexy. A rumpled primal male, confident,

arrogant. And if the tenting of the sheet was any indication, ready to mate.

"And I'm staying dressed." She laughed as she slapped his hands away and tugged the hem of the top back into place. "We're leaving today, remember? I'm ready to go."

To reinforce the claim, Mo-Jo bounded to the bed, certain that the evil feline-smelling man was finally fair game. Megan jumped back, laughing as dog and man growled and snarled, bared teeth and fought for dominance.

"Damn dog!" Braden cursed as Mo-Jo nipped his ear.

A fury of Breed limbs and thick canine fur accompanied Braden's snarl. Megan stood back, laughing as he wrestled the huge dog to the bed and bit him back.

The look of canine amazement on the dog's face was hilarious. His brown eyes widened, his expression going slack for all of a second before a surprised doggy cry left his lips and he twisted forcefully from Braden's hold.

He jumped from the bed, casting the two humans a disgruntled look before snarling back at Braden and stalking to the corner of the room. He plopped down on the air-conditioning vent before batting pitifully at the abused ear.

"Do we have to take that mutt?" Braden flashed his incisors at the dog, who only sniffed in disdain before rising enough to turn his back on them, then settling back on the vent.

"Love me, love my mutt?" She gave him a pointed look before a surprised yelp left her lips.

Braden had gripped her wrist, pulling her to the bed before catching her beneath his weight and staring down at her, obviously not amused at her response, or her laughter.

Laughter that his lips caught as they covered hers, that his tongue tasted as he licked at them wickedly. When he raised his head, his expression was somber, filled with arousal and enough emotion to cause her heart to clench in response.

His hand raised, his fingers touching her lips with the gentlest of caresses as he watched her. At that moment, she

told herself that being at Sanctuary wasn't all bad. The nights
were incredible. The days had been a pain in the ass. Being
poked and prodded at by anything or anyone other than
Braden was guaranteed to put her in a really pissy mood.

"You've been ready to go." He reminded her of her earlier statement as his thumb smoothed over her lips and he
continued to stare at her, his gaze possessive, warm.

The Mating Heat had supposedly been stilled with the
alteration of her DNA. God, she hated that word. But damn
if she still didn't get so wet just from the touch of his thumb
against her lips that she debated changing her panties.

"And you haven't?" She arched her brow, lifting her
hands to stroke her fingers through his hair.

She watched his lashes lower, watched the pleasure that
filled his expression as she ran her fingertips over his scalp,
scraping against the sensitive flesh. A heavy groan rumbled
in his chest and his cock began to prod her thigh.

"Down, boy," she ordered lightly, though her head
turned for his lips to caress her neck as his hands buried in
her hair. "I say we leave first and have wild sex later. I'm
being smothered, Braden."

And she was. Not for breath—for freedom. For adventure. The mission Callan and the Breed Ruling Cabinet had
requested they take sounded like a blast. Braden lifted his
head, his gaze solemn as he sighed deeply.

"Wild animal sex later then." A smile curved his lips as
he continued to watch her, as though he couldn't believe
she was truly there.

"I love you, Megan." He whispered the words slowly,
unused to the freedom to feel, to expect emotion in turn.

Her savage, beautiful lion was still a shade uncertain in
that regard, which continued to surprise her. The emotion
in his face clenched her chest and tightened her throat with
tears as she smiled tremulously, basking in the savagery of
his pride and his possession of her.

The horrors he had lived through in those Labs still gave

her nightmares. The stories the Breed females had related to her and the reports she had read were horrifying. They were still events Braden refused to talk about. It was how he lived with it. How he retained that playful, amusing side of his personality.

"Oh Braden," she whispered, tearing up despite her best efforts not to as she glimpsed the fears in his gaze. The fear of losing her, of having the gift he believed she was, taken from him. "I love you. With all my soul, all I am. I love you. Forever, Braden."

He lowered his head, touched his forehead to hers, his eyes filled with the heat of emotion, hunger, need. All he felt for her, all he was. And in that they were equal. Because he had all she was as well.

"Forever," he whispered, his voice soft, husky. "I may have left my mark on your shoulder, Megan, but you marked my very being. Forever, I'm yours."

Forever.

"Now, let's get the hell out of here." He bounded from her and the bed, leaving her to stare at him in surprise. "I'm ready to hit the road, woman. What are you doing lazing around? Don't we have a mission to complete?"

Megan tossed her pillow at his back as he chuckled in delight before disappearing into the bathroom, the taut line of his buttocks drawing her gaze as she moved from the bed.

Maybe they had a little bit of extra time after all, she thought as she began stripping off her clothes and following quickly. Yep, definitely enough time to love her mate before they headed out. There was always time for that.

◆   ◆   ◆

Jonas stared out at the gated driveway leading from Sanctuary, a frown creasing his brow as the newest in the line of law enforcement/military vehicles headed toward the main road.

The plain black model-eight SUV appeared as harmless as any other on the road. The stealth and armed advancements to it were anything but harmless though. The computerized display screens engaged quickly, with voice or manual commands; the small computer that folded into the dash had a secured link into one of the most advanced satellites orbiting in space. A nice little gift donated to the Breed community by a benefactor with more money than he knew how to spend.

The vehicle was occupied by the latest Mated pair of the community: Braden and Megan Arness.

Jonas tucked his hands into his black slacks, his head lowering as he watched the vehicle drive out of sight and the wide gates close securely behind it.

He remembered the last time he had watched such a vehicle leave Sanctuary. The ever-present pain sliced through his chest as he thought of Aimee.

He hadn't suspected that she had Mated with Mark. There had been no signs of it until the autopsy was performed. The Mating mark hadn't been placed on her shoulder as normal, but rather in the tender flesh of her upper breast. Mark's had been placed similarly. And the marks hadn't been fresh.

His fingers balled into fists at the thought. She had Mated with the other man years before, even before their rescue from the Labs, and never revealed it. Neither Breed had shown a sign of Mating, only one of a very close friendship.

His lips tightened at the thought, his teeth clenching with enough force to send a jarring ache through his jaw. He had cared . . . He shook his head, pacing from the window and staring around the neat, expensive office he inhabited.

Head of National Breed Security Affairs. He had an office in Sanctuary as well as one in Washington. He had a personal assistant, the latest in gadgets and the freedom he had always longed for. But the woman had eluded him. She had chosen another.

Not that he blamed her. He had been unable to protect her in the Labs when she had come of age. What would have made her believe he could have protected her now?

He snarled as the fury bit at his soul. So many wasted lives. He had been his Pride's leader; it had been his responsibility to protect the younger females, to deflect the Trainers and guards and to lessen the horrors of their lives.

He blocked the memories. Years of practice had taught him how to blur the edges of that night, how to push it back into the recesses of his mind. But he never truly forgot. It was always there, waiting to strike, ready to destroy him.

"Mr. Wyatt?" His personal assistant knocked timidly at his door, her voice hesitant.

"Enter," he snapped, doing nothing to hide his impatience at the distraction.

The door opened slowly as the normally confident, balls-busting secretary stepped into his inner sanctum. Her cool gray eyes flickered over him with only a hint of nervousness, her composed features never shifted, the emotionless mask never dipped. She was as cold as an iceberg and as efficient as a robot. And it was all a very brilliant, very impressive façade. He could feel the nervousness, the hint of fear that raced through her.

To give her credit, she hid her fear of him much better than others did.

"We received a message from the liaison in Washington. You're needed back at the office for a meeting first thing in the morning with the Oversight Committee regarding Senator Cooley. Senator Tyler is requesting that you take care of this personally. He'd like to get the amendment to the Breed Articles pushed through quickly to allow for the dismissal and prosecution of Agents Farrow and Harding."

Farrow and Harding. Sanctuary's Washington liaisons would never see the inside of a court for their crimes. They would never be seen again, period.

"And have Farrow and Harding been found?" Their disappearance had raised more than one question within the law enforcement community.

Mia regarded him steadily. "Agents Farrow and Harding have not yet been located," she informed him. "We have several patrols out looking for them though."

A waste of fucking manpower, but necessary. Farrow and Harding were enjoying their entrance into hell, via a drop into the burning lava of an overseas volcano. If nothing else, the Council had taught the Breeds how to dispose of bodies properly.

"Very well. Gather what we need together and we'll leave after dark. I want a profile pulled on the two liaisons in Washington as well. I want to know every detail of their fucking lives right down to their last fart. And I want it yesterday. This will not happen again." He was aware of Mia's flinch as he growled the final sentence and he didn't really give a damn. He wasn't there to make anyone comfortable, least of all his PA.

"Right away, sir." She nodded with a quick little jerk of her head before leaving and closing the door behind her.

And once again he was alone.

Jonas stared around the room, the antique cherry desk, the large chair behind it. The carefully polished bookshelves and the leather couch and chairs. The room reeked of class and formidable power. Power that the Breed community was slowly amassing and putting to use to secure their place in the world.

The Feline Breed Ruling Cabinet worked quietly, outside the public eye, to secure their place in the world. There were so few Breeds, and procreation wasn't an easy process. Unfortunately, it would appear that the longer life spans would cause them more problems than anything else.

Especially considering the leak in Sanctuary by one of their own.

He paced back to his desk, picking up the file he had gathered together and staring down at it grimly. Killing a few non-Breed agents with delusions of the riches to be gathered by betraying the Breeds didn't affect him either way. Killing another Breed for turning the Mating results over to the Council was another story. Especially a female Breed.

He breathed in deeply as he shook his head in regret.

And reminded himself, there could be no regret.